"IT'S A DEL_____ _____E."

Mrs. Amaury leant forward then, her face serious and showing all of her seventy years. "But I have to tell someone, and you, with your...peculiar...abilities might be able to help me."

It was true enough that during his years "in the wilderness" since being struck off by the Law Society he had found the work of an inquiry agent congenial to his talents, but now that he had been reinstated by the same august body—partly as a result of his being instrumental in solving certain cases of crime—he was not sure how such talents could be of use to a respectable client such as Mrs. Amaury.

"My services are at your disposal in every way, Mrs. Amaury," he remarked somewhat formally.

Rose Amaury looked at him very straight, and, although her lips trembled as she brought out the words, yet her voice was firm. "You see, Mr. Kemp, I think my life is threatened. Someone is trying to kill me."

───────────── ★ ─────────────

"An intelligent, absorbing mystery, full of elegantly crafted surprises."

—*Drood Review*

"A light, poetic and moving touch remarkable in this genre."

—*Publishers Weekly*

Also available from Worldwide Mysteries by
M.R.D. MEEK

HANG THE CONSEQUENCES

Forthcoming Worldwide Mysteries by
M.R.D. MEEK

THE SPLIT SECOND
A WORM OF DOUBT
A MOUTHFUL OF SAND

M.R.D. MEEK
In Remembrance of Rose

WORLDWIDE.

TORONTO • NEW YORK • LONDON • PARIS
AMSTERDAM • STOCKHOLM • HAMBURG
ATHENS • MILAN • TOKYO • SYDNEY

IN REMEMBRANCE OF ROSE

A Worldwide Mystery/March 1989

This edition is reprinted by arrangement with Charles
Scribner's Sons, a division of Macmillan, Inc.

ISBN 0-373-26002-4

In
Remembrance
of
Rose

ONE

'I CAN MANAGE perfectly well, Paula. You'd think I had one foot in the grave already...'

Paula Warrender's reaction was to tighten the firm grip she had on her mother's arm.

'I'm only making sure you don't have another fall like you had last week,' she said in a voice intended to be soothing but which came out none the less on a stern note. Her personality was ill-adapted to soothing. She had no instinct for nursing but assumed that she had it as part of her womanhood. She placed Rose Amaury carefully in a chair, and fussed with the cushion.

'Stop thinking of me as an invalid, my dear.' Rose turned to their visitor. 'Now, Mr Kemp, it's good of you to come out to Castleton House to see me. I could quite easily have attended at your office. I hear Gillorns have branched out into Newtown, and that you're very modern and up-to-date.' She gave Lennox Kemp a smile which in a younger person might have been called arch.

He smiled back.

'A new town needs new ways, Mrs Amaury, and even the practice of law has to change with the times. The partners felt the firm's talents had been too long hidden away in the City. We're venturing out into Indian territory.'

Rose Amaury's grey eyes were appreciative of his lightness of touch. She did not look her age, which was seventy; her soft brown hair was only faintly streaked with white and her cheeks, under the dusting of powder, scarcely lined.

'Mother could not possibly have gone into Newtown in her present condition, Mr Kemp. It is the making of her will you are to discuss.' Paula spoke reprovingly as if to put the conversation on its proper level, and the solicitor firmly in his place.

'You would seem to link my frailty—as you call it—with the need for a last will and testament,' Rose observed tartly, 'but as you and Lionel insisted, I asked for Mr Kemp.'

Kemp himself wondered why Paula Warrender treated her mother as though she were dimmed in her wits and far advanced towards senility; this at a time when many women of Rose Amaury's age were standing on their heads in all walks of life, competing in beautiful grandmother competitions and sailing round the world in small boats. Perhaps it was the ambience of the Edwardian house inhabited by the Warrenders, Paula and Lionel and their family, which dictated their attitude. Mrs Amaury was accommodated at their door in what they might have liked to term the Dower House, except that such had long been pulled down and replaced by a modern bungalow—the equivalent in other circles of a granny-flat.

'There was no need to engage someone new, Mother. We have always dealt with Gillorns at Clement's Inn, and Lionel could have had Mr Archibald out to dinner—they're old friends—and the matter could have been discussed in a civilized manner.'

'I know. I know.' Now it was the older lady placating the younger; Rose wanted peace within the household. 'It was I who insisted on Mr Kemp. I have my reasons.'

In her own way Rose Amaury could be stubborn, a quality she had evidently passed to her daughter who used it with much less grace. Paula's haughty expression was possibly one she could not help, given the arrangement of her features; the brow seeming to look down upon the nose and it in its turn to be contemptuous of the mouth while her chin had no option but to recede, there being no other position it could take. The result was an aristocratic mien, devoid of mobility. Only the eyes were like her mother's but lacked the spark of humour and the warmth.

For Kemp the interview went smoothly enough. Mrs Amaury was obviously a rich woman but one who had an attitude towards fortune which deprecated the money itself; she spoke of responsibility, even of stewardship, and her calm acceptance of the changing times was reflected in the instructions she gave Kemp for the drafting of her will. There was to be a measure of equality, but with a fond leaning towards the younger generation.

'We have been fortunate people, Mr Kemp,' she told him. 'I had a certain heritage, my husband worked hard all his life but had the advantage of being a professional at a time when merit was adequately rewarded...' Dr Amaury had died some five years ago, not long after his retirement; he had been a consultant physician, a serious man dedicated to his calling, who had done well in the post-war London medical world. There were two children, Richard, also a doctor but at present out of the country, and Paula, the châtelaine of Castleton House.

The first trip wire came with the appointment of executors. Naturally Richard Amaury was to be one but Paula demurred at being the second. 'I would rather Lionel took it on,' she said, 'It's not something I care to do and he's the proper person so far as our side of the family is concerned.'

'Richard and Lionel don't see eye to eye on many things, Paula,' Rose Amaury observed mildly, 'there's no reason to suppose they'll be any different after I'm dead. Much better to have someone outside of the family, then... Would you be an executor, Mr Kemp?'

'Come now, Mother, don't be so foolish. There's no need to have a complete stranger.'

'But Mr Kemp's no longer a stranger. He's learned a great deal about us this afternoon, haven't you, Mr Kemp?' She gave him another of her winning smiles. He was delighted, but tried to keep his own face straight as he explained to a stiff-backed Paula that it was not unusual for an executor to be appointed from one of the partners of the firm—perhaps she would agree to Mr Archibald Gillorn? Mollified by

the mention of that august name, Paula agreed. Kemp knew
well that the old man wouldn't take it on. He was on the
verge of retirement and had the good sense not to enter into
any further trusteeships, but there were plenty of younger
men available.

There was a knock at the door, and a parlourmaid entered with the tea-trolley. Paula rose and crossed the room
to take charge, and under cover of the delicate clash of china
Rose Amaury spoke swiftly to Kemp in a low voice.

'I want you to be my executor, Mr Kemp.' Kemp nodded; he had no idea why the old lady should make such a
request but her wish must be his command.

'I really don't see why you have to bother with these
charity bequests, Mother,' Paula observed, handing cake,
'particularly the local ones.'

'Most of them are to medical foundations, my dear. Your
father supported them and he would have wanted it. As for
what you call local ones, just because we have a new town
at our door doesn't mean we don't still have poverty...'

'Nonsense! They're all well-housed and well-fed, and
what do we get? Crime and vandalism. A lot of layabout
louts lounging about the streets. Newtown's a disgraceful
place.'

Kemp turned the conversation by admiring Castleton
House itself, a move which caused Paula Warrender to un-
bend a little. He was to understand that Castleton House
had been rooted in the land long before Newtown was even
a gleam in the eye of the planners, and the Warrenders had
been there too and now wished to have nothing whatsoever
to do with this upstart child of the post-war development
era, this conurbation which had sprouted and been left to
spread like a happy weed right up to their park walls. Not
that the Warrenders had done badly out of it, Kemp
shrewdly surmised. Paula might talk of the loss of the home
farm and fields but their sale must have brought in a small
fortune. Lionel, as a stockbroker in the City, would see that

it was wisely invested. Or would he? Not all stockbrokers were wise.

'I will telephone you when the will has been prepared for signature,' he told the ladies when he took his leave.

'I shall come to your office to sign it,' Mrs Amaury said firmly, disregarding her daughter's exasperated frown, 'and see for myself how the legal profession is advancing its frontiers...'

Kemp grinned. He and Mrs Amaury had established a comfortable rapport despite the disapprobation, mute but unmistakable that showed in Paula's attitude. Paula, it seemed, approved of little that had occurred without her consent during her forty years, so that Kemp felt in no way diminished by being curtly dismissed at the door as if he had been an errand boy delivering a parcel.

In fact he was rather pleased with himself—it was the effect Rose Amaury had on people—and he skipped down the four moss-grown steps from the terrace to the grey gravelled forecourt where he had left his car. The sombre leaden urns on the balustrades should have upheld offerings to sylvan gods but only harboured granite chippings and cigarette ends; perhaps they knew such gods had withdrawn their beneficence. There were no flowers either in the severely cut-out beds and the grassy slopes of the gardens were not particularly well-tended. This absence of colour gave the mansion itself an austere, somewhat utilitarian aspect for all its grandeur. Yet it had an Edwardian exuberance of its own. Built at a time when builders were apt to get carried away by sudden flights of whimsy, it was embellished by odd little towers and turrets which must have been endearing once, when the grounds would have been nurtured by a team of gardeners and the lawns stretched green velvet right up to the home pastures.

Now the place was hemmed in; the roar of traffic on the main road just beyond the truncated drive assaulted the ears, as the blue-slated roofs of the nearest council estate

visible on the skyline behind the row of dying elms gave
similar affront to the sight.

Briefly, Kemp sympathized with the Warrenders.

He slowed his car before reaching the ornate iron gates,
and glanced in at the neat white bungalow tucked in among
the laurels and rhododendrons. Here at least someone loved
gardening; although it had been a cold spring the daffodils
were brave, crocus covered the earth, and round the door of
the little house hyacinths bloomed in soft, splendid har-
monies of colour. He guessed it was Rose Amaury; the tiny
garden reflected her special qualities; a contentment within
a small sphere, and an acceptance of restricted boundaries
neither of which had apparently blunted a natural sharp
awareness disinclined to the sentimental or cosy view often
attributed to the aged. Indeed, sitting that afternoon amid
the decayed elegance of the drawing-room at Castleton
House, Kemp had already experienced a sense of the generations being a-slip, the ages out of kilter. The Warrenders—certainly Paula who still hunted and spoke more
feelingly of her horses than she did of her own offspring—
seemed to have regressed into some historical backwater of
their own choosing, whereas Mrs Amaury had moved forward keeping step with the years. They, not she, it seemed,
had lost their nerve as well as their land when the changing
times had spawned Newtown on their doorstep.

As he drove back to the town through a network of streets
between tidy little blocks of red and white houses, trim green
verges set with unlikely groves of almond and cherry now
hopefully budding in this their first spring, he found himself whistling:

> 'The rich man in his castle,
> The poor man at his gate . . .'

He wondered if it still had relevance.

TWO

ROSE AMAURY was as good as her word. Two days later Lennox Kemp saw the entry his secretary, Elvira, had made in his diary for this morning. The draft will had been sent, approved, and Mrs Amaury had made her own appointment for its execution. Kemp hoped she would like his modern office.

He himself was not sure about the huge gold lettering which emblazoned the windows looking down upon the newly cobbled square of Newtown's main shopping centre. The words 'Gillorns, Solicitors' certainly met the eye with no modest assurance. But Archie Gillorn, the senior partner had had no qualms: 'If a thing's worth doing, it's worth doing well...' Which also meant grasping with both hands the advantage granted by recent legislation to permit advertisement in a profession hitherto conducted with gentlemanly reticence.

All right for him, Kemp reflected, the old man's remaining snugly at base in that Dickensian building behind Clement's Inn, where no doubt business will still pussyfoot along as it did in the days when to advertise was to sin, and concepts of marketing and competition were strictly for tradesmen.

'Just the place for you, Kemp,' Archie had grunted, 'out there in Newtown. Give you scope. Seems you need it...from your record...'

Kemp had demurred.

'It's been some years since I practised law,' he had said, trying to find the eyes in the tortoise-like creature before him. The scaly lids rose and he found them, sharp and bright and looking straight at him. 'Law doesn't alter in practice, for all these new fangled ideas about it,' said the old man. 'A lot of daft legislation about... Our job's to make sense of it... You'll manage. You've been outside it a while. Could be an advantage. A ha'porth of common-sense's sometimes worth volumes of statutes. Got another wife yet?'

The abrupt change of subject only the very elderly can get away with had startled Kemp.

'No.'

'Humph... A good wife settles a man.'

Kemp was willing to believe it, but could take the matter no further. Useless to say that the only ladies he seemed to fancy were either married to someone else, or were half his age.

Or getting on for double it, he suddenly thought impishly as his client was shown in. My God, if she was thirty years younger, I'd marry Rose Amaury!

She was not alone, however. Elvira also ushered in Paula Warrender who hovered over her mother like a disgruntled hen.

'Paula drove me in this morning, Mr Kemp...in case I met contagion on the bus.' It was said with such sweet irony that even her daughter could take no offence. Kemp pulled forward another chair which Mrs Warrender took without acknowledgment, remaining gloved, hatted and stiff with propriety. She allowed her gaze to wander over the beige synthetic carpeting, the angular steel furniture, and the electronic equipment on Kemp's black glass desk, only pausing momentarily at the soulless plastic curtains. Kemp had never really noticed them before; he did so now as Paula's eyes shrank in disapproval.

Elvira produced coffee in flowered cups, not the beakers in general use; she had an instinct for the better class of client. Being thin and rather anaemic, she had a delicate air and gave an impression, as she saw herself, of gentility despite downright plebian origins, but she was a hard-working girl none the less and now laid competently before Kemp the

immaculately typed will, the drafts, the inscribed but un-
dated envelope, and Mrs Amaury's slender file.

'When you are ready, Mr Kemp,' she said in her refined
voice from which she had ironed out all but the merest trace
of East London accent, 'if you will call me I'll bring in the
clerk for a second witness.'

Mrs Amaury watched her seemly withdrawal with amused
eyes.

'I like your up-to-date surroundings—and the service,'
she said, sipping her coffee. 'Do your criminal clients get the
same treatment? You do have criminal clients?'

Kemp laughed.

'They're not criminals when they're in this office, Mrs
Amaury, nor I hope when they leave the Court if I do my
job properly.'

Paula Warrender sniffed audibly.

'I'm sure Mr Kemp wants to get on with our business,
Mother. You're wasting his time.'

Kemp read the will through to them carefully, clause by
clause.

'That last is merely a charging clause which is necessary
since you have named either myself or one of the other
partners as one of the executors. That is the usual thing . . .'

Rose's eyes met his. Paula stared straight ahead.

'Now is the will just as you wished?'

Rose nodded.

'Then it is ready for you to sign.'

'Has Tullia Cavendish's name been spelt correctly?' asked
Mrs Warrender. It was an unnecessary interjection but
Kemp gave her a polite affirmation. Tullia Cavendish was
one of the few personal beneficiaries, outside of the family.
He recalled Paula's evident satisfaction at her inclusion.

'Mrs Cavendish is a dear friend of mine,' Rose had explained. 'She's been good to me, and I owe it to her. She's
fallen on hard times, poor Tullia . . .'

Paula had not been pleased at this divulgence.

'The Cavendishes are a very distinguished family—they have owned land round here for generations...'

'Well, they don't now. They sold it to pay their debts and Tullia hasn't a penny to her name—no matter how distinguished that name may be,' Rose had remarked with one of her occasional bursts of asperity. She had reminded Kemp momentarily of old Archie Gillorn; that same prerogative of the elderly which they share with the very young to say outright the normally unspoken. The young use it out of ignorance or from a desire to shock, the old from carelessness, or an impatience wilfully blind to the effect produced. Whatever it was in Rose Amaury, it had its disconcerting side.

The witnesses being summoned, the signing proceeded, and the formalities were quickly over. Mrs Amaury leant back in her chair while Kemp and Elvira completed and dated the drafts.

'I understand you wish the will kept here? Elvira will make a photocopy and send it to you...'

'With the account?' Mrs Amaury was laughing at him again. He handed the file to his secretary and she and the young clerk left the room.

'Well, I'm glad that's done,' said Rose, turning to her daughter. 'Perhaps you and Lionel were right, my dear. I should have thought about my will earlier but there always seemed something repellent to me in preparing for the inevitable end. It was only that fall in the garden which made me think...'

Kemp took the opportunity to make his usual conventional little speech.

'Now it is done, Mrs Amaury, you can put it out of your mind and live for many more happy years.'

'My mother is frailer than she looks, Mr Kemp,' observed Paula sternly as though his common enough remark constituted a breach of the peace, 'and this visit has been a strain, and could have been avoided if she'd had the sense to sign the will out at Castleton.'

'But I've enjoyed my trip into the town,' said Rose placidly. 'I feel I have done my duty, and doing one's duty should incur a little personal hardship, should it not? I feel I can even face Mrs Roding better knowing that I have not forgotten her...'

From the look in Paula's eyes Mrs Roding had been better forgotten altogether. That had been another sticking-place when the contents of the will were discussed at Castleton, and had given rise to another altercation between mother and daughter.

'I would like Mrs Roding to have a small annuity,' Rose had told Kemp. 'She's my daily. Does the rough work, as we used to call it...'

'Really, Mother,' Paula had protested, 'I see no reason why she should get anything. Lionel and I don't trust her—or those boys of hers. And you've given her quite enough as it is.'

Rose had turned her mild eyes on her daughter. 'It is my wish that she should have some benefit on my death. Like Tullia Cavendish, she has not had an easy life.'

Paula Warrender had risen angrily at that point. She strode over to her mother, ostensibly to rearrange a fallen cushion but it was Kemp's feeling that, had Mrs Amaury been a child, she'd have had her fingers soundly slapped.

'How can you speak of Tullia Cavendish and that dreadful Roding creature in the same breath, Mother? Why, one of the Roding sons is already in jail!'

Rose had brushed aside Paula's fussing hands. 'And where do you suppose Tullia's husband, the gallant Major, has been all these years?' she had murmured, under her breath.

'There are things we don't speak about...' Paula had hissed the words in the old lady's ear as she pushed the offending cushion roughly down the back of the chair.

Kemp had sought to sooth over the situation with the suggestion that the annuity be made conditional upon Mrs

Roding still being in the employ of the testatrix at the relevant time, and the moment had passed.

It was now Paula who rose first, and went briskly over to Mrs Amaury. 'Come along, Mother, we don't need to take up any more of Mr Kemp's time.'

But Rose Amaury sat firm, gently disengaging Paula's delicately manicured fingers from her sleeve. 'You go on down to the car and wait for me, Paula my dear. I have a word to say to Mr Kemp—if he will spare an old woman a few minutes...'

'Of course,' said Kemp politely; one could not be other than courteous with this lady whose natural manners were in so much better shape than her daughter's.

Mrs Warrender hesitated, irresolute.

'But we've finished here. We can't have anything further to discuss with Mr Kemp.'

'But I have, Paula,' with the faintest stress on the pronoun.

Kemp opened the door for Mrs Warrender and shook her limp hand, giving her no option but to leave. She shrugged her tweed-clad shoulders in reluctant toleration of such whims, and threw her mother an exasperated glance which was not given any response.

Kemp came back to his seat with a sharp look at his client. It couldn't be anything to do with the will; that had been effectively put away until the ending of her life—which he genuinely trusted would be a long time in coming.

Rose Amaury had watched him close the door behind Paula, and the grey eyes were still on him when he settled in his chair. Only her hands, the transparent skin mottled with brown age spots, betrayed nervousness as she toyed with the clasp of her handbag.

'Take your time, Mrs Amaury,' he said gently. 'There's no hurry.'

'You know that I insisted on seeing you, Mr Kemp. Did you not wonder why?'

'I am aware that your daughter and son-in-law would have preferred Mr Gillorn himself—he has always been the family solicitor. It would have been the natural thing.'

'I had heard of you, Mr Kemp. From a friend of mine—Grace McCready.'

'You know Mrs McCready?' Kemp was surprised; he would not have thought they moved in the same circles.

'We are on the same charity committee. I also know that her husband who is a retired police officer runs a detective agency in Walthamstow. I asked Grace a discreet question—she is a very discreet lady herself—and she mentioned your name. How providential it was to find you were actually with Gillorns in Newtown!'

'I don't know much about the workings of providence, Mrs Amaury, and I still don't understand how my previous employment comes into it,' said Kemp, picking his words carefully.

She leant forward then, her face serious and showing all of her seventy years.

'It is a delicate matter, you see. Something I cannot speak to the family about . . . I could be wrong, and distress might be caused. But I have to tell someone, and you with your—peculiar—abilities might be of help to me.'

Mrs McCready must have given him quite a character, thought Kemp without resentment. It was true enough that during his years 'in the wilderness' since being struck off by the Law Society he had found the work of an inquiry agent congenial to his talents, but now that he had been reinstated by the same august body—partly as a result of his being instrumental in solving certain cases of crime—he was not sure how such talents could be of use to a respectable client such as Mrs Amaury.

'My services are at your disposal in every way, Mrs Amaury,' he remarked somewhat formally.

Rose Amaury looked at him very straight, and, although her lips trembled as she brought out the words, yet her voice was firm.

'You see, Mr Kemp, I think my life is threatened. Someone is trying to kill me.'

THREE

A WEEK LATER Kemp sat gazing out of his office window but seeing nothing; he had just received the news of Rose Amaury's death. Paula, quite understandably, had been too distressed to speak but Lionel had not been lacking in the terrible words.

'Struck down in her own sitting-room by some scoundrel who broke in last night. It's so typical, so damned typical, of the frightful world we live in—the world those left-wing planners have brought on our doorstep. They're to blame for letting these hooligans loose among decent people... What happened, you ask?' For Kemp had managed to stem the flood of invective by inserting a query. 'What do you think happened? She disturbed the intruder, and was murdered for it... The police? Oh, they have their usual claptrap... Determined to apprehend the criminal responsible... Well, you know better than I do, Kemp, what all that jargon means...'

'They have their methods, Mr Warrender,' Kemp responded as equably as he could while trying to swallow the choking reality. Rose Amaury was dead. He had liked her, sympathized with her, listened to her, yet she was dead. He had been unable to save her. None of this could he say to Lionel Warrender. Only a lame compliance with convention. 'It's a dreadful thing. Please convey my deepest sympathy to your wife and family. I'll be in touch.'

After that he sat back, and stared in front of him. Beyond his window a nervous pale sun was trying to break the mists, the chilly moist air of an indeterminate spring. The plastic curtains hung in unforgiving folds. And there is no health in me, thought Kemp bitterly. One week. Seven little days. It had not been enough, and now a world of time could accomplish nothing.

He willed his mind back to what she had said.

'You see, Mr Kemp, I think someone is trying to kill me.'

He closed his eyes, concentrated, and listened, the words coming as on a broken tape for even he, adept at listening, had only picked up the signals getting through.

'That fall Paula spoke of... the reason I had to have you out to Castleton... it didn't happen exactly as I told her. I said I'd slipped on the steps in my upper garden while carrying a trug full of weeds. They thought I hadn't been careful, but I had. Afterwards I saw the wire stretched across the top step. I didn't tell them. I said my ankle gave way. Why, Mr Kemp? I don't know. Do you mean why didn't I tell them, or why should such a thing be? Because that same morning there had been another incident. I had been going to walk to the shops. You know my little house is at the end of the drive up to Castleton but I have my own gate at the back leading on to the main road. As I came out of the gate I did listen for traffic. Paula insists I'm deaf, but I have very good hearing... A car came from nowhere, and I had to jump back into the hedge just in time. Perhaps that was simply my impression that it came from nowhere, but when I saw that stretched wire...'

The memory of her voice faded. Kemp shut his eyes to admit of no distraction, shook out a cigarette, lit it, and forced himself to recall her words. Come on, he told himself, you're supposed to be good at this. It's only a week ago, and a mere two days since you saw her for the last time. Get hold of that line to her, pull it straight and don't let go.

'Why didn't I tell them? You've seen what Paula thinks. I'm a frail old woman, fit only to be packed away in lavender bags. As for Lionel, his conception of age is based on his own mother—and she was old before he was born. To him, seventy is the depths of decrepitude—he thinks of me as a geriatric—he hates the word pensioner—who should be nodding by the fire in a wheelchair...' The echo of her silvery laugh made Kemp wince as he heard it again. Forget how much you liked her, he told himself savagely, just remember what she said.

'They would have treated it as an old lady's illusion. You have such an imagination, Mother, Paula would say—having none herself. She's not like me in that, poor Paula, she never had any time for it. Perhaps in the past I may have given them cause to think that I had too much... And Richard wasn't here so I couldn't tell him. I told no one. But I'm not a fool, Mr Kemp, I did what I could. I wanted a discreet investigation made. It wasn't easy... After my fall the doctor insisted that I should remain in bed for a few days, and even when I was allowed to get up I was not to go out. Paula would have liked to have me up at Castleton House where I could be an invalid—and at her mercy.' Rose had given the ghost of a smile, then sighed. 'I should not speak of her so, but...she doesn't understand I love my little house, Mr Kemp, and my independence, and I'm afraid I too was stubborn in my refusal to leave it. Paula only agreed on condition someone stayed with me all the time, night and day. I suppose she thought I'd grown tottery on my feet, had the kind of dizzy spell old ladies are believed to be subject to... And I couldn't bring myself to tell her about that wire.'

From what Rose Amaury told Kemp, Paula had taken her daughterly duties seriously, and indeed had rather enjoyed organizing a rota so that her mother was never alone in the bungalow during the week following the accident.

'I couldn't complain, of course,' Rose had continued on a plaintive note, 'but it was difficult to get even a moment to myself. And, I don't know whether you'll understand this, being bedridden and dependent on others is one of the horrors we face when we become old...' Her voice had faltered, and Kemp had glimpsed the fear behind the gently spoken words. 'And not having time to oneself is a privation. It was only by sending poor Tullia out on an errand that I managed to telephone Grace McCready. I thought perhaps Mr McCready might recommend one of his employees at that Agency of his. It was then she told me about you, Mr Kemp. Paula and Lionel had been anxious for me to make my will, and it seemed such a wonderful opportunity to see you. That was my first little outing, that day you came to Castleton House. I had asked for you specially... Paula insisted she take me up there—I think she wanted you to see the splendours of Castleton rather than my bungalow as a first impression of the family! She sets great store on such things... But of course she was pleased that at last I was making my will.'

The will. Kemp now gave some thought to it. If Rose Amaury was right, if the wire across the path and the speeding car were attempts on her life, they had both been before the will was made. Had she died intestate then everything would have been divided between Richard Amaury and Paula. But it was they who had been insisting on the will being made. Despite her mother's protestations, Paula had telephoned Richard in America where he was on a lecture tour, and he had spoken to Rose himself, relieved that the fall had not been serious but agreeing with the Warrenders that she must not put off any longer the making of the will. They all gained handsomely under it as it now stood, except for the very generous provision for their offspring—surely, as parents, they would not grudge that?

There were the various charities. But who would strike down an old lady just for charity? Then there was Tullia Cavendish of the distinguished if impecunious name, with the dubious military husband about whom no one was to speak. She would have gained nothing if either of these attempts had succeeded. Had she known she was now a beneficiary? And Margaret Roding, rough cleaner and mother of at least one jailbird? Rose had assured him she knew nothing of the will.

Kemp cast his mind back two days: his last visit to Rose Amaury. Delivering the copy will had been a good pretext for seeing her again. Now he screwed his eyes up and concentrated, trying to reconstruct every little incident, recall every scrap of conversation.

It had been a sunny morning when she had telephoned, like a conspirator. 'Paula is in London for the day,' she said, 'and even dear Tullia has parish business to attend to. They know it's one of Mrs Roding's mornings so I won't go falling about... But in case one of the Castleton servants should see your car I can simply say you brought me the copy will.' Mrs Amaury had seemed delighted by her subterfuge, and, amused, Kemp found himself carried along with it.

A small spare woman let him in at the door of the bungalow, a duster in her hand and a strong smell of wax polish about her aproned figure. Her pallid face bore depressing marks of that hard life of which Rose had spoken, and the blurred eyes had seen trouble and become inured to it.

Rose herself had come forward into the hall, only limping slightly, but as she did so Mrs Roding took out a strong ebony stick from the hallstand, and thrust it into her hand. 'You know what Mrs Warrender said, you're to have support for that ankle of yours...' Rose had taken the stick, and smiled at Kemp.

'You see how I'm looked after? This is Mrs Roding, my good helper. Margaret, will you bring coffee for Mr Kemp and me into the sitting-room?' Thus effecting such introductions as she deemed necessary. 'I'm sorry the word "parlour" is out of fashion,' she went on, 'it would be appropriate for this room, don't you think?'

Kemp agreed. The place was not as cluttered as one might have expected in the home of an old lady of means. There were small items of silver, and china figurines in a glass cabinet, family photographs on the tiny bureau but otherwise few ornaments to detract from simple bowls of primroses, and a large pottery jug stiff with daffodils. 'I've never been a collector of objects,' she told him, looking round with an air of complacency. 'For the first ten years of our marriage Gervaise was still in the RAMC and I learned to live out of Army boxes. You can't imagine how delightful it was to have our first London home, and to spread ourselves. But now . . . I'm back to a box again!'

'It suits you,' said Kemp, laughing with her, 'Contentment in a little room . . .'

'How perceptive of you to understand,' she observed, looking at him earnestly. 'Few people do. They speak of loneliness. I have never considered it. Why, only today I've managed at last to shake off Paula's insistence that I should have someone with me at night. Now I can get back to my beloved solitude.'

As her words came back to him, Kemp felt a thrust of pain. Paula had been right; someone should have stayed with the old lady. If they had, if Rose had not been so stubbornly determined on her independence, could the tragedy have been prevented?

He wrenched his mind back to the bungalow on that sunny morning. Over the coffee he had been direct: 'Does your Mrs Roding know that you intend to benefit her under your will?'

'Certainly not. I wouldn't dream of telling her. I won't buy loyalty that way. But surely, Mr Kemp, you can't suspect Mrs Roding of having anything to do with these incidents?'

Kemp had persisted. 'These sons of hers . . . Your daughter doesn't like them?'

Rose Amaury made a helpless gesture. 'Paula doesn't trust anyone in the Rodings' class. She reacts very sharply to my efforts in helping them. Mrs Roding's husband deserted her years ago, and I understand he spent a lot of time in prison. It's the old story. She was left to bring up the lads herself, Ted and Kevin, and I'm afraid it's true they haven't turned out well. Ted's in prison himself now, and Kevin's already been in trouble and is on probation. Oh, the usual things—stealing, breaking-in, taking away motor-cars. Sometimes poor Margaret's at her wit's end . . . I am so sorry for her.'

'Violence?'

Rose looked suddenly frightened. 'I wouldn't know about that. Kevin used to help in the garden here. I did some pruning at the end of the winter and I'd get him to gather up the branches in the wheelbarrow and set the bonfire going. He's a bit surly, but lots of youths are like that. I'm sure he's not really bad.' Her voice trailed off. It seemed she found it difficult to speak ill of anyone, particularly of anyone in what she had, unconsciously perhaps, termed the Rodings' class.

She had shown Kemp the garden, and the small flight of steps from her upper piece of lawn. It was easy to see where a wire might have been stretched between the cushions of aubretia to cause an elderly lady to catch her foot on the top step, but the earth below was soft. Was it just an attempt to frighten her?

'I landed on the weed-basket, but my ankle turned under me. I lay for a moment. I suppose I was dazed, and it was then I saw the wire. It had sprung back to the side. Look, I've still got it.' She'd taken him into the little toolshed. An ordinary piece of plastic-covered wire from a coil. 'We used it to tie up the creepers on the wall round Castleton House. It wouldn't have looked out of place lying at the top of the steps... But it was stretched across, Mr Kemp. I know it was.'

From the back door of the bungalow a path led over the upper lawn to a wicket gate in the hedge.

'I use it to go to the shops. There's a short cut to the parade on the other side of the main road. It saves me having to open the big gates on the drive. Of course Paula doesn't like me using the little gate—says it's dangerous. But I'm always careful... I look and listen... And I did that day. I didn't expect a car to come so fast—without a sound...'

Kemp swung the gate. The hedge on this side came close, but when he walked up the narrow grass verge he had seen the lay-by. Anyone could have waited there; anyone with patience—and a deadly purpose.

His intense concentration on that last meeting with Rose Amaury was shattered by the telephone. A worried Elvira. Did he know clients were waiting? Kemp sighed. Work had to go on; other people's burdens were on his shoulders, other dramas in lives linked professionally with his had to be resolved. None of his present clients might be famous, nor even rich, but at least they were alive. It was a cynical view but a clear-sighted one. He answered the phone, and put Rose Amaury out of his mind.

She came back to him that night before he slept.

'I've led a happy life, Mr Kemp. I've harmed no one that I know of...' She'd said that as she poured his coffee. He pondered sleepily how much there was to be learned amid the gentle clatter of cups. Women's talk as they fiddled with teaspoons. Do you take sugar?—to hide their racing thoughts. Have some cake—as they re-arranged their answers. It was all table-talk, but now he must remember because he would never hear that voice again...

'Tell me about the children, Mrs Amaury,' he'd said, 'Paula's children and Richard's.'

She had been concise, restricting herself to fact, giving no indication of bias, favour neither to one or other.

The Warrenders had two children: Lettice, twenty-four and a cartographer with Newtown Development Council (that had raised Kemp's eyebrows), and Roger, twenty-two and as yet undetermined as to career. Both had been privately, and expensively, educated.

Richard had married an American girl, Giselle, and they had one child, named for his great-grandfather, Torvil Amaury. Rose had smiled in response to Kemp's inquiry.

'The Amaury name must be truly Norman—that funny mixture of the original Norsemen with the French when they finally settled down. My husband had no great interest in his historical forebears—such romantic notions he left to me... And Richard is like his father in that, but Giselle loved the name.'

Torvil was twenty-six, and newly qualified in the same profession as his father and grandfather. He was for the present in a lowly registrar's position at the North Middlesex Hospital, and a frequent visitor to Castleton House.

'Paula likes him. He's a very respectable young man.'

The comment by his grandmother seemed to Kemp to lack warmth.

Drifting off to sleep, remembering her voice, he formed a picture of the family, blurred like a faded old sepia photograph; the Warrenders, the Amaurys, three generations gathered on the grey stone terrace in front of the Edwardian mansion, and looking down on the Rodings, coarse menacing louts waving blunt instruments out of council house windows.

FOUR

A MAGISTRATES' COURT at ten in the morning was no place to attempt classification of its itinerant population. The bodies who jostled and pushed in the cramped spaces provided gave no outward clue as to their identity as criminals or witnesses, supportive hand-holders or members of the harassed administration of justice. That dishevelled young man with the worried look in the company of a burly constable wasn't necessarily in his charge; he might equally be a local reporter, or a solicitor's clerk on his first day and desperate to get it right. The girl with the orange hair and preposterous earrings huddled in conversation with the cardigan-and-pearls matron might be explaining her deprived childhood for a social report, but it could well be the other way round; middle-aged shoplifters wore good clothes if they'd been successful—even if success had recently eluded them. The men and women who sat blind to each other but bound still by the children running heedlessly between them were the now polarized elements in what must have once been the solid state of holy matrimony. Policemen, burdened by charge-sheets and armfuls of paper-work and looking like worried sheepdogs, rounded up their particular bands of errant youth, while the youths themselves smoked and laughed and stamped their feet, taking their tone from one another and their bravado from their numbers. Soon get them sorted out, the Sergeant thought, eyeing them with satisfaction, once they're inside those Court doors. Behind those doors it was quiet; there was order, procedure, that process which would soon separate the discordant components and put them firmly in their place.

Across the bobbing heads, and the bustle of bodies, Lennox Kemp glimpsed the bulk of Inspector Upshire. This might be a stroke of luck. He took a quick look at the day's list. His own case, asking for an adjournment in a matrimonial, was down for just before lunch, and immediately preceded by the criminal cases. There was a long string of licensing applications, and a fair load of motoring offences for the Bench to get their teeth into before then.

He went over and tapped Upshire on the shoulder.

'Time for a chat, John? We're both on late.'

The Inspector had a word with the Sergeant of the Court, who nodded.

'Just as long as I'm back to see Jackman and Roger safely remanded in custody,' he said as he followed Kemp down the steps and into a quiet corner of the car park. 'If it wasn't for them I'd not be down here wasting my time.'

'I did wonder.'

'They're the pushers in that gang we apprehended last week. They've got some smart alec of a lawyer from London to oppose bail, and by God they're not going to get away with it ... What can I do for you?'

'Mrs Amaury.'

'What's your interest, Lennox?'

'I'm her executor. Can you give me the details?'

Inspector John Upshire was round-faced and snub-nosed with baby-blue eyes set wide apart which made him look both ingenuous and jolly. He was neither. He had risen through the local force and a hard spell with the Metropolitan Police to his present position through sharp intelligence and an instinct for spotting essentials. He ran a tight ship here in Newtown—as he was over-fond of saying—but was respected, if not altogether liked, by his men. Kemp had found him on the whole cooperative, if handled with care, and they had become friends.

'Bloody awful thing to happen,' said Upshire as the two men lit up. 'Couldn't be worse. Of course the family's making a hell of a stink, and I can't say I blame them. That poor old lady, she never stood a chance...'

'Take it I know nothing. What happened?'

It was soon told. The break-in had occurred just before midnight, and showed all the usual signs of that type of burglary. Whoever it was had waited in the shrubbery—there were cigarette stubs and trampled earth—presumably until the lights went out. The door lock had been wrenched with a jemmy or similar instrument. The desk had been rifled for money, some banknotes taken but cheque-book and credit cards left untouched, small items of silver and china lifted from the cabinet, a camera and a pair of binoculars removed, and the radio.

'Anything that was immediately saleable,' said Upshire, 'then a quick getaway—that was all he was after. And I wish to God he'd done it. But he must have made a noise—there was a smashed vase on the floor. Was Mrs Amaury not deaf?'

Kemp shook his head.

'Well, she heard him. She seems to have come out of her bedroom—that's at the rear of the house—and reached the door of the sitting-room where she was struck down by a single blow to the head. It was her own stick, great thick ebony thing...'

The Inspector took out a handkerchief and mopped his brow.

'I ought to be used to it by now, but you never do...'

'Violence is a thing by itself,' said Kemp, sickened at the thought of that one blow, the soft brown hair spattered with her blood.

'But unnecessary violence,' Upshire exploded angrily. 'That's unforgiveable... Why couldn't the stupid young bastard just push her to the ground and run? It was only burglary, for heaven's sake! Even if she did recognize him... Senseless bleeding panic, that's all it was.'

Kemp considered the words he had heard.

'So, you know who did it?'

Inspector Upshire turned his wide blue eyes on him.

'Kevin Roding's not been home since. Scarpered. What d'you expect? But we'll get him, never fear... The word's gone out. It's not a difficult case for the police. Not up your street at all, Lennox,' he added sardonically.

Kemp took his meaning. Don't complicate matters.

He hesitated, remembering what Rose Amaury had said. 'Please, Mr Kemp. I am trusting to your discretion. I want you to promise you'll say nothing of this to anyone. No matter what happens... If I have been mistaken...if I have imagined these things, don't you see how terrible it would be if they were talked about? I might be wrong...' She had given a wan smile. 'Paula sometimes says that my imagination runs away with me. So I want you to promise.'

And he had promised. This was not the time to break her trust. Not yet. Executorship also implied trusteeship.

So he said cautiously: 'It was just straightforward burglary, then?'

'Nothing's straightforward in crime,' said the Inspector primly, 'but, yes, if you like to put it that way. There was nothing fancy about it. He went for money, of course, knew she kept it in that desk. What he didn't know was that Mrs Amaury never kept much in the house—from what Mrs Warrender tells me, only enough for casual shopping and to pay Mrs Roding's wages... Aye, and her son's too from time to time when he did odd jobs in the garden. Easy as pie, I'll bet he thought it was. When there wasn't much in the way of cash he started in on the other things. But it happens all the time,' he went on wearily. 'Old ladies get mugged now for their pensions—in back streets, in council flats, in the suburbs—but this one has to happen here on my patch and the old lady in question has to be a connection of the Warrenders. That's all I need...'

He looked at his watch. 'We'd best get back. I'll be on soon.'

But although the crowd had diminished, the Sergeant shook his head. 'They're only half-way through the traffic violations.' They sat in his room and Kemp persevered with his questions. He got the gist of the medical report. Rose Amaury had died around midnight from the effects of one savage blow. Death would have been instantaneous. She had been found by her grand-daughter, Lettice Warrender, who called at her bungalow at eight in the morning on her way to work.

'And the Rodings?' asked Kemp carefully.

'You will probably know as much about the habits of our local villains as we do—burglaries, break-ins, damage to property, stealing from shops, garages, even churches. You name it, the Roding brothers and their pals have been at it for years. Big Ted's a hard man and into the London rackets—we managed to get him put away for a while but he's out soon, alas—and Kevin got off with a piffling probation the last time only by the skin of his teeth—and courtesy of a woman magistrate who was sorry for his mother, God help her.'

Kemp couldn't be sure on whose behalf the Deity had been invoked.

'The burglary at Mrs Amaury's had all the hallmarks of a Roding job, except for the last bit of wanton violence,' the Inspector went on. 'My men were round at Kevin's place, double-quick. Ma Roding was hysterical, but she knew all right. We've searched the house since, of course, although it was pointless; he never went back there after what he'd done. He's gone into the Smoke. Won't do him any good. He'll never get rid of that paltry stuff he pinched—it's all been itemized and circulated. He hasn't any money worth speaking of, and murder's the word that's out . . . He'll get no help from the underworld. It's only a matter of time before he's nabbed. If you're seeing the Warrenders, get them to shut up, there's a good chap.' He looked more closely at Kemp. 'This business has really got to you, hasn't it? But these things happen, and you know it. Remember what you quoted to me in my office one day—that speech by the Duke of Wellington a hundred and fifty years ago, wasn't it? The historical perspective you called it. I don't think you should try that one on Lionel Warrender when he's on his "don't know what this country's coming to" hobby-horse—at least not in the present circumstances.'

He'd scored a point, thought Kemp ruefully as he followed the Inspector back into the Court. It had been a month ago during a discussion on the crime rate and the incidence of mugging that Kemp had tried to strike a placatory note—playing Devil's advocate—by insisting that robbery with violence was nothing new; his words had come from the Duke's speech on the Metropolis Police Bill: 'Scarcely a carriage could pass without being robbed; and frequently the passengers were obliged to fight with, and give battle to, the highwaymen who infested the roads...' And there were no ambulances to take you to hospital then, he'd said; people just died in ditches after being beaten up, or they crawled home to perish later in agony from the septic wounds caused by shots from rusty firearms.

Kemp couldn't recall now what he had been trying to prove; what he did know, what he could not shake off knowing, was that there was a world of difference from mere theory once you had known the victim; that was the thrust that now went home.

John Upshire had made no objection to his visiting Mrs Roding. 'She's a beneficiary,' Kemp told him.

'Oh yes?' The blue eyes hadn't wavered. 'You'd better have a word with Detective-Sergeant Cobbins first. He's in charge there...'

THE FRONT WINDOWS of 32 Runnymede Crescent, the council property occupied by the Roding family, were blind to the afternoon sun, and the curtains were drawn.

'She'll be in,' DS Cobbins had assured him grimly. 'She's not going anywhere.'

Two households in mourning, reflected Kemp as he pressed the bell. For whom it was worse, the bereaved Warrenders up the hill, or the runaway's mother as she slowly came to realize the waiting and the pain, the glare of publicity, and the agonized hope, dying day by day, that her own flesh and blood might escape, might even not be guilty?

He looked gloomily at the small smudged garden, the dash of bright paint on a trellis, the net curtains and the fancy door-knocker. Even the poor have their pride—sometimes they have nothing else—and here, though the efforts had a tawdry pathos, Mrs Roding had apparently striven for the barest respectability.

His ring was answered promptly enough but without noticeable welcome. Indeed, the swart broad-beamed woman who stood, arms akimbo, in the doorway would have daunted the most courageous visitor.

'What d'ye want? If ye're from the press, get bloody lost.'

There was only one way to deal with this gipsy-type who looked as if she'd faced bailiffs, eviction officers, and inquisitive social workers, not to mention the forces of law and order, with that same implacable trap of a mouth as ready for verbal abuse as the set of her barrelled hips was prepared to resist manhandling. Kemp had met her like before, in the East End, these fierce, dumbly belligerent women, protecting their own kind. There was but one thing to do; a reasoned approach would go for nothing.

He took a step backwards, and rushed her.

He got a cuff on the side of his head but he was through, into the narrow hall and at the half-open door to the living-room. By the time the gipsy plunged in, breathless but still cursing, Kemp had Mrs Roding's hand in his. He had found her huddled in an armchair. In a corner the television set blinked despondently without a sound. The blinds were down and the room almost in darkness. Kemp took a firm grip on Mrs Roding and waved his other hand at her protectress.

'Ssh...' he admonished her. 'Can't you see Mrs Roding's upset? Go and get her a cup of tea...' He ignored the clutter of mugs already on the table.

The wind taken out of her sails, she hesitated, war welling up in her massive bosom, but she buttoned her lip and stood mute as Margaret Roding spoke in a quavering voice. 'She's my Cousin Bessie . . . She's come to look after me.'

'How are you, Bessie?' said Kemp pleasantly, 'I'm sure we're all grateful for what you're doing for Mrs Roding.'

'What's yer name, then? An' what's yer business with 'er?' But she was fighting a rearguard action and she knew it.

'I'm a lawyer, Bessie. I have some good news for your cousin. Go and get us some tea, there's a dear—and keep any of these prying reporters away.'

He recognized in Bessie one of these females ever on hand when misfortune strikes, part of the solidarity of the slums—that banned epithet though the traits persist—when the poor closed ranks and sat it out. His appeal to her protective instincts worked, and she flounced out taking her outrage with her.

'Mrs Roding, I have nothing to do with the police. Nor with your son. I represent the estate of Mrs Amaury.'

As she began to sob, Kemp rose and pulled up the blind. Sunlight flooded in. It lit the furnishings, comfortable if not luxurious. It lit too Mrs Roding's worn features, the red-rimmed eyes and weak quivering mouth. All she needs, he thought through a helpless pity, is a return to normality, the minute by minute normality by which people like her have to live. The drink of tea, the familiar domestic solace, the touch on the lips of milky fluid, the feel of a crumbling biscuit, no taste in the bite just the feel against the lips, the reassurance of daily bread.

He came back and sat beside her. 'I know how sorry you must be about her death but I want to tell you that she remembered you in her will. She left you an annuity—the sum of £10 a week will be paid to you from now on. It will be a little help to you, I'm sure. Things are not going to be easy... I just want you to remember that Mrs Amaury thought of you and did what she could for you. Now, that's all I've come to tell you.'

She shifted in her seat and turned to him with staring eyes. It wasn't the news she wanted to hear but it would sink in, given time. He left her to her thoughts, and neither spoke until Bessie bustled in with two steaming mugs on a tray. The larger one was inscribed 'Our Mum' in big black letters surrounded with pink hearts.

'Get that down yer throat, Maggie, an' stop that bloody snivellin'...' She glared at Kemp and went out, slamming the door. Britannia of Billingsgate right enough, he thought, but her command had its effect. Mrs Roding swallowed a mouthful of the hot strong brew, and wiped her eyes. The first thing she remembered was her manners, learned from a lifetime of service.

'What must you think of me, Mr Kemp. It's good of you to come yourself and tell me. She was a nice woman, Mrs Amaury, ever so friendly...the best I've worked for. It should never have happened to the likes of her... What they're saying, I mean. I'm sure Kevin never meant it...' Her hand flew to her mouth as if to take back the words. 'I mean, I'm sure it weren't our Kevin there that night.'

'Then why hasn't he come home, Mrs Roding?'

'Oh, Kevin's always going off. He has friends all over.' But Kemp knew she was only grasping at straws, and he had no desire to take them from her. He changed the subject.

'They tell me your Ted will be home soon.' The information had come from DS Cobbins in different form: 'The elder Roding's due to be released from the Scrubbs in a couple of weeks—and we'll be waiting for him. It took a lot of hard grind to put him away and we're going to keep tabs on him. There's never been a reformed Roding yet.'

Mrs Roding didn't seem especially encouraged by the prospect of seeing her elder son. 'Ted's always been difficult, Mr Kemp—he takes after his dad, in and out of jail. That's what I couldn't stand, that's why I came to Newtown, to get away from all that... And Ted's not been a good influence on Kevin.'

'They get on well together, your two boys?'

'Oh yes,' she said eagerly, as if brotherly affection could compensate for everything. 'They've always been ever so close, my Ted and Kevin.' As close as thieves were the words that sprang to Kemp's lips but not uttered. 'Kevin was so thoughtful,' she went on, 'going to visit his brother the way he did, to save me having to go.'

Margaret Roding was crying again. Kemp could see how it would be. There was the long desolate journey, the sordid waiting-room, and the all too short interview, and what could be said anyway within those bleak walls? Mrs Roding had indeed had a hard life; more could not have been required of her even by the most vengeful of gods. She had already been beaten into the ground.

'They had the same friends, Kevin and Ted?' he said casually.

'Well, not here in Newtown. Ted was that much older... He'd left school when we were still in Stepney. I thought coming out here would make a difference, Kev going to the Comprehensive, like...'

A fresh start—which hadn't worked. How many had come to Newtown in that same hope? It wasn't fair to press the poor woman further; finding Kevin Roding was police business, not his.

'If you need help, Mrs Roding, here's my card. You know where to find me.'

Bessie was standing by the stove in the kitchen staring out at the back garden.

'You're doing a grand job here with your cousin, Bessie,' he told her. 'She needs all the help she can get at a time like this, and it's only going to get worse—because they're going to find him, and then the hullabaloo will really start. You know it, and I know it, so keep at your post...'

The black eyes gleamed and an unbecoming flush arose in her cheeks. It was a long time since anyone had paid her a compliment, and she'd never expected one from the forces of law and order. She would remember it.

FIVE

THE DISTANCE BETWEEN Runnymede Crescent and Castleton House was short but in making the journey Kemp knew
he was passing from one world into another; Disraeli's 'two
nations' were still as far apart as ever.

He had a four o'clock appointment with the Warrenders, and his fellow-executor Richard Amaury. He understood Richard and his wife had arrived from the States and,
although no formal reading of the will was envisaged since
Paula could tell the family what it contained—and must
have done so by now—he had thought it advisable to meet
Rose Amaury's son as soon as possible.

He left his car in the lay-by and opened the big iron gates.
He'd like to get a look into the bungalow later. He walked
up the drive, crossed the forecourt, and was admitted to the
other house of mourning by an unsmiling parlourmaid in a
seemly black dress which did nothing for her yellow com-
plexion.

The family were gathered in the drawing-room. Here too
the shutters were half drawn, yet sunlight filtered through
and filled the green-and-gold room with soft radiance. Tea
was served as though no ripple of outside events should be
allowed to disturb the proper observance of the civilities,
and custom must be followed.

Richard was a large, capable-looking man but he had
Rose Amaury's quizzical, gentle eyes. His grief for his
mother's death was evident but, in the presence of a
stranger, not to be extravagantly expressed.

Lionel Warrender was all that Kemp had anticipated. A
short sturdy figure with a ruddy face, and reddish hair fast
receding from a forehead pink as a baby's, he looked what

he was: an outdoor man forced by circumstance to labour in the City instead of striding his manor like a squire. Whatever had been his feelings for Mrs Amaury, they were overlaid by the strength of his anger which sprayed out in all directions—at the ineptitude of the police (but he would be having a word with his friend the Chief Constable about that which would soon bring them to heel); at the Development Council who had now learned the lesson responsible land-owners had been trying to teach them for years, that they couldn't just plonk down hordes of East Enders in the fair English countryside and expect them to reform their villainous ways; and, finally, at the world in general to which the Socialists were rapidly bringing ruin and the collapse of civilization. Kemp listened to his diatribes with half an ear; he'd heard it all before, and anyway political theories bored him. He was more interested in people and, for the moment, the people in the room.

Giselle Amaury, he noticed, seemed a little out of it. She was a tall woman with a pleasant, open face, if a little uncertain in her smile when they were introduced, and the tanned brow below her mass of tawny hair was creased as if with the same doubt.

Torvil resembled her but with an arrogance in the line of his mouth which either spoiled his otherwise handsome looks or enhanced them, depending on the sex of the beholder.

Lettice Warrender surprised Kemp. She looked every bit as formidable as her mother but in a different way. Small and compact, she had resolute hazel eyes, a direct, almost challenging look and an air of stubborn determination which for a fleeting moment reminded Kemp of Rose Amaury. Lettice would be a force to be reckoned with, and he wondered if her character had been forged in the battle for independence which she must surely have had to wage before achieving her present employment in the bosom of her father's anathema—the Newtown Council.

As Kemp murmured the conventional words of sympathy he could not help adding: 'It must have been a shocking thing for you, Miss Warrender, finding her that morning.'

Her lips tightened, in the manner of her mother.

'It was a moment I shan't forget.' Her voice carried the words without inflection but her eyes glistened and she turned away abruptly as if to shield herself from too close a scrutiny.

'Roger is the only member of the family not here, Mr Kemp,' Paula announced smoothly when the tea ceremony was over, 'but I'm sure that doesn't matter. He's still up at Cambridge...' Her phrasing was nice, thought Kemp, who knew that young Warrender had been merely playing around with various unsuccessful courses at the Polytechnic in that city for the last year or so. 'Now I've told everyone about the will in general terms,' Paula was continuing, 'but I would be obliged if you could read it to us. That would be proper, would it not?'

'Of course, Mrs Warrender.' Kemp read out the contents of Rose Amaury's last testament. The only interruptions that came during his recital were a murmur of appreciation at the mention of Tullia Cavendish, and an explosion when he arrived at Margaret Roding's annuity.

Ignoring both, Kemp proceeded to the end and turned to Richard.

'I don't know whether you are returning to the States, Mr Amaury, but if you have the time I'd be grateful if you could call in at my office so that we can get down to the business of sorting out the assets: and perhaps I could be given access to your mother's papers at the bungalow—or we could go through them together?'

'Paula can let you have the keys, Kemp.' Lionel looked inquiringly at his wife, and she took some keys from her handbag and handed them over. The horror of her mother's death seemed to have softened her attitude towards the lawyer, or might simply have suspended it.

'I've cut short my tour,' said Richard heavily. 'It was
nearly over anyway. I only wish I'd been back sooner...that
I'd been here. Anyway I shall be working in England now
so I'll be available whenever you like. There's the inquest,
of course...and the funeral...' Richard had difficulty in
saying more, and there was an uneasy silence for a few
minutes as if in tribute to the dead. The demands of civilized behaviour precluded tears being shed by people of their
class and upbringing; stiff upper lips were expected of them.
But shock and horror at the circumstances of the death
could be expressed, and were vociferously and in varying
degrees, now that the normal procedure had been con-
cluded. Questions were asked of Kemp in the expectation
that he would have the ear of the investigating officers. He
answered with caution, knowing full well that the search for
Kevin Roding had already been widely broadcast, and in any
event, the Warrenders had servants who would be seething
with the local gossip.

'I've watched him stand there in Mother's sitting-room
while she went to her desk to get the money she paid him for
gardening. His eyes would be everywhere...' Paula was
saying to Richard, 'I warned her time and time again about
those Rodings.'

Richard shook his head. 'You'd never change her. She
trusted people. That was her nature.'

'Somehow one doesn't expect this awful kind of thing to
happen in England,' Giselle remarked to Kemp. She had
kind eyes that were troubled now as if safe ground had suddenly yawned open at her feet.

'Can this Roding woman really get her hands on that annuity Gran left her? I thought criminals weren't allowed to
benefit from their crimes?' Torvil demanded.

'Mrs Roding's not a criminal,' replied Kemp calmly.

'Of course she is. They were in it together. Sticks out a
mile...'

'I don't think so.' Kemp looked at the young man coldly.

'Have you seen her since?' It was Lettice who spoke, wasting no words; straight to the point, like an echo of her Grandmother.

'Yes.' Kemp was short with her.

'Why?' asked Lettice.

You're pushing it a bit, young madam, thought Kemp, reluctant to answer.

'She's a beneficiary. It was my duty.' He turned to Mrs Warrender. 'And, by the way, I ought to see Mrs Cavendish.'

'She keeps house for her brother at the Vicarage,' said Paula, 'and it's Miss Cavendish. I have—er—already told her... Did I do right?'

'Saved me a journey, Mrs Warrender. There's no reason why she shouldn't have been told.' But just when did you tell her, he would like to have asked.

Lettice was still following her own line. 'And how has Mrs Roding taken the news of Grandmother's death?' she persisted, with a rough edge to her tongue.

'I'll bet it wasn't news to her!' burst out Torvil.

'She is very grieved,' said Kemp, keeping his tone level, and he rose to go before anything further could be added.

There was a bitter taste in his mouth. Too much tea-drinking. The strong brown brew handed over by Bessie, that self-styled guardian of the oppressed; weak and delicately flavoured from this heirloom cup, gold-banded, thin as the veneer overlaying this urbane table-talk. They would be a vengeful lot, these Warrenders. Scratch the surface, threaten their way of life and they would give no quarter.

Kevin Roding hasn't a chance. But then, why should he have? To strike down a defenceless old lady, even if done in a moment of panic—there could be no mercy for such an act. Rose Amaury herself would have forgiven the attempt at theft, found excuses for the lad she'd befriended, of that Kemp was sure almost as if he heard her speak... But she'd not been given time...

Useless speculation, he told himself savagely as he strode down the drive under the blank, contemptuous stare of the high windows.

He paused at the white bungalow. There was no sign of police. He had the keys, but the front door gave under his hand and he walked in, to the same faint smell of lavender polish although this time there were no bowls of spring flowers in the little parlour—only an empty stillness. He had entered quietly and as he stood, almost seeing Rose Amaury there, he heard a sound from the back of the house.

He went quickly down the corridor and pushed open the bedroom door.

The woman kneeling beside the bed might have been praying; indeed, the swift sure movement that brought her to her feet showed her as not unaccustomed to such pious activity. Perhaps as sister to the Vicar it had become simply a matter of reflexes. For Kemp was certain that this was Tullia Cavendish, the well-born lady who had come down in the world and was now as poor as a churchmouse—a creature which at this moment she resembled. She looked as if she would have scuttled back under the floorboards if she could.

'Miss Cavendish?'

She nodded, and stood blinking large, vague, washed-out blue eyes at him, her hair falling over her narrow forehead in disarray; a guilty thing surprised. And with good reason, for on the bed lay a large suitcase which she had been in the process either of packing or unpacking.

Piles of clothes, and bundles of papers were laid out neatly on the counterpane. With a hurried movement she put those she held in her hand back in the case, and brushed down her skirt.

'I was sorting out some of Rose's dresses...Paula said we might use them...for the church, you know. We have jumble sales... Well, not just jumble...good things, like these.' She gestured towards the open wardrobe. 'I have Mrs Warrender's permission...' Despite the flustered, rambling delivery her voice carried the authentic accent of authority, the ingrained assumption that whatever she had to say would be listened to, whether by the Mothers' Union or other, less worthy audience.

'I'm sure you have, Miss Cavendish. And did you find anything suitable for your jumble sales in that?' Kemp went forward, picked up the items laid out on the bed, re-packed them in the suitcase, noting that there were levels she had not yet reached, and slammed down the lid. He gave a sharp look at her empty hands; she wore a straight shabby dress that had once been tailor-made, no pockets.

She came out from behind the bed, and brushed past him. He picked up the case and followed her.

'My name is Lennox Kemp. I'm the late Mrs Amaury's executor.'

'I assumed you were Mr Kemp.' She had paused by the front door as if to take a stance. Her guilty confusion was less apparent now that she had regained composure. But guilt there had been. She was not the sort to be so intimidated by a stranger in the house of an old friend. As she tucked the strands of her grey-streaked brown hair into an old-fashioned slide at the back of her head, she looked more herself; a faded gentlewoman at that uncertain time of life between forty-five and sixty when the years begin to run faster than the days. 'Paula has already told me that dear Rose remembered me in her will. I suppose it was all right for her to tell me . . . after that terrible thing happened? My brother and I were so shocked. We both loved Rose. Ever since she came to live here we have been close friends.'

'I will come and see you at the Vicarage in a few days, Miss Cavendish. In the meantime I have things to do here.'

She was not used to being dismissed so curtly. Good manners forbade an absolute refusal to budge but the lines of her long face deepened, and the vagueness in her eyes shifted to sudden awareness.

'My brother and I will look forward to that,' she said stiffly but with a touch of condescending graciousness as though she were putting the final word to an impending visit of a minor curate. It irritated Kemp; he couldn't understand why he had been so brusque with her. Perhaps her explanation was true. One ought to have trust in relatives of the cloth no matter how suspiciously they acted.

He watched her go down the path, the ungainly figure in an outmoded woollen frock, severe stockings and sensible, flat-heeled shoes seeming to embody a certain type of English countrywoman bent on good works and the continuance of tradition.

He went back and searched the house. Rose had been right; she'd never been a hoarder. When she gave up their London house on the death of her husband she must have divested herself of much in order to squeeze into this boxy little bungalow, and what she had kept was merely of use or comfort. Her private papers would be in the Bank, but he took a good look at the contents of the bureau. There was nothing there. Had she left him no clue? He cast his eyes over the bookcases. She had obviously been an avid reader, good novels of the last fifty years predominated, with a surprising amount of detective fiction among them. He took down a *Writers' and Artists' Yearbook*. It was an up-to-date edition, an odd acquisition for an elderly lady. Perhaps it wasn't hers. The pages fell open at literary agencies, and there were pencil markings.

He put it in his pocket, picked up the suitcase and went back to his car.

SIX

KEMP TOOK ROSE AMAURY'S suitcase back to his flat when he finished at the office. He had evaded Elvira's bubbling curiosity about Kevin Roding when she brought in the mail for signature, and hovered. 'Let's leave it to the fuzz, shall we?'

Elvira winced at the slang; it wasn't the way solicitors were supposed to talk but as Kemp had elevated her also when he brought her from the seedy detective agency in Walthamstow where they'd both worked, she was still too jubilant at her rise in wages and status to take exception to anything this odd, fascinating teddy-bear of a man either said or did. As she confided to one of the new girlfriends she'd made since coming to Newtown: 'The thing about Mr Kemp is that he always treats me like a lady.'

'Lucky old you,' muttered the other.

'Come to think of it,' added Elvira, on reflection, 'that's how he treats his women clients too, no matter whether they're rich matrimonials or real scrubbers up on a drugs charge. He's the first boss I've ever had who talks the same way to everybody. Know what I mean? It's like he sees no difference in people. Funny, isn't it?'

Had Kemp heard her he'd have been surprised; it wasn't something he'd ever given any thought to. His manner was the natural outcome of an inclination never to judge by appearances—and a certain laziness. He simply found it easier, professionally, to ignore a man or woman's position in the social scale, their means or lack of them, and whatever pretensions they aspired to, or felt were required of them. That way he could catch more readily the nuances, the evasions and small deceits, the blurring of truth and fiction

which were inevitable in any tale they told him. With so
much role-playing going on in front of him he never saw the
need to put on any act of his own. Courtesy, costing nothing, could cloak perspicacity besides keeping the wheels of
business oiled.

Now he threw the suitcase down on the purple and gold
uncut moquette settee, and went to make his supper as he
usually did from whatever was available. Sometimes he
thought his domestic habitat resembled a badger's sett—
simply a place to crawl into at night, in which to eat a little,
sleep a little, and think long thoughts. It didn't worry him;
the years when he had been alone since his divorce from
Muriel, the years of estrangement from his profession (for
an act of folly deliberately done and never wholly re-
pented), these years had wound a cocoon round him that
could hang from any twig for a home.

He switched on the television, and learned that the Metropolitan Police had a lead on Kevin Roding—a car found
abandoned had been earlier reported stolen in Newtown.
The police sounded confident; Kemp surmised there had
already been whispers from the grass. He turned the set off,
thinking briefly of the sad little screen flickering in Mrs
Roding's room. Why did she have it on? Habit, he supposed, like the consoling cuppa. But there would be small
consolation coming out of that box tonight as solemn-faced
cops assured a battery of cameras that the manhunt was on,
and would be successful, it was only a matter of time. All
good people could sleep safely in their beds.

Later he poured himself a whisky as compensation for a
meal of almost frugal simplicity, and sat down on the lu-
ridly-coloured settee—the furnishings in the flat were not of
his choosing and he was oblivious to them. He pulled over
the sofa-table and carefully unpacked the top layers of Rose
Amaury's suitcase; folded blouses, handkerchiefs and
scarves, faded photographs, old birthday cards carefully
kept because they had been equally carefully chosen, thea-
tre programmes too artistic to be discarded and perhaps

sentimentally cherished for the occasions they recalled; a hotch-potch of articles of no value except to her who had owned them. Finally, under a sheet or two of pretty wrapping paper and a roll of Sellotape he came to a large bulging brown envelope. Kemp looked at the items he'd laid out on the table beside him; unless Tullia Cavendish had been re-packing the case when disturbed, she hadn't got this far.

The envelope wasn't sealed. He spilled out the contents on to the table. There were several student notebooks filled with writing he recognized as hers; the same small, neat, school-girlish script as in the notes she had given him for the draft will. He riffled through the pages; they seemed to be rough outlines for stories. Along with the notebooks there was a bundle of manuscripts written by the same hand, on quarto paper, a bit ragged at the edges, fastened with clips that had made brown indentations in the corners, and there were yellow creases along the folds. Some of the manuscripts bore printed rejection slips, mostly from women's magazines, others had letters attached, short regretful letters saying the same thing. There was a letter from a literary agency, dated a few months ago, and addressed to Mrs Amaury. The writer had been kindly but, no, the material submitted was not, in his opinion, saleable.

Kemp felt himself smiling, and an amused regretful pity, strong though transient, pierced and startled him. The sharpness of the emotion gave him pause.

So Rose Amaury had written stories. Well, her daughter had said she had too much imagination. Here she was trying to channel it. She'd read a lot, she liked novels. In time such reading brushes off, strikes a spark. Rose must have been lonely in the years since Gervaise died. She didn't share the Warrenders' interests so she had found a cosy little interest of her own, harmless, absorbing—an old lady's hobby.

Kemp gave the tales a quick read. He was no critic of fiction—save for the gloss on reality sometimes offered to him by his clients—nor was he any judge of modern literature. Rose's stories weren't bad; she had a nice turn of phrase.

They were dated, of course, somewhat O. Henryish, the twist in the endings, the careful characters, the contrived plots. He picked up the letter from the literary agency.

> ...they are quite well written, you have a fair style but I'm afraid the stories lack the necessary punch... The one called *The Bystander* is interesting and perhaps you could work on it, but remember that the modern reader needs to identify with at least one of the characters... We would also suggest that if you are serious about finding a market you must submit typewritten material; editors these days will often refuse even to consider handwritten manuscripts...

The advice was run-of-the-mill, the praise just faint enough not to damn, just hopeful enough for perseverance. Kemp wondered if Rose had been disappointed. He didn't think so.

Hell, he thought, it's me who's disappointed. This blasted imagination of hers, this story-telling, had it in fact caused her to let slip her grasp on everyday life? Had there really been two attempts to kill her, or were these incidents just part of that too vivid imagination? There were a lot of crime novels among the books on her shelves...

He looked at the agent's letter again. He went through the manuscripts, and the notebooks. None of the stories was called *The Bystander*, none of the notes seemed to apply to such a story. Perhaps she'd destroyed it in order to start again... But why should she? It had been the only one picked out as showing promise.

He pushed all the stuff back in the brown envelope, replaced it in the suitcase, and re-packed the other items on top as he had found them. Then he sat back and looked at the suitcase. Perhaps he ought to be questioning his own view of Rose Amaury. He had only known her a very short time, he had taken her seriously and on her terms. He could be wrong about her. The feeling nagged at him.

He ran over in his mind all that he had been able to do in the short time separating her astonishing statement, 'I think someone is trying to kill me', from her actual death.

Grace McCready, that shrewd Scottish spouse of his former employer, had said: 'I only know Mrs Amaury through our Cancer Research committee, Lennox. But she telephoned me the other day. She went round and round the subject before coming to the point, which was that she wanted some private inquiries made—discreetly, of course. Oh, I jaloused perhaps one of her family had got into trouble—that kind of thing. Perhaps one of the grandchildren was mixed up in bad company. Anyway, she lived out Newtown way so I suggested she have a word with you. She was delighted, said Gillorns were their solicitors. No, she gave me no hint as to what it was about. Do what you can for her, Lennox, she's a rare nice lady.'

That telephone call only confirmed how she had got hold of Kemp in the first place. Had she simply been trying to find out how private eyes worked—for a story she was writing maybe? But why insist on having Kemp as one of her executors? Didn't she trust her own relatives?

A gentle probe at Archie Gillorn had produced nothing relevant. 'I've known Gervaise and Rose Amaury for years. Rose was a GP's daughter herself. Nice people, both of them. Quiet-living and content with their lives. Yes, very well-off, but they deserved to be. I'd be glad if you'd take on that executorship for me, Kemp, though I'm sure Rose will outlive many of us.'

Well, she hadn't. He would have to see Archie again one of these days, and carefully scrape the surface of family relationships but Kemp knew he would first have to show cause; Archie Gillorn was no gossip. More to the point, a discreet chat with a stockbroker friend had produced the information that, although Lionel Warrender was a partner in a good firm, he was not highly regarded for his business acumen nor for his investment advice. 'Hasn't got the flair, old chap. You need that in the City in the 'eighties. It's no longer enough that your grandfather was squire of all he surveyed. Personal standing? I wouldn't know about that. Lots of fellows like him take tumbles from time to time. There was money there once... Might be getting spread a little thin by now...'

Had Lionel been short of the ready? Castleton House and Paula's hunters must take some keeping up, and that young man playing careers in Cambridge might well by now have run himself out of Education Grants. The local Newtown garage hand who attended Kemp's own second-hand Cortina had waxed eloquent on the subject of Roger Warrender's cars: 'Likes 'em fast and drives like a maniac when he's round here...' Had Roger been 'around here' the day Rose Amaury had come out of her little back gate? There'd been no time to find out although Kemp had been to the lay-by once more and taken a closer look at the tyre marks and the concealing hedge without finding anything to show whether a car could have started up and hurtled straight at her in the way she had said. It was a busy road, cars flashed by every few minutes. Like many elderly people, Rose could have had a moment's inattention; she could have imagined any fast car that came close to the hedge and which she did not hear was a deliberate attempt to run her down.

Damn her imagination, thought Kemp wearily. Tomorrow I must have a talk with someone who knew her, someone who can tell me whether that imagination overflowed into that placid, contented existence of hers.

SEVEN

NEWTOWN DEVELOPMENT Council's Planning Department was housed deep in the entrails of the administration building—so deep in fact as to give an impression of shamed concealment. And not without good reason, for the office block itself looked as if it had been perpetrated by the Soviet committee responsible for the reconstruction of Minsk, on land steam-rollered by the ravages of war. Here the massive concrete erection pressed heavily down on what had been fair Castleton pasture and brooded on its accomplishments like an inflated elephant only temporarily out of breath.

Kemp found the maps department after a tedious walk through a subterranean warren of corridors, and her name on the door—Miss L. Warrender.

She looked her part, unfussy shirt-blouse and the ubiquitous jeans, trying hard to be businesslike behind a grey steel desk, but a little defiant with it as though the role was still new to her. She had her father's sturdy frame, and something of her mother's prissiness but her young face was as yet untried.

Lettice Warrender was in fact caught in a limbo of her own making; her transition from pampered childhood and Benenden schooldays had been dramatically accelerated when she had insisted on higher education at a polytechnic, and met, head-on, the surge of a new world. The stubbornness inherited from both her parents had backfired on them as she went forward under her own impetus with all the energy of a runaway train. That she had ended up here in the bleak nerve-centre of that new world she had craved so formidably was to her in some measure satisfying; she had set out to prove something; what it was she had still to find out.

'Yes, Mr Kemp? What can I do for you?'

Kemp looked at his watch. 'It's nearly twelve o'clock. Can I take you to lunch?'

She was startled by his direct approach.

'Well . . . why?'

'I want to talk to you about your grandmother. We can't talk here.' He gestured at the map-hung walls, the blotched charts like half-finished tapestries, the frowning impassivity of metal filing cabinets.

'All right.' She made some show of tidying an already tidy desk, gathered a jacket and shoulder-bag, and walked out in front of him, a trim figure, head perhaps a little too large for the body, an imbalance which maturity would correct when it came. But she had nice ankles and small-boned aristocratic feet in expensive sandals. There's vanity there, thought Kemp as he followed her into the corridor.

'I don't suppose you fancy our canteen, Mr Kemp?'

'Not if it's anything like this. Let's try one of your precious butterfly pubs. The Cabbage White defies its name.'

Some whim of the Council's had saddled local hostelries with the nomenclature of lepidopterous insects—a winged fancy guaranteed to be quickly brought to earth in the rich soil of the East Enders' ribaldry.

But The Cabbage White, with its scrubbed pine tables and climbing plants already rampant across the ceiling, proved quiet and the food fresh and good. Kemp noted that Miss Warrender ate with a hearty appetite, as they pursued innocuous conversation.

'I hate my name,' she observed, helping herself to salad, 'too much like this rabbit food. But it was in the family from back in Elizabethan times.'

'Of course. Lettice Knollys... Well, she didn't stay green and crisp for long.'

She only smiled faintly; apparently she alone was allowed to make jokes.

'You wanted to talk to me about my grandmother?'

'Yes. Did you know she wrote stories?'

'What? Granny?'

'She did. Not very successfully, I'm afraid. But you didn't know?'

'I'm sure nobody knew. What an extraordinary thing!'

'Not so extraordinary, Miss Warrender. She liked reading fiction. Thought she'd have a go at it herself.'

Lettice chewed her food properly like the well-brought-up schoolgirl she still was. She had yet to learn affectations. Her mother would have said she lacked 'finish', that final stage of a young lady's emergence, although Lettice herself was unaware of her lack of the quality—had indeed reneged on the French or Swiss process to that end spelled out to her.

She frowned now, concentrating. 'I never thought of Gran being like that. How very odd. You mean she actually wrote stories? Why didn't she tell us?'

'Writing's a fairly secretive occupation—until you're successful. It's not a thing you talk about.'

'But ... Granny. Of all people.'

'Why'd you say that?'

'Well, she always seemed so down to earth. So sensible. What on earth could she find to write about?'

'Your mother says she had too much imagination.'

'Oh, Mother...' Lettice dismissed her mother with a quick flip of her lip. In the same manner she lined up her knife and fork just off-centre on her plate and disposed of that also by pushing it impatiently to one side. 'Mother never sees anything beyond the tip of her nose...' Conscious perhaps that it was not quite proper to discuss her parent thus with a stranger, she reverted to her normal brusqueness; she saw herself as a direct, no-nonsense modern woman. 'How did you find all this out, Mr Kemp?'

'By reading your grandmother's notes—and some of the stories.'

'What right have you to meddle?'

He grinned, and offered her a cigarette which she took after slight hesitation, although her bright hazel eyes retained guarded hostility.

'Easy now, Lettice... May I call you Lettice? Just take it that I have the right. And I do want to know more about Mrs Amaury. I think you were closer to her than anyone.'

Her eyes dropped. She was silent for a moment.

'I don't know if that's true. About being close to her, I mean. We don't talk about such things in our family. At least not in an—emotional—way. I suppose it's not our style.'

'I'm aware of that. But I still want you to talk about her. You can talk about her?' Lettice was gazing out of the window at the orderly geometry of the Newtown rooftops. Eventually she said: 'It's not easy... and not because she's dead. I think perhaps you're right—about me being closer to her than anyone else. But that's because I was just beginning to think that I was like her—or like what she was when she was young.'

'Your grandmother wasn't old.'

She looked across at him, surprised.

'You noticed that, too,' she said eagerly. 'I'd just begun to think it. When I came back after college it struck me... Granny was the only one who seemed to appreciate what I'd gone through. I thought at first she was only being kind because the parents were being so rotten about it, and Roger... Roger was just... nasty. He never used to side with Ma and Pa but he did over me and the job I'd taken on. Called me a turncoat, a baby Marxist. Roger can be horrible when he wants to...' She broke off suddenly. 'Why should I be telling you all this?'

'I don't know. Getting it out of your system, I guess. Like your grandmother when she took to writing... Trying to make sense of an interior life while leading an everyday one.'

She stared at him. 'Say that again.'

He did, adding: 'It's not just imagination that makes a writer, though it helps. It's an appreciation of the complexities that face us daily, a synthesis of things that happen.'

Lettice Warrender was quiet for a long time, so long in fact that Kemp wondered if he'd lost her. When she finally spoke, however, he knew he had got through despite the restraints laid on her by her education and breeding.

'I don't think Grandmother imagined things,' she said slowly, as if learning to speak a new language, 'not the sort you associate with books—and certainly not fantasy. But she was interested in people, ordinary people in all walks of life. She didn't patter on the way most old ladies do. You know, who they've met, what they wore, what their husbands did, how successful their children were. Gran didn't seem to care about such trivial conversations. How can I put it? She always got the nub. Could be very disconcerting at times.'

'So I'd gathered. Go on.'

'I used to talk to her about college and the friends I had there. I didn't think she'd be interested but she was. She'd ask me about them later when to tell the truth I'd forgotten all about them. It was as if she really cared what happened to them. Not only my lot, but everybody she met or even heard about. And she was very shrewd in summing up situations, people's motives...and you couldn't shock her. Does this make sense?'

'Yes, I think it does.'

Lettice reined herself in as if she had said too much.

'I don't mean that Grandmother gossiped. You mustn't get that impression. I'm sure she never repeated things she was told. That wasn't her way. She really hated gossip. I've heard her being quite sharp with Tullia when she used to bring out some awful tale of somebody's misdeeds in her sanctimonious way.'

Kemp raised his eyebrows.

'I've only met the lady briefly,' he said, watching Lettice's face.

'Oh, I know the family thinks Tullia Cavendish is God's gift to the parish, but... There, you've got me doing it—gossiping!'

'You're giving me an opinion. That's not gossip. Why don't you like Miss Cavendish?'

'I don't dislike her. I don't really know her very well, though she's always been around. I just find her creepy, that's all. The Rev. Clive's rather a pet but its his sister who runs things. I don't go to Church any more,' she finished defiantly, 'and that's another bone of contention in the family.'

'Your grandmother was fond of Tullia Cavendish.'

'Gran had sympathy for anybody whose life had gone wrong. That's what she used to say about Tullia—her life had gone wrong.'

'She's known by her maiden name, Miss Cavendish. But she has been married?'

'Oh, you know about that? I thought it had all been covered up. Anyway it was ages ago, years before I was born. I don't know much of the story, I was never really interested. I think her husband left her soon after the marriage—he was in the Army. Wouldn't surprise me if he just couldn't stand her—found out he'd made a dreadful mistake. You'd think she'd have got over it by now—lots of people do. Deserted wives are no big deal these days, but according to Julian she's still bitter. Fancy, after over thirty years!'

Kemp reflected that no man was going to be allowed to make a fool of Lettice Warrender.

'Who's Julian?'

Lettice's cheeks had a healthy glow but the red colour had crept up to her forehead.

'Why, their nephew of course. Julian Cavendish. He lives with them. Teaches at Culverwood—you know, the boys' prep school.' She glanced at the clock. 'Heavens, I'm over my lunch-hour. I really must go.'

'I'll walk back with you.'

All the way he was debating whether or not he should tell her. She seemed a sensible girl and was on the point of growing up into a nice woman, the fires of independence would not be quenched too soon and her ideals would withstand the inevitable battering they would receive as reality bit. But was she ready yet for such a disclosure as he might make? By the time they had reached the portals of the administration building he had not made up his mind. He decided on the most tentative approach.

'I did want to ask you something else, Lettice, about Mrs Amaury's death.'

She looked apprehensive. 'Not about me finding her...please. I've told the police. I could almost draw from memory the room that morning...everything. But I want to forget it.'

'No, it's nothing like that. It's about that fall your grandmother had in the garden. It seemed unlike her not to be careful.'

'She was careful, Mr Kemp. But she did fall—she said herself she tripped. Anyway, what does it matter now?'

Kemp tried to sound casual. 'I just wondered if it's possible someone had been playing a trick...'

'What on earth do you mean?'

'Well, if there had been a piece of wire or string across the top of those steps...'

He was totally unprepared for the effect of his words.

Lettice Warrender turned, her eyes blazing with fury. She swung her shoulder-bag so that it caught him full in the chest and pushed him backwards.

'You...you snooper! You bloody snooper! All the time you've been talking to me you've been prying into my family...getting me to talk about them! And all the time...you knew! I'll tell my father... I'll warn them... You horrible little man...' She was incoherent, scarlet in the face, almost in tears.

She blundered into the doorway, and he heard her sandalled feet racing down the corridor.

Kemp stood staring after her—an object of some curiosity to the council employees drifting back after the lunch-break. At last he shook himself, and walked slowly back to his own office trying to work out where he had gone wrong. He thought of her exact words: 'And all the time...you knew!' Knew what? He didn't know anything. That was his trouble.

EIGHT

THE FOLLOWING WEEK was a busy one for Lennox Kemp and he had little time to think of Rose Amaury. As the intervention of other business might affect even his retentive memory he had followed good lawyer's practice and committed to paper all she had ever said to him, as well as conversations about her. Simply a precaution, he said to himself; the actual putting down of words brings back the timbre of voices, recalls the small hesitations and evasions, the changes in tones which mean things unspoken are running swiftly across the mind. Then he put his notes carefully away; they were for his eyes alone.

Richard Amaury and he were cooperating smoothly in the procedural steps to obtain probate, and towards administration of the estate. There had been few problems. Kemp had found Richard friendly, and grateful for the work being done by Gillorns. Like his father before him, he had a London practice and acted as consultant at one of the teaching hospitals and he had little time to spare, but a few days after Lettice Warrender's curious outburst he had called at the Newtown office to sign some papers, and Kemp was relieved to find no change in his manner. Whatever cause she had to be so upset had evidently not reached her uncle's ears. Nor had Kemp heard anything further from Castleton House.

On Monday morning as he was reading his mail there was a telephone call from Inspector Upshire. 'Knowing your interest in the Amaury case, Lennox, I thought I'd have a word before it gets into the Press. The Amsterdam police got on to the Yard at the weekend. A body was taken out of one of their canals. From the papers on him it was Kevin Roding...'

'Are you sure?'

'We are now. Ted Roding was whisked over there—he was due out anyway. He made the identification—didn't seem fair on Mrs Roding to make her do it. Oh, it's Kevin all right. Bloody young fool. He'd been trying to flog some of those bits of silver in one of their markets, somebody clouted him and pushed him into the water. Ironic, isn't it, him being mugged...'

'How did he slip the Yard's net?'

'Must have hopped it over the Channel before his description got circulated. He'd have nearly twelve hours, remember... And that car he nicked in Newtown—it was found abandoned near Harwich.'

'Still'—Kemp considered the time scale—'that's pretty fast for one of our local young tearaways. And it would need money, and a passport.'

Upshire snorted.

'Kevin Roding's been petty thieving for years. I'll bet it's never been entirely unprofitable. He'd have something stashed away—and a trip to Holland's cheap enough. Once he knew he'd killed the old lady—and he knew all right before he left her house—he wouldn't hang about. Not with a murder charge on him. And he had a passport. Brother Ted treated him to a holiday in Majorca before he himself got put inside the last time. Shake up your ideas a bit, Lennox, these aren't homespun yobbos we're talking about—they know their way around.'

'All the same, to get abroad that quick he'd need help...'

'What of it? Ted's not talking, that's for sure. Besides, what's it matter now? Kevin's dead. He's no longer even in the category of a man the police wish to interview...' Inspector Upshire mimicked the official euphemism. 'He's simply a corpse—and accounted for. Superintendent Quennell at the Yard is satisfied. I'm more than satisfied.

The case, thank God, is closed. Finis. Right? Just thought you ought to know.'

'Thanks.'

Kemp put the telephone down and looked at it while he tried to get himself inside Kevin Roding's head. It was an exercise he sometimes practised when attempting to understand the inner workings of those predisposed to crime. He didn't do it from a psychological point of view; merely as a plain man's guide to the questions that should be asked, or avoided as the case might be, when the accused stood before the Court. With most of his young villains, getting inside their minds was easy enough, disentangling the rag-bag of rubbish therein was more difficult, and ultimately depressing. Small wonder the majority of their nefarious little schemes to outwit the forces of law and order went miserably astray. Perhaps, he often reflected, he didn't get the best type of criminal. From all he'd heard of Kevin Roding—whom he'd never actually met—it seemed unlikely from his record that he'd ever aspired to the master class.

Would he, for instance, take along his passport when going to rob an old lady whose open house was a pushover? Of course he could have gone back to 32 Runnymede Crescent for it, and money, once he'd realized he'd killed Mrs Amaury. Was that why poor Margaret Roding was hysterical the next day when the police arrived? He'd stolen a car, he'd made for Harwich; an early daylight sailing to the Hook before the hue-and-cry was raised? It was possible.

Kemp sighed. Poor young devil. As John Upshire had remarked: ironic that Kevin Roding should himself end up mugged, his body rolled into the dark waters of a Dutch canal. The police had lost their man. Mrs Roding had lost her son.

Kemp was interrupted by Elvira. 'You won't forget, Mr Kemp, that you're seeing the Reverend Cavendish and his sister this afternoon. Four o'clock. I'll let you have the copy will before you leave. Now, have you got any tapes ready for me yet?' She looked at him accusingly, suspecting him of daydreaming again.

Fortunately he was a fast worker when he channelled his mind into the task, and he dealt with the business of that day the more expeditiously under his secretary's implied rebuke. She knew his tendency to be distracted from the often tedious paperwork of his profession and sometimes wondered if he regretted leaving McCready's Detective Agency where there had been greater scope—though less reward—for his somewhat unusual talents.

Later, as she handed him the Amaury will file he grinned at her. 'Tea at the Vicarage, Elvira. How's that for the ultimate in respectability?'

CASTLETON PARISH CHURCH of St James stood apart from Newtown's semi-urban sprawl on what remained of the old village green, now a mere scrap of rough grass inhabited by one lone tethered goat, and surrounded by dying elms. The church itself seemed also to be dying. It was not picturesque and no one came to see it as an example of Early English or indeed any other interesting period of architecture. It was red brick and solidly Victorian. If there had ever been an earlier foundation there was now no trace of it, unless in the deeper, boskier corners of the large graveyard behind the church where no doubt the ancient forefathers slept under grassy mounds with few, or fallen, headstones to mark their passing.

It was upon this untrodden area that the Vicarage windows looked out with discouraging blankness. It was a big building and looked older than the church. It did not appear to have suffered any attempts at modernization.

The Reverend Clive Cavendish greeted Kemp in the draughty gloom of the hall where the bright May sunshine tried to squeeze in behind him, but when the door closed the place was in darkness and it was only when they moved into what was obviously the drawing-room that Kemp was able to see his host properly.

Clive Cavendish was some years older than his sister. He too was tall but poked his head forward between hunched shoulders like a heron at rest. He had a smooth bland face with a voice to match. He wore a dusty black suit, and a long grey cardigan, the sleeves a little too short, which left the frayed cuffs of his white shirt exposed, lending a touch of pathos.

'Ah, Tullia, my dear, here is our guest. May we have some tea?'

Miss Cavendish greeted Kemp this time with composure, but made no attempt to hide the fact that she had met him before. She showed him to a straight-backed chair beside the sofa on which she had been sitting while she attended to the kettle set on a trivet before the very small fire smouldering in the marbled grate. She, like her brother, was soberly dressed in what appeared to be several layers of woollen clothes. Kemp wasn't surprised; the room was very cold.

On a round table in front of the fire—and taking from it any heat there was—tea was set on a lace cloth with old but well-polished silver, a cakestand bearing a sad sponge cake, four rather lumpy scones and an equal number of slices of currant bread. That's one each and one to go, thought Kemp, who was hungry.

He remarked on the size of the Vicarage and Clive responded by reciting a catalogue of its faults; the difficulties of heating, the inconsistencies of the plumbing, and the terrible cost of repairing the roof which leaked every winter.

'Of course we cannot use all the rooms,' said his sister, turning her large sad eyes on Kemp as though she saw, not him, but the emptiness of the upper floors.

'When it was built the incumbents were expected to maintain quite an establishment,' said the Vicar mildly, helping himself to a scone, 'and they had large families. Have you been into our church, Mr Kemp?'

Kemp had, but reserved judgement upon it. Having satisfactorily presented his Christian credentials, he merely remarked that the considerable ironwork and brasses must require much cleaning. This led Miss Cavendish into further lamentation.

'Even our church workers are a depleted force, Mr Kemp. The new town has not risen to the occasion. I do what I can with my women's groups but the young people take no interest. And now they are building this so-called community church...'

Kemp knew all about that since Elvira's husband, also moved out from Walthamstow, was a carpenter on the site.

'An interesting shape,' he remarked carefully.

'Vulgar, I should call it,' said Tullia Cavendish decisively, 'and it will probably be used for bingo sessions more than for worship.'

Clive spread his hands in a placatory gesture. 'These are modern times, my dear. Even the church must follow...'

He sounded unconvinced.

Lennox Kemp had not associated much with clergymen, his concepts haphazardly based on reading Trollope and, more recently, the novels of Barbara Pym. In his working life his contacts with them were few, their modest criminal activities confined to minor sexual offences while their means generally inhibited civil litigation. They tended to be a well-disciplined body, not merely by conscience alone but by the terms of the hierarchy. He had a certain admiration for their calling, appreciating that their poverty, though accepted in the spirit, must weigh heavily on their housekeeping.

That the present incumbent was no exception was evident from the surroundings. There had been money once—the heavy curtains hanging in ample folds from the pelmet festooned with gold Russia braid were of soft velvet, faded to old rose; the strewn rugs were Persian, their patterns long-dimmed to indeterminate colour; the silken lampshades were paper-thin; even the delicate china was chipped and the silver teaspoons in danger of disintegration. Yes, there had been money once. Now all was threadbare with use and the passage of time. There were still some splendid ornaments. On a massive sideboard two Chinese vases stood together as though it would take more than death duties to part them, and on a piecrust table at Kemp's right hand there was a collection of silver frames holding family photographs, the staring faces defying the flux of the days with mute indifference.

Tullia caught Kemp looking at them. 'That was my mother,' she said, singling out the foremost. Kemp took it up. A beautiful young woman in a white gown, with the ostrich feathers of a Court presentation. 'Yes,' went on Tullia simply and without noticeable arrogance although it was implicit, 'she was presented at Court. Of course when my turn came it was wartime. There were no Courts.'

'Alas, dear Tullia, those spacious days are gone,' said Clive, offering Kemp a piece of sponge cake, 'but your work in the parish will bring you a higher reward.'

Tullia Cavendish made no comment. Perhaps she did not share her brother's faith. He had turned to Kemp.

'I don't know what I would have done without my good sister all these years. She has been a tower of strength. The things she does single-handed! Even our humble parish magazine. We were given an old Gestetner copier and Tullia taught herself to type and she cuts the stencils and runs off the copies. Such things, my dear sir, are quite beyond me...'

'Oh, come now, Clive, it's not so much to do, and Julian helps when he has time...'

As she bent down to replenish the teapot the fire flared and showed up the pinched, self-disciplined mouth and the harsh lines of her face. She has eaten sour fruit, reflected Kemp, remembering what Lettice Warrender had told him.

Almost as if she'd read his thought she straightened her back and returned to her seat. She addressed him severely as though he had voiced an indiscretion.

'And are you married, Mr Kemp?'

'I was. I'm divorced.'

The word fell with a plop like a stone thrown in a pool.

The Vicar cleared his throat, and reached for Kemp's cup. 'Do have some more tea?'

'Thank you, no. I really must get down to the business that brings me here. I don't know whether you've been told the amount of the legacy, Miss Cavendish?'

She shook her head.

'Mrs Amaury has left you ten thousand pounds. Free of any transfer tax—that was the way she wanted it.'

A flush rose in Tullia's cheeks, and her eyes filled.

'Oh, my dear, how splendid!' The Reverend Clive went over and took her hands. 'Don't be upset. Rose was thinking of you...'

'I didn't know it was so much,' Tullia stammered. 'Do forgive me, Mr Kemp.'

'You deserved it, Tullia. You were a good friend to poor Rose, and she did not forget.'

'You too were not forgotten, Mr Cavendish,' said Kemp, giving her time to recover. 'There is a bequest to yourself as incumbent of Castleton St James of five thousand pounds. You understand, of course, this is not a personal bequest,' he hastened to add, 'otherwise it would not create a charitable trust... But Mrs Amaury expressed a wish it should be used towards the repair and maintenance of the church and its buildings. As you are probably aware, Mrs Amaury took an interest in various local charities in Newtown itself, and these have also been provided for very adequately.' He did not feel it either necessary or tactful to reveal that Rose Amaury had not neglected the new community church, nor the needs of Newtown's young people. She had been even-handed with her fortune, discriminating against no one.

'Dear, good Rose... I'm quite overwhelmed.' Clive Cavendish placed his fingertips together and brought them up towards his face in an attitude of deep thought, or prayer. He spoke almost to himself. 'I should not have grumbled so... But she was such a comfortable listener when I spoke of the needed repairs to our poor church ... I should have remembered these are but material things ...'

Kemp felt a sermon was brewing, and rose to take his leave. Miss Cavendish came from her seat by the fire, her eyes reddened but her face composed. The Vicar grasped Kemp's hand.

'Thank you for bringing us this news ... out of such sorrow there is hope. I cannot speak of her death. It was too dreadful. May God forgive her murderer!'

'He might just have done so,' said Kemp.

He was aware of the silence his words brought, but before he could make up his mind whether they were both digesting his use of the Deity's name—which in this house might be considered their prerogative—or whether they were merely working out the tenses in his remark, there came an interruption. The outer door slammed, there were footsteps in the hall, and a young man entered the room.

In fact Julian Cavendish was not as young as all that, being thirty-five, but a quickness of movement and a certain, thrusting stride made him appear so. He was of middle height, thick-set, with an alert look about him as though he were used to catching small boys out in punishable pursuits without losing his own concentration. Introduced to Kemp, he took him in with sharp dark eyes, and then went forward to scrutinize the remains of the tea-table.

Tullia Cavendish fluttered around him.

'We were not expecting you back so early, Julian. I'll make you some more tea.'

'I was cold,' said Julian, 'standing about the field with those wretched fourth-formers at rugby practice. I'd had enough, and so had they... I understand you're in the Newtown office, Mr Kemp. You'll know Mike Garrod?'

Kemp nodded. Mike was one of the younger probation officers, still idealistic, his belief in the possibilities for redemption a triumph of hope over experience.

'I help out now and then at the Youth Club,' went on Julian. 'Try to instruct the local lads in manly sports . . . I did a bit of boxing once.'

'Very commendable,' said Kemp.

'Makes a change from cramming French verbs and German grammar into my other lot of privileged little perishers.'

Kemp looked at him thoughtfully. Although he spoke of his work in the deprecating tone common to many schoolmasters, Julian Cavendish did not seem to conform to any conventional classroom image.

'Now, now, Julian, you know very well Culverwood's a fine school. You went there yourself, and so did Roger Warrender,' Tullia Cavendish fondly admonished her nephew as if he were merely a child acting up before visitors.

'Ah, my dear Aunt, and how that privilege still weighs upon me!' said Julian gaily. 'Allow me to hand you the kettle.' He swept it from the hearth and presented it to her with a bow.

'You talk a lot of nonsense,' she said, but she was smiling as she followed Kemp into the hall. Evidently Julian was a favourite of hers.

The Vicar had opened the front door to the sudden wealth of golden sunshine.

'There was one thing, Miss Cavendish, I wanted to ask you, if I may,' Kemp called to her as she went towards the kitchen. She paused, but did not turn round.

'Did Mrs Amaury ever ask you to do any typing for her?'

Tullia's back stiffened. There was a hard explosive crash as the kettle hit the bare wooden boards, and water splashed out across her feet. Clive Cavendish gave an exclamation of horror but seemed rooted to the spot so that it was Kemp who reached her first as she slid to the floor. He whipped off her shoes and pulled at her stockings. At least they're not tights, he thought as he wrestled desperately with the suspenders, I won't be upsetting her modesty. He uncovered her ankles and drew the stockings gently off. There were red marks across both insteps, but no sign of serious scalding. Kemp put his hand on the kettle. Fortunately it was only lukewarm though the water would still have been hot.

'I'm so very sorry.' He looked up at Clive Cavendish who was hovering ineptly but in some distress over his sister. Julian had rushed from the drawing-room, and now brought a cushion to put under her head. In a moment her eyelids flickered, then opened.

Kemp got to his feet. 'She'll be all right,' he said, 'there's no burn.'

Julian took his place beside his aunt. 'You simply dropped the kettle. There's no harm done. I'll help you up.'

'I'm sorry,' Kemp said again to the Vicar, and meant it. 'Perhaps I startled her...'

'My dear chap—it wasn't your fault. I don't know what could have happened... It's so unlike Tullia... But then she's been under a great strain these last weeks... Thank God there wasn't boiling water in that kettle... Perhaps you could give Julian a hand...'

Together they half-carried Miss Cavendish to a chair where she sat looking down at her bare legs.

'My stockings... Where are my stockings?'

'They're here, Aunt. And your shoes. But don't put them on yet. Just rest, and I'll get some cold water. There's no burn but the skin will be tender for a while.'

'Who took off my stockings?'

'I did, Miss Cavendish. I was afraid you'd been scalded.'

She looked at him then. He would not have thought it possible that such faded eyes could hold so much concealed hatred. Was it simply because he had touched her bare legs? There was certainly something old-maidish about her, and it was the second time in their brief acquaintance that he had violated her dignity.

Yet, as he left the Vicarage, he found that he was shaking. It wasn't easy to be the cause of what could have been a painful accident, and he knew himself to be that cause.

Although the Vicar had been unaware, Julian Cavendish had given Kemp several searching glances from those alert eyes of his. Had he heard the question put to his aunt? The drawing-room door had been open, and schoolmasters have well-trained ears.

It was all so obvious to Kemp. Who would Rose Amaury turn to if she had wanted one of her precious stories typed—the one that had shown such promise? Who but her dear, close friend who typed well enough to put together the parish magazine.

NINE

THE UNTIMELY DEMISE of Kevin Roding brought a sense of dissatisfaction into Newtown as well as to those concerned with Castleton House and the family there. Nobody likes an unfinished story, and many felt they'd been robbed of the final outcome—an exciting chase, trial and TV coverage. Lionel and Paula voiced their disapproval of police ineptitude in allowing the escape to Holland, though they would have bitterly resented any accusation that there was an element of frustrated vengeance in their feelings.

Roger, who had returned from Cambridge for his grandmother's funeral—a private ceremony attended only by the family—was not so inhibited. He and Torvil Amaury had had a wary rivalry in boyhood, hardened now into veiled animosity, but they were at one in condemning young Roding for taking the soft way out, ignoring the official view that he had been coshed. They were both strong adherents of capital punishment and declared he should not have been allowed to get away with it without paying his debt to society. Hearing of this from Richard Amaury, Kemp, who had known more murderers than either of them was ever likely to meet, was unimpressed. The cousins would soon come into a sizeable fortune, and it was not apparent that they had paid much attention to their grandmother in her later years.

Richard himself was simply glad the whole thing was over, and showed a doctor's wider tenderness.

'Tell Mrs Roding I'm sorry...' Kemp promised to do so; it would be the only message passing between the two houses.

He had heard nothing from Lettice Warrender, and chafed at her silence as much as he wondered at her anger. He badly wanted to see her again.

In the meantime, on a rainy morning he found himself attending Kevin Roding's funeral. Fortunately for the Reverend Clive Cavendish, who could well have been faced with an impossible duty, it was held in the Methodist Chapel. There was no police presence—it was hardly their business any more, though Kemp caught a glimpse of Mike Garrod well in the background.

Kevin might have been no great shakes as a criminal but Newtown turned out in force to give him a last farewell. The chapel was crowded, and certainly the younger element, shuffling their feet and uncomfortably buttoned up, hadn't come to hear the Minister's homely address which was a model of tactful elision, leaning more to the woes of the bereaved mother than to any notorious activities of the deceased. His life had been short but he should none the less be mourned as a son; the manner of his death was not referred to.

Nor was there any indication in the floral tributes laid out by the grave and inspected by an inquisitive Kemp that Kevin Roding had been other than a blameless youth: 'From Len and Ron', 'Auntie Dolly and Bob', 'Aunt Bessie Higgins and Cousin Steve', 'From all your pals at the Club, Kev.', 'In sadness from Gloria', 'To my brother from Ted', and of course 'From your loving Mother...' The rain splashed down and the ink on the little cards trickled into the drowning blooms.

Margaret Roding stood by the graveside, flanked by Bessie on the one hand and stalwart Ted, uneasy in a midnight blue suit a size too small for him on the other. Kemp looked at him with interest. The prison pallor was still on the man but he had none of the beaten look of his mother; his face was hard, and the set of his big shoulders gave an impression of contained power. There was nothing particularly thuggish about his features, which in fact resembled his mother's, but he looked capable of mischief. Around him were several of his cronies who glanced at him covertly as he stood until the final rites were over, and they followed him as he turned away with his arm round Mrs Roding.

Kemp went towards his car, more saddened than he had expected to be. It's probably the rain, he thought, conscious of a dripping collar. He was about to drive off when there was a rattling on his window and the face of Bessie Higgins appeared. He opened the passenger door.

'Get in,' he shouted to her, and she came round and wedged her great bulk in beside him.

'What'd you come for?' she demanded, belligerence as natural an opening to her as politeness is to others. Recognizing this, Kemp didn't bother to answer.

'Anyway... nice of you, all the same. Maggie said so. Them others, well, they're all pals of Ted's, aren't they? And Kev's, of course. Stands to reason they'd come. Proper respects, like, despite what's bein' said. He weren't a bad lad, our Kev... not really.'

'I didn't know him, Bessie. And I'm not a judge.'

Her black eyes glowered at him.

'None of that other lot came... Maggie could have done with a gesture at least... All that time she worked for Mrs Amaury...'

'Come on, Bessie, be sensible. It wouldn't be possible.'

'They think like what the police do...' Bessie was resigned to an acceptance of the way of the world as she had found it. 'They' were authority as they'd always been; they believed in law and order—their order, every man in his place according to his function, and she, Bessie, the Rodings and their like were at the bottom of the heap and must be kept there lest society break down. It was clear enough to Kemp. Oh, they even quoted Shakespeare to their point these days as they had once pointed the finger at the French Revolution: 'Take but degree away, untune that string, And hark, what discord follows!'

But Shakespeare's Ulysses was an arch old twister any-way; he'd have sold his mother down the river to make a political point with his fellow Greeks.

'What did you want to see me about?' he prompted Bessie, relinquishing mere philosophy for more basic realities.

'Not me. I don't want no help.' She bridled, pulling her raincoat tight round her bodice. 'It's Ted.' She finally got the words out as if having a tooth extracted.

'Ted wants to see me?'

She nodded.

'Why'd he not come himself?'

She spoke slowly. 'Well, it's not like he just wants to see you... That was my idea... on account of the things he's been saying...'

Kemp waited. There was no use trying to hurry her. He offered her a cigarette.

'Given them up, haven't I? Dirty habit, but you go right ahead, Mr Kemp.'

'What if we go somewhere warm and dry and have a cup of tea, Mrs Higgins?'

'Not anywheres around here...' She looked as startled as though he'd suggested an apéritif preparatory to rape.

'OK,' said Kemp, starting the engine. 'You're ashamed to be seen with me. We'll go to my place.'

Bessie sniffed at his household arrangements, took over the tea-making, and brewed a strong cup. She looked with favour at the contents of his biscuit barrel. Kemp knew she was only playing for time.

Settled at last, replete with tea and a handful of choco-late bourbons, she came to the point.

'What Ted says is, Kev was set up.'

'Set up?'

'For the job on Mrs Amaury.'

'You're saying he was framed?' That old delinquents' tale: 'Please, sir, it weren't me...' Right out of the school-room, or the Juvenile Court for that matter.

'Call it what you like. Ted says Kev was set up.'

Kemp sighed. 'Brother Ted's only saying that to make it easier on his mother. Believe me, Bessie, the police had a watertight case. They even got his fingerprints, you know, from that glass cabinet... Kevin was there all right.'

Bessie was silenced, but not for long.

'Ted says... Ted's not denyin' he might have been there,' she said, stubbornly. 'Look, I'm only goin' on what I hear...the talk between Ted and his mates. I listened...then I tackled him. He says it were a set-up, that Kev was played for a patsy... Kev got money...'

Kemp pricked up his ears at that. He hadn't believed the police theory that Kevin had money stashed away. Kevin Roding was a spender. Kemp's pet garage-hand—a mine of information in this field—had told him young Roding had just bought another motorbike. The police had found it in the shed behind 32 Runnymede Crescent, but it hadn't been used on the night of the killing—he'd stolen a car. Panic? It looked like it.

'Where'd Kevin get this money from?'

'Ted's not saying. Will you see him, Mr Kemp?'

Consorting with known criminals—particularly one just out of jail—was scarcely the best way to build up a respectable practice. Kemp hesitated.

'Kevin was on probation, wasn't he? Was that his officer at the funeral—Mr Garrod?'

She nodded. 'He were fair to Kev—I'll say that for him,' she said grudgingly. 'Got him in at the Youth Club...somewhere to go, like, when he were on the dole. Kev didn't like it much, said it were only for kids. Kev was near grown-up...'

'He was twenty-two and had already set out on a life of crime, Bessie,' Kemp remarked sternly. 'That reminds me, I didn't see any sign of any father Roding today?'

'Died in prison, didn't he? Just after Maggie and the boys come to Newtown. He were a nice man, Josh Roding, but he never enjoyed good health...' she added reminiscently.

It was a fitting, if uncensorious, epitaph for one who'd spent most of his years behind bars, but Bessie, like Kemp, never set herself up in judgement.

Kemp made up his mind. 'I'll arrange through Mr Garrod for Ted to come and see me at my office. Now I'll run you back to Runnymede Crescent—or you'll miss the baked meats.'

More drink than meat was being taken at the crowded little house as Kemp pushed his way in behind Bessie Higgins. He ignored Ted—better that any words between them should be handled professionally and Kemp intended to be scrupulously circumspect in that—and made straight for Margaret Roding. She sat with the women, a damp handkerchief clutched at her work-weary hands. She looked up at Kemp with eyes that had cried themselves blind.

'Thank you for being in chapel,' she said simply.

'I came to tell you that Richard Amaury sends you his condolences. He is very sorry about your son, Kevin, and wishes me to tell you so.'

He turned away before the tears came again. With a brief nod at Bessie he walked out through the cluster of youths draining beercans and munching sausage rolls in the passage, and went to his car. He still had an afternoon's work to get done.

Even after six o'clock he stayed on, smoking, drinking coffee from the new dispenser, and sorting out his thoughts. Tomorrow he would have a word with Mike Garrod.

He no more trusted Ted Roding than he would a king cobra but there would be no harm in listening to what the man had to say. Besides, he was curious; there were many things about the death of Rose Amaury that still left him uneasy. In his mind he went over the police case, spelled out to him in various conversations with Inspector Upshire. It was true what he'd told Bessie about Kevin Roding's fingerprints on that cabinet. Upshire had been terse: 'Bloody idiot—took off his gloves to fiddle with the latch...' Kemp remembered the pretty showcase, the gleam of silver behind the glass, the china figurines, the small but precious mementoes Rose had cherished, the filigree inlay of the lock, and the tiny key. Yes, too delicate to open with gloves on... He could have smashed the fragile case but that would have made a noise. It was the crash of the fallen vase which had wakened her, brought her, stick in hand, to the door of the parlour.

But the police had no doubt that Kevin had been there that night. Mrs Roding had polished the furniture the morning before. So much she had told the police—with sullen pride. Yes, she'd always kept the place clean. Of course they'd not said a word to her about fingerprints, so that when she said her son hadn't been to Mrs Amaury's for weeks—there'd been no heavy work in the garden for him to do—she wasn't aware of the trend of their questions.

Inexorably the police had built up their case. The stolen car had disappeared that same night from the car park of the public house in the shopping parade just across the main road from Castleton House. The owner had been in the pub until closing time, decided he'd drunk far too much, and walked home a law-abiding citizen—and blistering mad the next morning to find his car had gone.

Carefully Kemp considered all aspects of Kevin Roding. It was possibly just within his scope to have tied that wire across the steps, or driven a car at Rose when she emerged from her small gate. Or both. To cause an accident, get her out of the way while he rifled her house? When these stratagems failed did he simply wait till she was at last alone at night? He would be one to know, a casual inquiry of his mother would give him that information. It all fitted very nicely. Kevin Roding was a dead ringer for the job. Very apt.

'The Dutch police?' Inspector Upshire had shrugged his shoulders, 'It's just another mugging to them... Path. report showed he'd been coshed and was probably unconscious when he went in the water. Cause of death was drowning. None of the stuff he took was found but it'll turn up sooner or later. It wasn't of any value...'

Neither apparently had been Kevin Roding's life. Now that the young malefactor lay in the churchyard the case had been buried with him.

TEN

TED RODING SHOWED UP in Kemp's office two days later with Mike Garrod in tow—not the other way round. In fact young Garrod looked distinctly uneasy; he was an energetic and enthusiastic officer with the local lads in his charge, but a hard man from the London end whose contempt for the whole probation service was blatant presented a challenge Garrod didn't altogether relish. He slipped a folder on to Kemp's desk—Ted's record.

'Thanks, Mike, I don't think you need stay.'

When he'd gone Kemp flipped the pages. He wasn't really interested in what Ted Roding had been up to in the past. It had only served as an excuse to see him; Kemp preferred to make his own assessment.

Ted leaned back making the chair creak. He spread his legs and rolled a cigarette, to make it plain the surroundings weren't going to intimidate him.

'Smoke if you want to,' said Kemp, 'I can give you fifteen minutes.'

Roding scowled, eased the heavy belt securing his check shirt inside his tight jeans, and remarked truculently that he hadn't wanted to come.

'Then why're you here? Nobody forced you.'

Ted's opinion of lawyers—if such as he could be said to have anything so intellectual as an opinion—was low. There had been occasions when they'd got him off; then he'd give himself full marks for cunning rather than give them the credit. More often they'd restricted their efforts to persuading him to cop a plea—in his view they were all in cahoots with the police anyway—and such mitigation as they could manufacture on the spur of the moment in Court before the inevitable sentence. In his erratic pilgrimage from the Juvenile Court, through several appearances before Inner London Sessions, and finally the Old Bailey, Ted Roding had gained wide experience of the legal profession, and thought he knew it all. Actually he'd learned nothing, save that they represented the Enemy.

For his part, Kemp was fully aware of the closed circuit; he could see right into Roding's thick head and out the other side. There wasn't much in between. He waited as a lion tamer waits, to see which way this big cat would jump.

'I'll pay you,' Ted said at last. In his world that always made the buggers sit up and take notice.

'For what?' asked Kemp carelessly.

'I'll pay you a fee, like...'

'I don't take fees. What I take are costs.'

Ted glared at him, shifted his black leather boots, and his ground.

'I want you to do a job for me, see?'

'No, I don't see.'

They weren't getting anywhere but Kemp wasn't in a hurry. He looked out of the window, and made no effort to suppress a yawn.

Ted dragged his chair up, and thumped the desk-top with a fist.

'Ain't you interested? I thought you lawyers took on all sorts of clients...'

'Well, I don't.'

'Look, Bessie said you were good. I've bin asking around. I found out about you. You were with an agency—private tec, like. Down in Walthamstow.'

'What if I was?'

'A private dick's better than lawyers any day. No crap with the old Bill, get me? A private dick has to go along with his client, the one who pays him, right?'

'You talking to yourself, Mr Roding, or do you want me to listen?'

Ted's scowl deepened. Whatever he wanted, the interview wasn't going his way. That didn't worry Kemp.

'What the hell!' Ted sat back and started to roll another
thin cigarette. Kemp pushed the ashtray forward to receive
the blackened stump of the last. He wasn't smoking himself. He rarely did in the office except when he was alone and
wanted to think, or sometimes when the company was congenial. It wasn't at the moment.

Ted just looked at him expectantly. 'Ain't you supposed
to be askin' me questions?'

'What about?'

'Jesus! Why d'you bloody well think I'm here?'

'I don't know. You tell me. But don't take all day.'

It erupted in the end like a burst water main. Ted slouched
forward suddenly, his bluster gone, his face caved in, the big
hands falling limply to his sides.

'It's our Kev... He didn't oughter go like that... It's gotta
be seen to. What I mean is...his name's gotta be cleared.
Our Mum...she can't live with that...not for the rest of her
life. Oh God, if only I'd known... Look, Mr Kemp, you've
gotta do somethin'...'

Kemp got up and retrieved the burning roll-up from the
carpet where it had fallen from the man's fingers. When he
got back behind his desk, Ted Roding had recovered enough
to take a dirty piece of tissue from his pocket and blow his
nose.

'Right,' said Kemp. 'Now we're getting some place. And
I'll ask the questions. What did you and Kevin talk about
the last time he visited you in the Scrubs? When was that, by
the way?'

'I'd just got the whisper, see? Day before he come...'

'When?' barked Kemp.

Ted's mind was no calendar; it was slow going getting a
date out of him. Prison time would pass in a grey proces-
sion of days, but Ted had been due for release and that must
have been a light at the end of the tunnel.

'It were urgent. A job wanted doin' out of Newtown. Nothin' much, they said...just a break-in. There'd be money. Not in the place, like, but afterwards...'

'How much!'

'One thou. Some before...for expenses. Then when the job was done there'd be more.'

'Getaway laid on?'

'Yus...money...in notes, and a car...'

'To the Continent?'

'I dunno, do I? All I'd to do was give them a name.'

'And you gave them Kevin?'

'I weren't to know, was I?' There was rising panic in Ted's voice. 'They said it was urgent, couldn't wait...' There was resentment too in Ted's tone, and illumination dawned on Kemp.

The whisper had come to Ted, Ted was due for release, there was a lot of money in it; Ted himself would have relished a job like that. But, suddenly, there was urgency and Ted still had time to do, so he'd given them his brother—keep it in the family.

And the date of Kevin's prison visit had been the day before Rose died. Anger drove Kemp's next question.

'Exactly what were you to tell Kevin?'

'He were just to wait at home, like. He'd get instructions.'

'Is that all?'

Ted shook his head vigorously. 'There weren't no more... Only that it had to be done quick, like... The whisper was that the coast was clear and they couldn't wait no longer.' The whine was back in Ted's voice. 'How was I to know the way it would go...?'

'Murder,' said Kemp coldly.

'Jesus!' Ted breathed. 'There weren't any talk of killing. D'you think I'd've told them our Kev? There weren't no talk of killing...'

'Just simple straightforward burglary? What did they want taken?'

'I swear I never heard. You've got to believe me, Mr Kemp. If there'd been any talk of harm to anybody, it's God's truth, I'd never have given them Kevin.'

Kemp looked at him thoughtfully. It was probably true.

'He'd not been in the game long enough, our Kev. He'd never been up on even a GBH. He weren't in that class. It were only a break-in, the job, like...'

'One thousand pounds is a lot of money to pay out for a burglary. Someone wanted something pretty badly. Any idea what it was?'

'I swear to God, I never knew. There was just this whisper...the place, Newtown... All they wanted was a guy who knew the place.'

'Funny the whisper came to you, Ted?' The time had come—if it had ever been—to drop the Mr Roding. Kemp was entering his own field; he could feel his antennae rising out of the bumps on his forehead, that stirring of the senses the huntsman gets when the dogs trace the scent. He repeated his words: 'Funny the whisper came to you, Ted.'

'Well, I'd come from Newtown, hadn't I?'

'And was the specific address given in the whisper?' Kemp watched his man closely.

'No...I swear to God...'

'Look, Ted, I think the Almighty's tired right now of checking out your credit.'

'Uuh?'

'Never mind. So you didn't know it was Mrs Amaury's house that was to be burgled?'

'No! I swear to...'

'OK. All you did was give the name of somebody you knew in Newtown who was prepared to commit burglary?'

'That's all it was. Only, afterwards, I were inside, weren't I? What the hell could I do? Sure, I heard about the old lady's death...at first it didn't connect. Then they were after our Kev. The bastards!'

'Who, Ted? The Police? They'd every reason.'

'Those other bastards... Them that put him up to it.'

'It was you that put him up to it.'

Ted Roding shook his head and shoulders like a bull at bay. Kemp could see he was running out of words.

'All right,' he said briskly, 'What have we got? Just a whisper. Where'd the whisper come from?' But Kemp knew there'd be no answer to that, even as Ted shook his head once more. Exercise time, shuffling men, feeding time, the clatter of mugs, the gabble of mouths, like calling to like, mastodons bellowing across a swamp... There'd be no names, no descriptions from that quarter. Kemp sighed, and got up wearily from his chair.

'I'll do what I can, Ted. No promises, and you'll pay what it costs my firm. That's all for today.'

Ted Roding got slowly to his feet.

'One thing,' Kemp said as he opened the door. 'Keep your lip buttoned about this. No blabbing to your mates that you've got a lawyer in your pocket. I want none of that kind of talk. Get me?'

'Sure, Mr Kemp. I won't say nothin' to anybody.'

'And if you hear any more whispers you're to come straight to me.'

As the door closed behind his latest and most unlikely of clients, Kemp thought grimly: If there's any truth at all in Ted's tale—if it's not made up of sawdust and ashes—then Ted's the one to scrabble around the shifting population of the Scrubs.

All the same, he considered, as he skimmed Ted Roding's record before handing it back to Garrod, these dates might be useful; and there's that chap at McCready's who specializes in ex-cons. He lifted the phone.

ELEVEN

IF LENNOX KEMP had been a proper 'private eye', or 'tec' or 'dick'—however Ted Roding's limited vision encompassed it—every minute of his time would have been spent scurrying about in pursuit of clues. But as his duty lay with Gillorns who paid him, the daily round and common task must furnish him with more prosaic demands. Room to deny myself, he muttered—his mind running to hymns—the pleasure of the chase.

Only in the evenings could he follow his own bent, indulge his propensity for doubt and his insatiable inquisitiveness as to motive and cause, and the general whys and wherefores of people's actions. Of course he could have elevated it all to a higher plane; the aspiration to shape things into some form of impossible justice. But, basically, he knew it was the ferret's instinct, to root about at ground level, or below it, to shake out a meaning from the matted web of inconsequential happenings.

As for justice, well, had there been really a miscarriage of that august concept in the case of Kevin Roding? He had never been charged; he was now beyond trial. Did that mean he was also beyond justice?

Kemp's rooting about, as he liked to think of it, had by the end of another week brought him only scraps. Bert Dobbs of McCready's Agency had indeed found a former cell-mate of Roding's who swore that there had been a whisper all right in the Scrubs. The amount of money for the job to be done in Newtown varied but it was large enough for it to be whistled at. Where the whisper came from, no dice; it might as well have arisen like a miasma from a crack in the prison floor. There were rumours about a gang going for the antique market, that it was to be a wages snatch at one of the factories on the industrial estate, a raid on Newtown's first department store, even the jewellers in the cobbled square opposite Kemp's office was mentioned, but not a breath of the name Amaury, or the address of either Castleton House or the bunglaow at its gates came through from Dobbs's various meetings with the criminal fringe who lapped in and out of prison like seaweed caught up in rock pools.

Yet, it confirmed Ted Roding's story—and that was enough to whet Kemp's appetite. He went over to the police station and bothered Detective-Sergeant Cobbins.

'Look, Mr Kemp, I've told you all we've got. You've seen our file—the rest's at the Yard. As far as we're concerned the case is over. You trying to make out Kevin Roding wasn't guilty? There weren't no sign anyone else was there that night. And it were just the kind of bungled job a young villain like Kevin would get up to. I'm sorry for his ma but I'd had trouble enough these last few years from her boys so I wouldn't waste sympathy on either of them. Go and worry Inspector Upshire if you must,' he finished plaintively, 'I've got enough on my hands...'

But John Upshire, too, was beginning to be exasperated by Kemp's insistence. 'Prison rumours!' he scoffed, 'I thought you'd more sense than to fall for that one. As far as that lot's concerned, none of them are ever guilty. What do you want the Yard's papers for? Quennell's satisfied. They've closed their file. My God, even Lionel Warrender's stopped firing rockets... What's got into you? You taking it personal because you knew the old lady? Forget it.'

'Couldn't you have a word with Inspector Quennell, and get him to let me have a look at their documents on the case?' Kemp was at his most persuasive. 'I'm still Mrs Amaury's executor. You could always say I wanted to clear up some minor point about the stolen items...'

'Richard Amaury has an inventory—you know as well as I do that the stuff was trivial. You're a persistent bugger when you get the bit between your teeth, I'll say that for you... OK, I'll get on to the Yard. And now, for heaven's sake, leave me alone!'

And then, quite suddenly, all avenues were blocked; the holes in the ground that a mole like Kemp could burrow into were stopped up by an earthfall from above.

It started with a call from Head Office.

'Mr Archibald is on the phone for you,' said Elvira the next morning. 'He wants to talk to you urgently.'

The Senior Partner's voice was cracked but clear.

'Kemp? I want you here as soon as possible—say, this afternoon at three o'clock.'

'I'm due in Court in half an hour. Might take all day.'

'Get someone else to handle it. You've got young Lambert out there. Use him. I want you here.' The line went dead.

Edwin Lambert was inexperienced in other than plain run-of-the-mill conveyancing, but he was keen. 'I'll come with you this morning,' Kemp told him, 'introduce you to the witnesses, set up the case for you—if it goes into the afternoon, you're on your own.'

By lunch-time they hadn't been called but Lambert was confident he could manage. Kemp was running down the steps of the Courthouse when he met Inspector Upshire coming up. Upshire caught hold of his arm.

'I don't know what the hell you've been up to, Lennox, but you're mighty unpopular all of a sudden. That request of yours to the Yard—sure, I passed it on. And got a blistering reply. On no account are you to get a sight of the Amaury murder file. Inspector Quennell was furious that you should even ask.'

Kemp stared.

'And what's more,' went on the Inspector, jabbing his finger as if to nail home the words, 'you're to get no more cooperation from my station either. I've been told off good and proper for letting you meddle in the first place. You've offended somebody very high up, I can tell you that much.'

And the Inspector stumped off, leaving Kemp standing with his ears buzzing. That was a flea in the ear, he thought to himself as he went for the London train.

Things weren't any better at Clement's Inn. Kemp's reception by Mr Gillorn was chilly. He had been sent straight in. The old man shook his hand briefly, then reseated himself behind the big mahogany desk that his grandfather had bought in the Tottenham Court Road over a hundred years ago. The rest of the furniture and the surroundings, to Kemp's eye, hadn't changed much in those hundred years. The panelling was dark oak, rising into the shadows of a yellowed ceiling where dusty stucco roses had looked down on a century of reasoned argument and patient endeavour, to say nothing of velvet-gloved chicanery, as clients and their affairs played themselves out to more or less satisfactory conclusions in the room below.

Kemp wasn't given much time to gaze about him. This was not to be the usual leisurely chat over cigars and good port. The eighty-year-old was sharp, and to the point.

'It's the Amaury case, Lennox. From what I've been hearing, you've been asking too many questions.'

'The Amaury case is closed. At least that's the official view, but..'

'And it must remain closed. Before too many people get hurt.'

'So that's it—the Warrenders. I didn't think they had so much influence.'

'I never mentioned the Warrenders. But think, just think for a moment, of the effect on them if you go on the way you're doing. Paula Warrender has lost her mother, the young people their grandmother...in hideous circumstances. Already they've had to face distressing publicity. All this modern nastiness of the so-called media...' The heavy-lidded eyes held anger and sadness. 'As if her death weren't unspeakable enough. Rose Amaury is at rest—they too must be left in peace.'

Kemp said nothing. You're breaking my heart, you old charlatan, he felt like saying but knew it neither wise nor polite to be flippant with the elderly. He did wonder, however, if the time had not come to divulge Rose Amaury's suspicions that her life had been threatened. So far he had told no one; he had thought to wait till he himself was certain. Surely that was what she had meant when she asked for his discretion? You could not take fresh instruction from the dead.

Yet it seemed unfair to burden this tortoise-like creature with a mystery he was himself unable to solve; so he said nothing.

'Haven't you anything to say? Lost for words, are ye? Humph...you've been saying plenty...to the police...and to others. Well, it's got to stop.' The head had shot out; now it retracted into the carapace.

Kemp allowed himself one word: 'Why?'

'Because I say so. Isn't that enough?'

'No.'

'Don't rile me, Lennox Kemp. I can make you or break you. I'll not be spoken to like that.'

Kemp held his rising anger.

'I'm sorry, sir. I really am. I won't go against you or the firm, you know that. I only want to know why I should not pursue inquiries of my own—inquiries which I think are warranted.'

The old man sighed. 'I should have known better than to employ someone like you, Kemp.' His voice was hoarse. 'Get me a drink.'

Silently Kemp went over to the cupboard and brought out a decanter and water jug.

'And for yourself, damn you.'

Kemp took the two glasses over, poured the drinks and sat down.

'I can't help it,' he said patiently as he watched the
gnarled brown hand shake as the tumbler was lifted. 'I have
to know...'

Archie Gillorn took out an enormous white handkerchief and wiped his mouth.

'Ye're a fool. You mean well, but ye're a fool. This time
you'll not get further. Oh, I know all about what you've
done in the past. Tenacity, they call it. But not with this
case. You must accept what I say—there are to be no more
inquiries into Rose Amaury's death, d'ye understand?'

'No, I don't understand.'

'Then accept it without understanding. I do.'

'What do you know about it?'

'Nothing. And I don't want to. She's dead, and the young
man is dead. We have only to consider the living.'

Kemp considered them, and was not satisfied.

'And what if I don't accept?'

'Then ye're in trouble. And so's my firm.'

'Why should the firm be in trouble if I make inquiries on
my own? What harm will that do?'

'More than you think. Don't try to bamboozle me, young
man. If you go ahead with what you seem to imagine can be
a private investigation, ye'll be digging your own grave—
professionally. Take my advice, leave it alone.'

Kemp drank the almost neat spirit he'd poured for himself and looked at the wrinkled face in front of him where
deep furrows made the waxy skin into the creased vellum of
ancient documents. There was wisdom behind that stretched
skull; a lifetime in the law, the example of his forebears had
made Archibald Gillorn a model of prudence. Yet he too
must have at some time taken his chances; that neck now
mere sinewy ropes must have been stuck out on behalf of
clients when they had cause. At his age he ought to be im-
mune to pressure.

'Is it the Warrenders?'

The scaly lids drooped. 'Lennox. You're fatiguing me.'

'I'm sorry. I shouldn't have asked.'

An impatient hand brushed his apology aside.

'You'll make me say more than I should. All I can tell you is that there are higher levels involved in this. A directive has come from certain quarters...'

'A directive? To us? What, through the Law Society?' Now Kemp was really startled.

Archie Gillorn shook his head. 'Not from the Law Society. But you're catching on. I'd a thought to stop you before you got this far. But, yes, a directive...from the powers that be.'

'Phew! I never realized we moved in such circles. How did they get on to Gillorns?'

Archie pursed his lips. 'The word was passed to me at the Club. And I'm not telling you by whom. My lips are sealed—if I may quote...'

'*That* high up? You'll be saying next that M15 is involved!' Kemp could not keep the note of sarcasm from his voice.

'M15 or 6—I can never remember the numbers—much prefer words... Anyway those chaps who deal with our security, heaven help us... Now ye've already made me say too much. Far too much for someone like you, I dare say. You have a faculty for making people talk, Kemp—it must be something to do with that innocent puggy face of yours...'

Kemp wasn't aware that his face was registering anything other than dumb amazement. Was the old man having him on? M15 indeed! Directives from on high? Was this supposed to be a joke?

But Archie was becoming petulant again. 'Why can't ye take an order like anybody else? Why'd I have to argue with you? Just have the goodness to accede to my request and stop meddling in the Amaury case.'

Meddling. That was the word John Upshire had used.

'I don't know what to think, sir. I'm just astounded, that's all. Are you seriously putting it to me that national security is threatened by my inquiries?'

'I'm saying nothing more. I want no part of it. I'm simply giving you an order, loud and clear, and you'd better
take heed of it. Do I get your promise?'

Kemp thought about it. They can't stop me thinking.
Who? Who are they anyway?

'What form should my promise take? Do you want it in
writing?'

He got a baleful glare.

'I should have thought as between professional gentlemen your word would be enough,' said Archie Gillorn
gruffly.

'And if I don't give it?'

'You'd disappoint me, Lennox.'

How adroit the old schemer was. He'd made the only reply Kemp could not get round.

But the promise thus extracted from him he made sure
was a guarded one: that their conversation would go no
further; that he would not involve the firm in anything to do
with Rose Amaury's death beyond his strict duty as her executor; that he would desist from any investigation on his
own. 'Unless,' said Kemp, taking a last stand, 'something
should perhaps come to my ears without effort on my part.'

'H'm, what's that supposed to mean? No, don't tell me.
If you choose to be insubordinate, on your own head be it.
Just don't come running to me if you get into trouble.'

Kemp grinned. 'That's a promise I can give without con-
ditions,' he said, rising. The interview was at an end.

AT LEAST I GOT the last word, he thought in the train as the
flat lands out of London flashed green and grey beyond the
carriage windows, but it was small consolation. He'd known
frustration before in previous cases but never to this extent,
never had the forces ranged against him brought such powers to bear. The police, his own profession, and now the
State, he reflected, his mind wrestling with the problems of
who, and why. All it needs is the Church.

That came too before the end of the day. Another visitation—this time from even higher Authority, if the Reverend Clive Cavendish was truly in the service of the Almighty. In fact he was off-duty when he met Kemp as though by chance in the cobbled square where the lawyer was leaving the office at seven o'clock.

'Ah, Mr Kemp, how fortuitous that we should meet. I was ... ah ... doing some late shopping in the supermarket. Not quite my field, I'm afraid. I find the music most distracting ...'

'You wanted to see me, Vicar?' Kemp wondered how long the reverend gentleman had been hanging around in the store watching the lights of the office.

'Well, now that by happy accident we've met ... What a nice little place they've made of the square ... I wonder if these trees will really ever grow out of the pavements—they don't look very pleased to be boarded up but doubtless nature will find a way ... Of course I don't usually shop in Newtown—that's my Tullia's province, but she's ... ah ... not well enough yet ...'

'I'm sorry to hear it. Is she not recovered from that accident?'

'Oh, I think so ... I really think so. It wasn't serious. But she's been under strain ... Mr Kemp, I have to ask you something.'

'Fire away.'

It was a somewhat peremptory request to make of a man who was accustomed to taking half an hour to reach the nub of his text but Kemp's weary brevity made the Vicar comply with it.

'My sister is at present very low in her spirit ... The death of her dear friend preys on her mind. It would be—er—inadvisable for her to be worried by any further visits from you.' Clive Cavendish suddenly stopped as though appalled at his own words. 'My dear chap, I meant nothing personal. Oh, dear me, no. That's not what I meant at all ...'

'I had not intended calling on Miss Cavendish again. Settling the legacies left by Mrs Amaury can quite easily be done by letter. She will not, I trust, be upset by my writing to her?'

Mr Cavendish looked as if the burden of Atlas had been taken from his shoulders. He straightened up and flapped his arms.

'Capital idea...yes, yes, that would be splendid. So good of you not to take it personally. Tullia is not normally so...um...sensitive.' He paused and stooped to pick up the carrier bag of groceries he had placed on the pavement beside him. 'I'm glad we've met, Mr Kemp, and that you have been so understanding. It has taken a weight from my mind. Now I must find my car...' He looked vaguely around as if unsure where he had left it.

'I should not have thought your sister unduly sensitive,' said Kemp, determined at least to get his word in. 'She seems to me a very competent woman and well able to handle most situations.'

'Oh, indeed so. Indeed she is. But she is susceptible to—er—gossip. In a place like ours, Mr Kemp, there does tend to be . . . gossip.'

'Gossip? What about?'

Clive Cavendish was not used to being pinned down by direct questions. He shifted his load of provisions from one arm to the other, and gazed at the lighted windows above the shops.

'Ah, now there you have me... Gossip...rumours...I take no notice, of course, but things like that worry Tullia. I believe she heard that there are—um—further inquiries being made... It's all so very distressing. There are some things better left alone, Mr Kemp. Let the dead rest... We cannot help them. Let not the living suffer...' His voice—high Anglican, upper register—dropped to a sonorous whisper; the beaked nose thrust itself forward a few inches above Kemp's head so that the shorter man felt he was about to be pecked by an eagle. 'I do beseech you, my dear chap, to have a care. What you are doing may be wrong...'

Kemp stepped back. There was no doubt that Cavendish was in earnest. Kemp had a moment of compunction.

'I've no wish to harm anyone, living or dead,' he said quietly. 'You have my assurance on that. Please tell Miss Cavendish I shall not call upon her again, unless invited to do so. And now, Vicar, can I help you to find your car?'

Relieved at last to be in the safety and privacy of his own home—for unpopularity cannot help but breed a certain paranoia—Kemp unwrapped his Chinese take-away and popped it in the oven while he got himself a long drink of beer. It had been a hard day.

Shredding the events through his mind, he pulled out the most important, the most portentous, and examined it in detail. Archie Gillorn was as meticulous in his use of words as he was in a discreet forbearance of them; his very reticence spoke for him. As for the wily old bird saying too much—experienced lawyers were in the habit of erring on the other side. So it had been a hint, the merest ghost of a hint but a hint nevertheless; the directive from on high had indeed come from those responsible for Intelligence—in the widest sense. It was also a hint to put Kemp on his guard while warning him off some dangerous ground, perilous territory, an area trodden only by those authorized to do so.

As he drifted off to sleep that night, an image troubled the edge of his thoughts, an image of barbed wire and sinister watch-towers. Although facts were his business, Kemp believed in intuition; when facts are scarce there is nothing else for it but that leap into the unknown.

TWELVE

AN ADVISORY LETTER had come into the office from the firm's stockbrokers necessitating liaison with Dr Amaury as to the sale of his mother's holdings. Kemp sent it on to him with a brief note expecting a reply at arm's length in view of the invisible wall that appeared to have been erected between himself and the Warrender family.

Not so. Elvira informed him that Richard Amaury would be coming in on Thursday to discuss the matter. Kemp sighed. Here goes, he thought; another chilly interview, another admonition not to meddle. Hands off my relatives.

But Richard, entering Kemp's room, appeared no different in his manner. He was as friendly as he had always been and their discussion proceeded equably and without argument.

'Well, that's settled, then. Thanks for your help, Mr Kemp. Are you free for lunch? I don't have to be back in London till late afternoon.'

They went to The Cabbage White, two men it seemed to Kemp, of like mind. He found Richard an easy man, totally absorbed in his work. Kemp felt he understood him; Richard Amaury would ignore trivia, brush off petty issues, the tittle-tattle which occupied minds less engaged; his battles lay in another field, his only enemy disease, his sole concern its cure or at the very least amelioration of its effects. He was in the line of his father and his grandfather, and had never wished to look beyond it.

The refreshing ordinariness of such company, the amiable suggestion of lunch, went a long way to restoring Kemp's peace of mind considerably dented by his becoming *persona non grata* in so many quarters. He had felt in need of some reassurance that he was not entirely put in quarantine. At the risk of alienating even this pleasant relationship he wondered if Richard might be the one to whom he could speak openly. After all, he was Rose Amaury's son and had his mother's tolerance.

They had been talking of crime and criminals—a subject which intrigued the doctor who had little experience of the world of the transgressor, the world of those prone to by-passing penal boundaries.

'If you're in medicine, unless its the forensic department, you tend only to see the flesh and bones, the ways the body reacts to illness. Illness itself, I suppose, is the crime we fight. We never have the time to consider whether a person's good or bad in the legal sense—to us, they're just patients.'

'That's the framework in which you work, as the law is mine. I don't like it when the law overlaps with morals or ethics. We haven't the time to be philosophers either, and it's not my job to apportion blame for the way people are. We try to see them simply within the spectrum of their strictly legal problems. All the same, even with the simplest cases I find my mind straying. I suffer from incurable curiosity.'

Amaury laughed.

'You're like my mother. We used to tease her about it. She was always wanting to know why people did things. As all the men in her life had been doctors, she never got any answers. My father was like me—intensely interested in his own work, he used to tell her he found the behaviour of microbes far more fascinating than people.' The doctor stopped. When he resumed it was on a more sombre note. 'As he was with the first medical team to enter Belsen, that experience only reinforced his view. He found it so shocking...that human beings could treat other human beings so... Anyway, I guess I'm like my father. I too prefer patterns under a microscope—they make more sense. But I suppose it made both of us dull company for Mother.'

'Perhaps that's why she took to writing stories,' remarked Kemp casually.

'Oh, you know about that? Well, actually it was Giselle who started her off. It was about a year or so ago Mother was dining with us and talking—as she did—rather well. She'd a nice turn of phrase, perhaps you noticed? A way of using words.'

Kemp nodded.

'Giselle loved the little bit of sparkle she said Mother could give to the most ordinary happenings... Anyway, she said Mother ought to try her hand at writing. She told here there was a market for romantic fiction, that kind of thing.'

'And your mother took it up?'

'Oh yes, but we were sworn to secrecy.' Richard smiled sadly. 'She was very sensitive about it. Didn't want anyone to know until she'd had something published. I used to ask her from time to time how she was getting on. She never said much, but I think she was enjoying her little pastime. How did you find out?'

'There's a suitcase with her notebooks and some of her stories. I'm afraid they'd been rejected—they were a bit old-fashioned, but I thought them rather good. She probably didn't appreciate what a modern publisher wants, but, yes, I agree with you it pleased her to write. It was a hobby she could work on alone. It's a mistake to think old people only want to knit or do embroidery, or go in for good works around the parish. Are you sure no one else knew about it?'

'Quite sure. Paula would have had a fit. My sister has very definite ideas on occupations for old ladies...'

'That's what her daughter said. By the way, I did tell Lettice Warrender. I hope you don't mind, and of course you can have the suitcase any time. I removed it from the bungalow, and it's in my flat.'

Richard had been recalled by memories. 'Poor Mother... How bright she was, and always so young at heart. No, I suppose her writing doesn't matter any more. I'm glad it was Lettice you told. She's a sensible girl, if a bit headstrong.'

'She was headstrong all right with me,' remarked Kemp ruefully, 'nearly knocked me down...'

'What on earth for?'

'Oh, it was some comment I passed...probably rather a stupid one. That fall Mrs Amaury had in the garden—I said I wondered if someone had played a trick on her, stretched a piece of string or wire at the top of those steps.'

Richard's eyes widened. 'You said that to Lettice?'

'Yes, I did.'

'And you'd no reason for saying it?'

'Not really. It was just an idea I had.'

'It's a wonder Lettice didn't knock your head off. Good heavens, man, had you heard the family tale? Did you know about it?'

'What family tale? I didn't know anything—it was only a notion of my own...that your mother might have tripped by something on the path.'

Richard looked grim for a moment, then he laughed.

'And Lettice threw a punch at you? I'm not surprised. You see, years ago...it must have been when she was about thirteen, we had a great Christmas party for the youngsters and their friends. They were doing charades in the big hall at Castleton. Lettice was to make a spectacular descent of the staircase all dressed up as an Elizabethan lady... I think that was it. Anyway she had this great dress on with huge skirts, and she thought she was the cat's whiskers as she came out along the gallery. Everybody was gathered in the hall below and we all clapped as she began to come down the stairs, but she tripped and fell headlong. Oh, she wasn't hurt but her dignity was quite demolished. It was only afterwards that the picture wire was found stretched between the newel posts at the top. Of course it was one of the boys, Roger or Torvil, or both of them together, but neither would split on the other... So I gave the two of them a good thrashing. I was furious at the time, but looking back I can understand why they did it. Lettice was being insufferably bossy with them at the time and inclined to put on airs. I think they were simply fed up with her. It was only a schoolboy prank though it was a dangerous one, and they were duly punished. So you see why she took it out on you, Mr Kemp. She must have thought you knew all about it.'

'Well, I didn't. Will you please tell her that, Dr Amaury?'

'Of course. Lettice flies off the handle rather easily, even now when she ought to know better.'

Kemp changed the subject with deliberate abruptness.

'Have you ever come across any of those guardians of our national security in M15 or had anything even remotely to do with the Foreign Office?'

Dr Amaury looked astonished. 'Good Lord, no. And I've no wish to. That's a dark area. One does wonder sometimes why it has to be so secret if their aim is the health of the State. One does read of cases, of course. One can't help wondering whether it's not a growing virus, the kind that feeds on itself. I'm glad to say I've never encountered any of its manifestations. Why do you ask?'

'No special reason.' Kemp was well satisfied with Richard's answer; there had been no hesitation, no fluffing of the lines, he had been speaking in generalities. 'Just one more thing: did your mother ever talk to you about one of the stories she'd written called *The Bystander*?'

'She never talked to me about any of her stories. Partly my fault. I never had the time to listen. Why do you ask?'

'It isn't with the others, and I wondered where it went.'

Richard rubbed his forehead. 'I wish now that I had taken more interest, but I'm afraid romantic fiction is hardly my line. You do ask the oddest questions. Now I really must get back to London. I've enjoyed your company. Sometimes it's good to get out of the practice and the hospital and meet sane healthy people—even those who suffer from insatiable curiosity like you!'

Kemp laughed. 'It's an itch for which there is no cure— I'm afraid I'm stuck with it.'

On that note they parted, each returning to the burdens of his particular profession.

'I JUST CAME TO SAY I'm sorry.' Lettice Warrender had appeared in Kemp's office the next day like a small Valkyrie, but she was nevertheless contrite. 'The way I bashed you with my bag,' she went on gruffly. 'It was a terrible mistake. I thought...'

'I know what you thought. Your uncle told me. Now forget it.'

She sat down very squarely in the chair opposite him.

'I've been doing some thinking. You wouldn't ask a question about a trip-wire or piece of string without good reason. I've checked up on you, Mr Kemp. You don't do anything without a reason.'

'True. What do you want to know?'

'Why you mentioned it in the first place.'

'Because your grandmother said it was there.'

The shock drove the colour from her face.

'But who could possibly...?'

'Who did it the last time—to you?'

'That's unthinkable! It couldn't have anything to do with that. It was years ago.'

'I know. A schoolboy prank. Which of them thought it up?'

Lettice Warrender's features registered every passing emotion as nakedly as though she were still a girl. Now she flushed, red on white.

'I never knew. Both of them together, I guess.'

'Shared animosity can be a bond. I gather they don't get on so well nowadays?'

She shrugged her shoulders, fiddled with the catch of her bag.

'Why should I discuss them with you? Oh, all right. Actually, they've just gone their separate ways, that's all. Torvil's older anyway, and he's clever, which Roger most certainly is not. Cousin Torvil sees himself going right to the top of the tree as the new breed of medico, computerized patients and to hell with people. Roger's going into business studies—well, that's what he says, though he hasn't got

very far. I suppose he envies Torvil, having money to spend
and being free of his parents...

Money matters a lot to Roger...'

'Money matters to everybody, Lettice. Even to you.
You've always had it to fall back on.'

She looked mutinous for a moment, then changed the
subject.

'Do you really think Granny was tripped up deliberately?'

It was Kemp's turn to shrug. 'She might have imagined it.
That would be what would be said.'

She stared. 'What do you mean—putting it like that?'

'Look, Miss Warrender—Lettice—I'm allowed to think
my own thoughts. No one can stop me. But I can't do anything about them. Your family has seen to that.'

'I don't understand you.'

'I thought it was plain enough. I've been headed off, told
to mind my own business.'

'Not by anyone in my family, Mr Kemp,' she rounded on
him.

'Someone with influence,' said Kemp carefully, 'in high
places. There are to be no more inquiries made about any of
the circumstances of your grandmother's death.'

'That's quite ridiculous. None of my family has that kind
of influence. Anyway, why were you inquiring into her
murder? I thought it was all finished. That Roding...the one
who killed her, he's dead, isn't he?'

Kemp nodded.

'Well, then? And he could have set that trap in the garden. Just to get her out of the way...'

'Yes. That's exactly what the police would think. But if
it was all as simple as that why has the word gone out that
I'm to be stopped from asking questions?'

Kemp watched the play of indecision and doubt across her
features where the high-bridged nose of her mother failed to
dominate the softer curve of her mouth. She's still un-
formed, he thought, and transparent in her efforts to be

both fair and stern. She must have been a terrific house prefect. He got a level accusing look from her hazel eyes. 'You want to link this thing with my family? Who're you working for anyway with these so-called inquiries?'

Kemp shook his head. 'You know better than to ask that.'

'But if it's going to upset us, then I want to know.'

'Why should it upset anybody if there's nothing to hide?'

'Of course there's nothing to hide... And what did you mean exactly—you've been warned off?'

'What I said. And there's an end to it, Miss Warrender. Now, I have other work to do.'

But her mouth was set in a stubborn line.

'You said we had influence in high places. That's absolutely nonsense. Pa can't even influence his own clients... He's not that kind of man...'

Kemp smiled. 'What about the Chief Constable?'

Lettice went red. 'That's only his talk. He's really mild as a lamb.'

'A lamb that roars. The word has come down the line that I'm to get no cooperation from the Yard or even the local force.'

'Then it wasn't through pressure by my father. The Chief Constable's a new man in every way—came up through the red-brick. He gave poor old Pa the brush-off when he tried to harry him about the police not doing enough in the early days... well, you know how Pa did rather go on about the iniquities of the Newtown hooligans.' She hesitated. 'Of course, I suppose he was right, Pa I mean... it was a Newtown hooligan who killed Gran...'

Kemp made no comment.

'You seem to have very funny ideas about my family, Mr Kemp. You think we have some kind of power. Oh, we probably had it once, centuries ago, but these days have gone. Besides,' she added briskly, 'if it were true that the parents were distressed by inquiries you were making, I'd have heard about it. There's not much I miss where they're concerned. I'm fairly perceptive about them—I've had to be in order to get where I am now without actually breaking away.'

It was an aspect of her which Kemp had not considered. He considered it now, and was puzzled. He had fully expected Lettice Warrender to be part of the conspiracy against him.

'Perhaps you've trampled on someone else's toes in whatever investigation you've been doing. Are you going to leave it like that?'

'I've no option.'

'But you have to finish something you started. Isn't that the way private eyes work? Leave no stone unturned till justice is achieved?'

'Not this time. And don't mock.'

'Aren't you curious as to who's stopping you?'

Mindful of his promise to Archie Gillorn, Kemp wasn't going to mention national security—whatever, in this context, it could mean.

'Of course I'm curious. I'm also frustrated. Your grandmother thought her life was threatened. She told me and trusted me. She died. I didn't save her.'

He watched her eyes widen in disbelief, then fill with tears, and he wondered at his own directness. But he was tired of hedging.

'So that was it. Gran told you ...'

'Yes.'

'And that was why you asked me about her imagination?'

'Yes.'

Lettice Warrender got up from her seat and walked over to the window, staring out. When at length she turned she seemed to have grown up.

'And you don't think the threat came from Kevin Roding?'

'No.'

'Yet now you want to leave it there?'

'I told you, I've no choice.'

'And you accept that?'

'I have to.'

She came and put both hands on the desk in front of him, resting the knuckles of her fists like a challenging school-boy.

'But *I* don't have to. No one has told me not to interfere. She was my grandmother. If there's something still to be explained about her death, then I want to know what it is. One thing I did learn at college was how to draw a straight line. I don't like anything crooked. I like maps and how the land lies. I like facts and where they lead, and I like things to fit . . . and I won't be put off.'

It was quite a speech.

'Miss Warrender—Lettice—you don't know what you're up against.'

'Then you tell me,' she said fiercely, 'after all, you started it.'

'Your grandmother did.'

She plumped down again in the chair. 'Well, it wasn't her imagination, I can tell you that. If Granny thought some-one was threatening her, then that was fact. You don't think it was young Roding, so who was it? And why should any-body threaten a harmless old lady?'

'Because she wasn't harmless to someone.'

Very slowly, because the thought was repugnant to her, she took in what she'd heard. Her eyes were large with hor-ror, but they were excited too. She spoke with deliberate emphasis, spacing the words, her breath coming short.

'You don't believe Kevin Roding killed her?'

Kemp hesitated. This wild pony given her head would take some reining in. He parried the question. 'I'm simply not sure . . .'

THIRTEEN

LETTICE WARRENDER was no Lorelei giving the come-hither from a rock, nor a siren singing men to their doom. Sex in her had not yet been found—certainly not by Lennox Kemp. Her feminine wiles were of a different order, if indeed they were wiles at all. Imagining herself an emancipated woman, and fast becoming one as she strove towards that ideal, she was formidable when she saw only one road ahead and went for it like an arrow.

Dragged along willy-nilly in her wake, Kemp found himself that evening in his flat while she ransacked the contents of her grandmother's suitcase.

'There may be a clue in all this,' she said, a pencil stuck behind her ear, her small hands scrambling about among the mass of paper. 'Something she wrote...'

'They're only stories. I've been over them.' Kemp played second fiddle, and made the coffee. She drank it without regard for taste or temperature, and munched biscuits.

'There's one missing,' she announced, frowning.

'I know. The one called *The Bystander*.'

'Then where's her notes on it? There's notes on all the others. And look at this, there's pages torn out of one of her scribble books. See? The pages are numbered but ten are missing. I bet those were the notes for that story. Did you notice that?'

Kemp confessed he hadn't. 'Perhaps Mrs Amaury tore them out herself.'

'Why'd she do that? And where's the story? It must have been important to her—the agent said it was promising. The only one in fact he'd a kind word for.' Kemp nodded but made no comment.

'She worked on it, finished it, and gave it to someone to type for her.' Lettice summed up her deduction with an air of triumph.

'Maybe.'

'Then who'd she give it to? Uncle Richard says she was very self-conscious about her writing so it must be someone she trusted.

'Giselle?'

'Don't be silly. She can't type, and anyway she was in America. I've got it—Tullia Cavendish. She made a great song and dance about the typewriting course she took. And she'd do anything for a bit of pin-money. Gran would pay her, and tell her to keep it quiet. Poor old Gran...she must have hoped it might be published. I wonder if dear Tullia still has it...I'll ask Julian,' she finished decisively, gathering up the books and papers and arranging them neatly before slipping them back into the brown envelope. Kemp noted she was a tidy worker.

'Why Julian?'

'Oh, he knows everything Tullia does. That's always been his trouble. He's let her swamp him.'

Kemp raised his eyebrows.

Lettice became slightly flustered but his questioning look made her take the matter further, which was what he had hoped.

'Julian has allowed himself to slip into the position of family pet in that household. A pity. I had great hopes of him once...' She went red. 'And I don't mean what you think. Well, I suppose at one time I did have rather a schoolgirl crush on him. He was really ever so bright, and he had all the right ideas...'

It sounded to Kemp as if Julian Cavendish had supported Lettice's youthful revolt against the parental mores, thereby earning a higher regard from an impressionable girl than perhaps was merited.

'He was so sympathetic when I went to college. He talked about the change in attitudes, how Society had to be turned on its head . . . Not exactly Marxism but . . . well, you know. Then when I came back to Castleton, what did I find? He'd gone into that job at the private school! Wangled for him by the Cavendishes, of course, and naturally it keeps him in line. You talked about the power of my family—you've no idea the power the Cavendishes still have.'

'Do they? I thought they'd lost everything.'

'Everything but their name. To them the Warrenders are just upstart Tudor gentry who got their lands playing political footsie with the first Elizabeth. The Cavendishes were around at the time of Ethelred the Unready.'

'H'm. Talking of history, what's Julian's?'

'Didn't you know? He's their orphaned nephew. Came to live with them when he was about six, and apart from going away to Public School he's been there ever since.'

'Where'd he come from?'

'No one would dare ask. You don't ask things like that of Tullia and Clive. It would be too much like *lèse-majesté*. To me Julian's always been around. He's very clever, and an excellent linguist, so it's quite ridiculous his ending up in that school for the privileged.'

Kemp was amused, and showed it.

'But you went to a privileged school yourself, Lettice.'

'I'd no choice. I'd much preferred to have gone to the Comprehensive.' She sat up and drained her mug. 'By the way, you make terrible coffee.'

'Why are you doing all this, Lettice?'

'Because someone has to. And you seem to be under an interdict of some kind. That doesn't apply to me.' She slipped on her jacket, ready to leave.

'I'll run you home. I suppose you walked to work today but it's much too far back to Castleton House from here.'

'Thank you. You live pretty starkly, Mr Kemp.' There was something of Paula Warrender's condescension in her inspection of his bleak sitting-room and kitchen arrangements.

'I never notice,' said Kemp truthfully. 'I usually live inside my head and that's more lavishly furnished.'

In the car she reverted to the subject uppermost in her mind.

'You know, I really believe what Gran told you. When I used to sit with her after her fall she wasn't herself. I'd never noticed her being nervy before but she was then... And this making of her will. Oh, I know Mother had been going on at her about it but Gran made up her mind ever so quickly. It wasn't like her to give in to Mother—usually she held out just for devilment.'

'It was the sensible thing to do, to make that will. And you all benefited.'

'You do get down to earth, Mr Kemp.'

'For heaven's sake call me Lennox. I've been calling you Lettice.'

'I suppose as we're in this together now we can drop the formalities. But this is serious, Lennox, what we're doing...'

'What *you* are doing.'

'Oh, I see. You want no part of it?'

'I want the truth.'

'Well, partners in that at any rate. Will you come in and see the family?'

'What, now?' Kemp wasn't yet ready to meet the Warrenders again *en masse*; Lettice really had got the bit between her even white teeth.

'Just to demonstrate to your sceptical mind that it's not us who've put the ban on you.'

'In that case...'

THEY WERE GATHERED in the green and gold drawing-room where firelight flickered on the faded furnishings, softening and lending grace to their time-worn elegance. A game of bridge had just finished.

'Kind of you to bring Lettice home. We thought she was working rather late.' Paula was herself, neither more nor less so. She passed Kemp a plate where a few sandwiches lay curled under celery stalks as if in hiding.

'Though what she finds to do in that monument to idiotic town planning beats me.' Lionel too was his usual bluff self. 'Don't you agree, Mr Kemp, that the whole of Newtown's a blot on our landscape?'

Unsure as to whether he himself was being elevated into a joint tenancy of the said landscape along with the Warrenders, Kemp demurred.

'It's where I earn my living, Mr Warrender.'

'And I'm sure that criminal element down there keeps you busy, eh?'

'There's more conveyancing than crime in Newtown,' said Kemp equably, accepting a whisky and signalling for more soda. 'I don't only associate with law-breakers.'

'That's not what I've heard,' muttered the young man who was putting away the cards at the other end of the room. Roger looked like the brother of Lettice but without her resolute chin. Seen together they were unmistakably two sides of the same coin, but one was true metal already stamped with value while the other remained indeterminate, acquiescent in whatever ore he had been cast. He had a sullen look but he came over and shook hands with Kemp.

'I'm Roger Warrender. We haven't met but I've heard about you.'

Judging by his *sotto voce* remark he'd heard too much, and Kemp wondered where.

Torvil also strolled over from the bridge table. Tonight he was splendid in fashionable buttoned-down mauve shirt and violet tie.

'Those Newtown houses look pretty dreadful to me,' he remarked, 'Can't imagine anyone buying them.'

'They've passed the Public Health standards,' said Kemp without a smile, 'they all have bathrooms, I understand.'

'Lennox!' There was a warning note in Lettice's voice, despite her giggle. Of course she might have been simply rescuing Torvil who had narrowed his eyes at Kemp's remark as if diagnosing an obscure and nasty symptom.

There was desultory conversation, superficial and unexceptionally dull. On the part of the senior Warrenders at least there was little trace of animosity towards their visitor so that Lettice, crisp and naturally at home, met Kemp's glance with a look that said, 'I told you so.'

For his part Kemp, who, when he thought about it at all, prided himself on being strictly an onlooker in the class war, was unjustifiably uneasy in the presence of the people at Castleton House. As a result, he was mildly irritable. What do I suspect them of, he asked himself as he joined in the polite give-and-take-nothing conversation? Murdering their elderly relative? A blanket cover-up to keep the family escutcheon unblotted?

Certainly something prompted Roger to say for no apparent reason, 'Saw that lout Roding in town the other day with some of his cronies. You'd have thought common decency would keep him off the streets for a bit. As it was, he just stood there staring at me. Jolly uncomfortable it was.'

'I think he looks like Oliver Reed in a bad mood,' put in Lettice mischievously. 'Do you know him, Lennox?'

Kemp caught the quick glance that passed between Torvil and Roger, and recalled his own comment that shared hostility can be a bond.

'We've met,' he said briefly, watching the reaction between the two young men. Was it the mention of Ted Roding, or was it Lettice's use of his own Christian name that made them wary? Did they think he was out to seduce the girl?

Paula Warrender moved her shoulders with a shudder of distaste. 'I quite dread meeting that awful Roding woman in the town but one can't help it when one has to use the same facilities. Why, even going into the Bank isn't safe any more...'

There ought to be special enclosures for the natives, thought Kemp; Paula would have been at home in the India of the Raj. Aloud he merely observed that the Vicar found the Newtown supermarket convenient.

'Poor old Clive,' said Lionel, 'he's having to do the shopping, is he? Is Tullia no better?'

'Julian's had a word with me,' said Torvil importantly. 'I've prescribed something for his aunt. He says she won't go to her own GP at the local Health Centre because Mrs Roding's never out of the surgery. I'm afraid Tullia Cavendish is on the verge of what you ladies call a nervous breakdown.' He spoke as though such a condition was beyond his professional comprehension, and certainly beneath his contempt.

'Tullia, a nervous breakdown? Nonsense!' exclaimed Lionel in robust dismissal of the notion. 'She's not the woman to have nerves. Julian's exaggerating as usual. He likes to be dramatic.'

'Tullia's jolly lucky getting all that money,' said Roger. 'Oh, I know she was fond of Gran but money's always a great consolation.'

'Now, now, Roger, I'm sure you didn't mean it but that remark was in very poor taste.'

'Sorry, Mater, but people do have to face up to realities.'

'And you're just the one to tell them that, aren't you, brother dear. You haven't done too badly out of Gran's death yourself.' Lettice had spoken with some asperity, and as Kemp had no wish to see her kitten claws in action, he announced it was time he went home.

Lettice showed him out. 'See?' she said. 'It isn't my family who's stopping you. I think even my mother is beginning to like you.'

'I'm clean, I'm sober and I don't frighten the horses. But I take your point. Is Cousin Torvil as good a doctor as he thinks he is?'

'Torvil's self-esteem was evident even when he was a little boy. In all our games he made the rules—and usually saw that he won.'

'To the extent of tripping up his opponents?'

'What? Oh, that . . . He might have suggested it, and got Roger to do the dirty work.'

'Was Julian Cavendish at this famous party?'

The red colour swept over her face.

'The Cavendishes were all there—they always came to our parties. That made it worse . . .' She hesitated. 'I told you I had this schoolgirl crush on him. It was terrible, me tumbling down the stairs like that in front of everybody—especially him. I'd wanted, I suppose, to impress him with that dress. I'd put my hair up . . . I cried for days afterwards.'

'Brave of you to tell me, Lettice. Anyway, it's probably got nothing to do with your grandmother's accident.'

'But you think it has?' She had regained her composure and her straight, clear-sighted gaze. It made her face look naked and vulnerable.

'Only that it might have struck a chord in someone's memory—given someone an idea.'

Kemp was conscious that the drawing-room door had opened, and he sensed that Torvil and Roger were standing watching them.

'Good night, Miss Warrender,' he said, and he went down the steps.

FOURTEEN

IT WAS SEVERAL DAYS LATER that Kemp began to suspect that he was being followed. He'd done enough of that kind of trailing himself to be aware of the shadowing presence of certain cars, and the inconspicuous figures who flitted on the edge of his vision when he was walking in Newtown. He took no overt action but carried on with his business as though in ignorance of whatever surveillance someone had thought fit to put upon him. He gave the watchers only three out of ten on the McCready scale.

He had one short telephone conversation with Ted Roding—though conversation was too urbane a word for the disgruntled exchange. It was Ted who called.

'I've not heard a dicky-bird from you, Kemp. What's goin' on?'

'Enquiries take time, Mr Roding, have patience. I've got other cases besides yours.'

'Yeah? Reckon you're not tryin' too hard. Was it you put the rozzers on to me?'

'No, it wasn't.'

'Stickin' around like bloody glue. I'm clean. I done my time. Why don't the sods leave me alone?' Ted's voice rose to a whine. Kemp sighed. Why can't inveterate villains get it into their heads that they're not pure as the driven snow once they come out? But it did sound as if the local force were giving Roding a lot of unwelcome attention.

'Did you want to tell me something, Ted?'

'I got summat all right, but I'm not tellin' you. Not now you're in with the nobs, like. Can't trust you no more, can I? Bloody lawyers, they're all the same. I thought you was different. Well, I was wrong.'

'If you've got something to say, then come out with it, or, better still, come in and see me.'

'Not on your nelly. You've done nothin' about our Kev. You're as twisted as the other lot. You're in with them, Kemp.'

'I'm in with nobody.' Kemp was getting weary; it was like talking to a half-articulate ape.

'You can stuff that for a lie. You're thick with the girl. You're on their side.'

'I'm on no one's side. Come in and...' But the phone had been slammed down.

Kemp made a note; it was time he visited Mrs Roding anyway.

Other events intervened. Young Mr Lambert's wife having produced their first infant, and his mind being understandably diverted from mundane transfers of the fee simple, he was about to take a few days off to recover it.

'The only really urgent thing,' he told Kemp breathlessly, 'is that auction of the Halstead property. I've drafted the particulars but I'd be grateful if you'd take a run out there and see if I've missed anything.'

'Oh, I'm sure you haven't,' said Kemp, 'but I'll take a look. Now off you go and learn all about changing nappies. I'm told it's trickier than an estate agent's brochure...'

That afternoon Kemp spun his old Cortina out along the wilder shores of Newtown to where the countryside still remained cosily hedged, and the wide fields were as yet undeveloped. Not for long. Halstead had acreage around the ramshackle old house recently vacated by a spinster now happily retiring to an Eventide Home, and the land-hungry speculators would be eagerly lining up for a cut at the land.

He left his car half way up the drive which was hung heavily with white May blossom, lilac and golden laburnum, the scents of summer taking their first breath of the sun's warmth. He walked up to the house studying the layout. Lambert didn't seem to have got anything wrong,

and his survey of the property was accurate. Kemp shook
out the bunch of keys, selected the one Yale, and opened the
front door to the smell of dust and the closed odour of
empty rooms. He wandered through, noting the peeling
wallpaper, the fireplaces still with their fallen soot, the
kitchen where wooden cabinets lurched rakishly beside an
old-fashioned sink and draining-board, the line of bells
above the door. No central heating, no concessions to
modern convenience. They would pull it down, of course;
the house wasn't worth saving. A pity; the ceilings were lofty
even in the bedrooms, though the two bathrooms were tiny
and the plumbing bared in all its writhing ugliness.

He came downstairs again, checked the mains—at least
it wasn't septic-tank drainage—locked up and went across
the courtyard to the outhouses. Nettles grew high about the
coach-house, a modest one but at one time they had been
people who kept their carriage. The stable had been con-
verted to a garage—the old lady had driven her car till she
was past eighty—but the corrugated iron roof had fallen in,
and garage was only a term for shelter for her vehicle. The
door hung off its hinge and creaked as he peered into the
musty interior.

He should have been more vigilant. He should have heard
the footfalls soft on the grass-grown cobblestones behind
him. As it was, the first blows struck him down before he
could turn, and then there was nothing but confusion and
pain. They went for his legs first so that he fell, gasping. As
he struggled to regain his feet he faced round, seeing the
sunlight in the aperture of the doorway and the figures sil-
houetted against it. He could swear there were three of
them, but with hoods pulled down across their faces, the
more menacing for that terrible detail so that they were not
men but alien creatures. More he could not take in as they
advanced on him, so in desperation he willed himself to see
their feet. As he was struck again, this time without mercy,
he saw one set of feet take a dancing step. A boxer's

stance—his last coherent thought as he slid into black oblivion.

'IT'S BEEN A LONG TIME since I heard a blackbird's song in the evening,' Kemp remarked conversationally, squinting into the dark through the windscreen of a car which was strange to him.

Glyn Norris glanced at him briefly.

'You got battered about the head as well . . . and that arm of yours looks bad.'

'There was a blackbird singing . . . and the smell of hawthorne...sweet and rich like dress perfume...' Kemp's voice to his own ears sounded far away like someone reciting poetry in an empty room.

'Yeah, you've taken a right battering.' Glyn Norris kept his eyes on the road. 'Lucky I came along. Saw your car in the Halstead drive so I stopped by. I mean, what the hell...I see the lawyer there and the auction only ten days away, so what do I think? I think trouble, that's what I think. Maybe the gippos got in, or someone's pinching the roof tiles...' Glyn had spent several years in the States and had adopted the tone; it helped sell houses even around Newtown—people remembered him for it—the agent with the American accent, it distinguished him from the others.

Kemp's eyes were slowly returning to their proper focus.

'Where're we heading?' It still didn't seem to be his own voice.

'Newtown Hospital.'

'Oh.' Kemp tried to raise his left arm to wipe the stickiness from his forehead, but the arm refused to obey the brain's summons. He looked down at it in pained surprise. It lay there, inert under his jacket sleeve, throbbing gently like a time bomb. Which reminded him. 'What time is it?'

'About half ten, I reckon. It was barely light when I saw your car, and damned lucky for you I did. I thought you'd be in the house, see? But it was empty so I scouted around and there you were laid out on the garage floor. You'd been properly done over—that cut on your head's still bleeding.'

'Shoes . . . What d'you call them, trainer shoes? Lace-up sports, white with green bands . . . And boxer's feet in them, side-stepping feet . . .'

'Thugs,' said Norris, 'and more than one, I guess.'

'Thugs,' said Kemp, his head swimming only just above swirling soupy water, 'now there's a word that's been debased. Weren't they once an elite sect?'

'I wouldn't know. But they sure did a job on you. With a stout stick, I'd say. Oh, they left this . . .' Glyn took a piece of paper from the pocket of his waistcoat, and pushed it over to Kemp who found that his right hand responded after a slow start. He held it up to his eyes. Even in the dark of the car he could read the big scrawled words as the car slid under the bright lights of the arterial road.

LAY OFF LETICE WARRENDER.

Kemp closed his eyes; they seemed happier that way. He heard the blackbird's piercing note again. Possibly it had been a warning but if so it had been in a language only St Francis would have understood. It came from a long way off, like the footsteps behind him. He tried to concentrate on the present as he crumpled the note and put it in his pocket.

'You're with Crowthers, that agents, is that right?' he said slowly, gathering his wits which he saw lying scattered on the ground like the hawthorn petals.

'Yeah, Glyn Norris. We've never met, Mr Kemp, but I recognized your car as being from Gillorns. I've only dealt with Mr Lambert but he's mentioned you—and your name's in your wallet which was on the ground beside you. No money in it, by the way . . .'

'And that bit of paper?'

'On top of you.'

'I owe you, Glyn. I owe you a lot. There's just one thing. that note, no need to tell anyone. OK?'

'I never saw it, right? Your business, eh, Mr Kemp?'

Kemp again tried to move his left arm. Pain shot through him.

'Don't try and move it. I'd a hell of a job getting you into that front seat. Your arm's useless. The scum that attacked you knew their business. Well, here we are. Take it easy, and I'll get help from Casualty...'

They had drawn up outside the Hospital. Glyn Norris leapt out and made for the lighted doorway. Kemp stayed where he was; any other choice had been very effectively taken from him. He slid into semi-consciousness which seemed a state of bliss half way between total oblivion and euphoric clear-sightedness. He could have described in microscopic detail the pattern of peeling paint on the walls and the configuration of the central heating pipes along the corridors; the washed-out stain on the white coat of the doctor on duty, the wisp of brown hair escaped from the starched cap on the nurse attending the stretcher, and the exact position of the handles on the swing doors as they pushed him through. After a while he gave up; there was too much going on, and he didn't think it was going to matter any more whether the messages from eyes and ears were getting through; his mind had signed off for the night.

FIFTEEN

NEWTOWN GENERAL HOSPITAL was used to emergencies, and saw Lennox Kemp as no different in species from the other victims of casual road accidents, muggings, domestic incidents and even—from the still idyllic farmlands around—tractor overturnings, that cluttered their wards.

In the view of the Staff Kemp came through tolerably well but he was not an ideal patient. For one thing he was angry. He would not lie down. He would not rest. He wanted to see people. He wanted to get up.

'How long have I been here?' he demanded once he had taken his bearings, knew where he was, and had, himself, examined minutely his injuries. He tried to move his left hand beneath the plaster.

'You've been here two days.' Sister was stern despite her pretty looks. 'You'll not use that arm for a while. The bone is fractured. It's been set. And you were unconscious when you came in, Mr Kemp. There is concussion. Dr Walters has advised complete rest. Mr Kemp! What are you trying to do?'

'I'm trying to get up to make a phone call.'

'You'll stay right where you are. Rest, Mr Kemp. As ordered by Dr Walters.' She stuck a thermometer in his mouth which silenced him—at least for the time being.

When she had whisked out Kemp lay back and considered concussion. They said it didn't last. Maybe you might lose an hour before, an hour or two afterwards. Kemp was determined to lose nothing; his time on earth might be measured out in coffee spoonfuls but every minute was precious because it was his own. Look to this day, he told himself, for it is life, the very life of life; in its brief course lie all the realities of your existence. He'd be damned if he lost even one jewelled second. He began to concentrate on tangibles; smell, hearing, sight, striving to bring them to the surface of his mind. For they were there, they had been experienced, and so would remain. He only had to dredge them up. The smell of hawthorn blossom, the sound of the blackbird's song, the sight of those dancing feet. One set of feet. But there had been others. Just standing as he turned, then moving forward. Shrouded heads, no faces. Three of them. How did he know there had been three? Silhouettes against the light. So he had been inside somewhere. What had Norris said? Laid out on the garage floor.

He took it back, step by step. The Halstead place. He'd been followed. Yet something was wrong. He remembered now. He'd kept a careful watch on the road behind him, that unused country road down to the property, no car had been in sight trailing him on that excursion. He'd checked, from habit. Norris had seen his car where he'd parked it at the end of the drive, but Norris had an interest in the place... The attackers' interest had been in Kemp himself.

He edged his good arm towards the drawer where they'd put his personal possessions, and rummaged through them, his wallet—less the odd thirty pounds which had been there—his watch, handkerchief, car keys. Nothing else. Slowly he pulled himself off the bed, and stood for a moment dizzily as the room swam before his eyes. He waited, taking deep breaths till the floor steadied. Then he groped his way over to the wardrobe. Fortunately the cubicle he was in was tiny and there were plenty of handholds. His blood-stained jacket was hanging there, looking lonely without him. In the right-hand pocket he found the note and carried it with him by painful progress back to bed.

LAY OFF LETICE WARRENDER. He wondered what Glyn Norris had made of it, and didn't greatly care. He stuffed it under the pillow as Sister returned, this time preceded by Dr Walters.

'How am I?' seemed a proper enough inquiry.

'You'll mend. The X-rays show that arm will heal all right but you'll not use it for a week or so. We did a good piece of work on it.'

'Congratulations,' said Kemp drily. 'Can I go?'

At a nod from the doctor Sister unwound the bandage from Kemp's forehead.

'H'm. That head wound isn't deep. The stitches can come out in a day or two. You sustained a heavy blow on the back of the skull which knocked you out so there may be concussion...'

'I think not. I remember what happened.'

'Do you now, Mr Kemp? Well, please let me be the judge of that—it's a medical condition...'

'It's my head. It's where I live. By the way, Dr Walters why am I in here and not in the general ward? Private room, eh?' He waved his good arm round the small cubicle. He saw Sister's eyes—which were green and rather beautiful— widen in astonishment.

'You talk too much, Mr Kemp,' said Dr Walters, shortly

'Is that a general observation, or just in these particular circumstances? Was someone afraid I might talk in my sleep?'

'I was told you were to be put in the amenity room—that's all I know.' Dr Walters was more at home with patients who were properly grateful for such favours, but Kemp in his present mood was not inclined to let him off.

'When can I leave this place?'

Dr Walters studied the chart hanging at the foot of the bed, and looked inquiringly at Sister. Kemp grinned at her to show he was capable of it, and was rewarded with a small answering smile. She and the doctor held a muttered conversation, then he returned to Kemp's side.

'If you behave yourself I might let you go tomorrow. Of course you'll have to come back to have that left arm attended to.'

'Not out today, then?'

'Certainly not. Now there's an Inspector Upshire waiting to see you—if you feel up to it, and you've another visitor—I understand she's your secretary...'

'Now I know why I've got a room all to myself. I hope this place isn't bugged?'

The doctor's fine nose looked pinched at the nostrils as he drew in his breath but he couldn't think up a suitable retort so he stalked out, followed by Sister. She turned in the doorway, and held up an admonishing finger at Kemp but her mouth was curled with suppressed laughter. Kemp was glad he'd amused somebody.

JOHN UPSHIRE took the chair beside the bed, glancing uneasily at the plaster cast. 'How bad's that arm, Lennox?'

'Fractured, but I'll live.'

'What happened?'

Kemp told him most of it, leaving out the warning note. He hoped he could trust Glyn Norris but reflected that Gillorns threw a lot of business Crowthers' way. Glyn wouldn't talk.

The Inspector closed his notebook. 'And you've no idea who they were?'

Shrugging shoulders was painful so Kemp simply said no, he hadn't any idea.

'Simple robbery? I gather you'd about thirty pounds in your wallet?'

'They didn't get much.'

John Upshire eyed him warily.

'You think that was it, then? You were mugged for thirty pounds? And it took three of them, you say?'

'I only know what happened. Conclusions are your business.'

Upshire rubbed his forehead. 'It was a vicious attack, Lennox. There must be more to it... Have you been up to something we should know about?'

'Look, John, I went out to inspect a property on behalf of a colleague. A perfectly innocent pursuit in the line of work. Whoever it was could have been hanging about. It's a lonely place, perhaps they were up to no good out there, and I interrupted some skulduggery. It's up to you to find them—if you're allowed to...'

'What the hell do you mean by that?'

Kemp's head was beginning to ache, some of the working parts were objecting to overtime. 'Forget I said it,' he replied, 'Sister says I've to be a good boy and not tire my brain.'

Upshire pushed his chair back.

'I don't know what to make of this, Lennox. You can't give us much description to go on, and I'm not buying your theory that they were there on a frolic of their own. I think whoever it was they were out to get you.'

'Well, they got me.' Kemp lay back and half closed his eyes. He decided to take advantage of his invalid position which had already given him a light-headedness surprisingly conducive to clarity of thought. Whatever he said now could be attributed to healing drugs or the aftermath of concussion. 'Don't go, John.' He put a weak hand on the bedclothes, 'I've been thinking...'

The gesture aroused Upshire's sympathy, and allayed his normal suspicion of Kemp as being a tricky customer. The officer was out of his depths sitting at a bedside, and as well as being bewildered by the circumstance he had also been considerably shaken by his friend's appearance. Used to Kemp's jaunty bearing and easygoing ways, Upshire was perturbed by his greenish pallor, the skin stretched across his bumpy temples as if to emphasize the frailty of the skull beneath, and the lines etched round the mouth giving it a hardness, even a hint of desperation.

'Tell me,' said Kemp, 'this thing you got from higher up... to stop my request for the Amaury file... where did the instructions come from?'

Upshire shifted uncomfortably. 'Well, you know how it is...'

'No, I don't. You get on well with the Yard, with Chief Inspector Quennell? Did he pull rank on you?'

'Of course not. It wasn't like that.'

'So the Yard wasn't responsible for the directive? How'd it come? Sideways?' There was more than a suggestion of feverishness in Kemp's continued probing.

Upshire nodded, his eyes on the ceiling. 'You could say that...'

'How high up?'

'Quennell says pretty high. The Deputy Assistant Commissioner, if you really want to know.'

'I really do. And he must be under orders from even higher?'

'For God's sake, Lennox...'

'Well, what's it all about, then?'

'I knew better than to ask. All I know is that all the files on the case, the investigations, everything, have been referred...upstairs. That's what Quennell told me and he ought to know.'

'And where's the case gone from there?'

Inspector Upshire spread his hands. 'Search me. Look, Lennox, I'm only an ordinary copper. If a case is taken out of my hands and I'm told not to ask any more questions—then that's good enough for me.'

Kemp changed his tack.

'Weren't your lot confused by other fingerprints found at the Amaury house?'

The Inspector's milky blue eyes turned bland as a baby's but the absence of surprise in them was revealing enough.

'Come on, John. One old lady and a cleaner who cleaned? Your men must have had a field day. And all you told me about were Kevin Roding's...'

'That's all we found—officially. You suffering from concussion?'

'Not half. There's nothing like a blow on the head to clear the mind. Aren't you even curious about this whole affair?'

'It's out of my hands.' The Inspector got up. 'And a blessed relief. At least it's taken it off my patch . . .'

'Don't be too sure of that. It was on your patch it began, remember.'

It was Upshire's turn to change the tenor of the conversation.

'Was it Ted Roding and his mates who coshed you?'

'Did the elder Roding ever do any boxing?'

'He was keen for a time in his younger, more innocent days, but he got thrown out of the Youth Club here when he brought in a London gang and caused a riot. He was up on a GBH on that one. God help us, what did the Roding pair think they were—latter-day Kray brothers? You haven't answered my question.'

'Frankly, I don't know the answer. Ted Roding's got no reason to assault me. On the contrary . . .'

'Yes?'

'Why're you keeping such close tabs on him?'

'Oh, come off it. Look at his record. And don't tangle with him, if you want my advice—which you've never taken in the past. Keep out of the whole thing, Lennox. Look what's happened to you.'

'I'm looking. Thanks for coming yourself, John.'

ELVIRA WAS WHITE-FACED. 'Oh, Mr Kemp, we've been so worried about you. Even Mr Archibald has been on the phone every day. I could only repeat what the hospital told me but you never know with hospitals, do you? They sound so comfortable—it's the only word they know. So I came myself.' She hovered uneasily, and held out a small box of chocolates. 'Flowers didn't seem right, somehow. Can you eat these?'

'I can eat anything. Sit down, Elvira. You look worse than I feel.'

She brightened up, however, as she assured him that the office was running smoothly despite his absence, thereby confirming an old view of his mother's that 'there's no man yet that can't be done without.'

'Someone phoned, you know, just after you left for the Halstead property,' Elvira remarked, 'said it was ever so urgent so I told them where you'd gone. Was I wrong to do that? I mean, it wasn't any secret and you were only doing Mr Lambert's work anyhow.'

'Did they leave a name? Was it Ted Roding?'

Elvira sniffed. 'That goon? I'd know his voice all right. No, they didn't say who it was. Just that they had urgent business with you and would like to see you that afternoon. It was an educated voice, Mr Kemp, you know—a gentleman, and very pleasantly-spoken.'

Elvira's penchant for ascribing accents was spot-on; she wouldn't allow herself to be caught out.

'No, you didn't do wrong.'

'And Mr Lambert's come back,' went on Elvira eagerly. 'Says his wife's mother has come to take over so he's been made redundant. Oh, and we've got the auditors in.'

Kemp frowned. 'What, again? They've not long finished.'

'I know. Mr Carruthers is most put out.'

Peter Carruthers the cashier was a retired Bank official and kept meticulous books, but unexplained visits from the auditors disturbed his routine.

'Well, ply them with tea and buns, Elvira, and keep them happy. Eliot and Roberts aren't a bad pair as auditors go.'

'It's not them this time. These are complete strangers and very stand-offish. Commandeered that room at the end of the passage and won't pass the time of day with any of the staff. They've even brought their own Thermos flasks and sandwiches as if they might get poisoned.' Normally Elvira rather liked attending the young men who came to do the audit; accountancy was a gentlemanly profession in her strictly classified code.

'Mr Lambert felt ever so bad about you being mugged at Halstead House, and asked if he could have your keys so's he can bring your car back from there.'

'Here, take them—and tell him it wasn't his fault.'

'Is there anything I can do for you, Mr Kemp?' asked Elvira before she left.

'Yes, you can go to my flat tonight, pack me some decent clothes, and come and collect me tomorrow. Better make it after twelve; I gather God makes his rounds in the late morning. Use my car—it's insured for anyone in the firm to drive.'

'Sure I'll come for you.' She was pleased. 'Seems funny you having no one else.'

'Like a wife, you mean? You're a darned sight less trouble. Off you go now, and keep Gillorns on the rails.'

When she had gone Kemp settled back, and to his own surprise but not to Sister's when she looked in on him, he fell into a deep sleep.

LETTICE WARRENDER CAME, quite properly, during the evening visitors' hour, waiting at the ward door with the herd until shown into his room by watchful Sister who appraised her from the top of her shining bob to the tips of her expensive shoes.

'Mr Kemp has not been long awake,' she remarked severely, 'don't stay long. He tires easily.'

Lettice edged in, and softly closed the door.

'I hate hospitals,' she announced, coming over to the bed.

'I'm not keen on them myself. They're very demeaning.'

'I didn't bring you anything.'

'You brought yourself. That's good enough for me.'

She sat gingerly on the edge of the chair.

'I phoned your office and they told me what had happened. Did it have anything to do with ...?'

'No, it didn't.' Kemp was determined to keep this girl out of whatever trouble he'd got himself into. He felt better after his long sleep although the establishment's supper had set him back—back, as he told Lettice, to childhood meals.

'I've not had to eat rice pudding since I had my tonsils out—and that was long before you were born.'

'You sound normal.'

'I am normal. You're all dressed up. Are you going somewhere?'

Lettice glanced down a the silk dress sliding round her knees beneath the short fur coat.

'I'm going out to dinner with Julian Cavendish,' she said with some defiance.

'Bully for you.' Kemp tried not to sound sardonic.

'It's because of what we decided... You know, about that missing story of Gran's. I phoned Julian the morning after I came to your flat. I said I would, didn't I?'

'Indeed you did. You believe in direct action, don't you, Lettice?'

'Anyway, I got him at the school and I told him about finding out that Gran had been writing. As Uncle Richard pointed out, it's not a secret any more. I asked Julian if Tullia did any typing for Gran. I made the excuse I didn't want to bother his aunt when she wasn't well but I wondered if she still had any stories of Gran's. I made it sound like a harmless inquiry so as not to arouse his suspicions.'

'Quite the little detective. And what did Julian have to say?'

'Not much, really. In fact, come to think of it, he didn't even answer my question. Just made some joke about his Aunt Tullia being a Tippex addict—then he asked me out to dinner.'

'An invitation you naturally jumped at?'

'Well, it's in the line of our business, isn't it? I can find out more by talking to him.' But her cheeks were pink and Kemp feared the excitement in her eyes had little to do with detective work. That schoolgirl crush went deep, he thought ruefully; Julian Cavendish could worm the heart out of her for all her liberated ideas.

'Be careful, Lettice. Don't say too much.'

'What? To Julian? But he's practically one of the family!'

'For that very reason.'

Lettice stared at him, her eyes shocked. 'The family? You still think my family's involved...in this?' She put out a hand towards his injured arm, then withdrew it and clenched it under her chin. 'I don't know what's wrong with Roger—he looked uncomfortable this morning when I said I would come in and see you...' She was following her own thought. 'Oh no,' she burst out suddenly. 'It couldn't be...they wouldn't...!'

Kemp was tired. He remembered other running footsteps on those cobbles...that was before the final excruciating blows, before he saw the trainer shoes. One had stood there while the others ran. In panic at what had been done to him? But the owner of the shoes had stood there, had finished the attack—with vicious deliberation.

He was so weary of it all now that he lacked his usual finesse. 'I don't want you blundering about, Lettice...'

His words made her angry. She pulled her little fur collar up round her throat and stood up. 'I'll do whatever I like. I can look after myself, thank you—which is more than you can, by the look of you. Sleep well. I think you need it.'

Kemp didn't agree. He wanted time to stay away and think, but hospital routine at bedtime was inimical to such an exercise, and within the house he had slipped once again into deep and dreamless oblivion as if he'd been pushed off the end of a diving-board.

SIXTEEN

'I'M GLAD YOU'VE DONE something at last about that awful suite in your sitting-room,' remarked Elvira as she drove Kemp out of the hospital early the next afternoon. A mild skirmish with Dr Walters had not delayed them long. He had arrived in Kemp's cubicle at precisely ten to two and found the inmate fully dressed, reading the morning paper. Elvira, sitting neat in the chair, had his suitcase at her feet and had already established feminine camaraderie with the green-eyed Sister based on mutual acquaintance in a flower-arranging class, and a shared sense of amused admiration for the patient. They each felt themselves to be in charge of his welfare.

There had then ensued a brisk exchange of non-compliments between the doctor and Kemp, ending in a reluctant admission that if Kemp was determined to discharge himself there was nothing the medico could do about it.

'It's no good me explaining to you that I'll accept no further responsibility,' said Dr Walters bitterly. 'You're a lawyer, you probably know all that. But you leave against my orders...'

'Right,' said Kemp cheerfully, 'I won't trouble your conscience, then. Thanks for the plaster, I'll return it when I've finished with it.'

He was glad to be breathing the polluted Newtown air from the open car window after the antiseptic sterility of the hospital. He supposed he ought to have felt grateful for the expert attention but gratitude was temporarily held in abeyance by less agreeable emotions. In any event he was scarcely listening to what Elvira was saying.

'I'm afraid I'm not with you. What suite are you talking about?'

'That awful purple and gold thing you've got rid of. I love real leather. Wish Bill and I could afford it.'

'I still don't know what you're on about.'

She gave him a quick sidelong glance, then steadied her eyes on the road. 'I suppose concussion does funny things to people. They say you can lose days...'

Kemp was silent till they reached his flat, and Elvira opened the door from the hall. The room looked quite different, lighter and less drab. He soon saw the reason. The blonde leather sofa and matching armchairs gave an air of opulence, even of luxury, with their soft cushions and buttoned backs. Kemp stood, staring.

'What the devil! Where'd these come from?'

Elvira was already in the kitchen unpacking groceries.

'There's tea, sugar, coffee and bread,' she said, counting them, 'butter and milk in the fridge, and I see you've plenty of cereals and biscuits.' She came to the kitchen door. 'I got in all you need for a few days, Mr Kemp. There's eggs and bacon, and I've put some steak in the fridge. What's wrong?'

'This suite of furniture, where'd it come from?'

Elvira looked at him with rounded eyes.

'Well, I suppose you bought it, Mr Kemp, and they delivered it while you were in the hospital. Bill and I saw one just like it in Cousin's furnishing department. I think it's really super. Great improvement on your old one. Now will you be all right? I ought to be getting back to the office.'

'Yes, off you go, Elvira.' Kemp wanted to be alone, to gather his wits.

'Here's your keys. Are you sure you're all right?'

'I'm sure. I gave you those keys yesterday. Did you let anyone else have them?'

'Of course not, Mr Kemp.' Elvira was affronted at what she saw as lack of trust. 'They've never been out of my handbag. Now if I were you I'd have a nice lie-down, and I'll come in later and make your supper.'

'You'll do no such thing. I can make my own supper.' He was aware he'd spoken roughly. 'Sorry, Elvira, and thanks.'

Elvira stood hesitantly on the threshold of the kitchen, methodically folding plastic bags. Her habitual decorum, which she considered proper to her role as secretary, could not quite suppress a desire to play nursemaid so that a certain motherliness crept into her tone.

'As I've said, concussion does strange things. They say you can lose your memory, Mr Kemp. But you're not to worry—it'll come back. Now I'm going to put your car away in the garage, and I'll pop the keys through the letterbox before I go, but you won't be driving for a while anyway. You're to rest...'

'Stop clucking like a hen, Elvira, and get back to your typewriter.' But he smiled to take the sting out of the words.

When she'd gone he lowered himself carefully into the soft depths of the new sofa, but its comfort threatened to ensnare him. He got up and prowled round the apartment, examining the door lock, and the window-catches. There'd been no break-in here; everything had been done in a civilized manner—which made it all the more sinister.

He sat down eventually and pulled the phone towards him. First he called his garage.

'I want to hire an automatic. Small but serviceable. For about three weeks. I've had an accident to my left arm—can't handle the gear level. Oh, so you'd heard? Didn't know I was that important... Yes, that sounds just the job. Could you bring it round tomorrow with the necessary papers?'

He made another call. Miss Warrender was not in, whether to the world at large or just to him he could not be sure.

He roamed the room restlessly, always confronted by the brash new suite. Whoever had bought it showed somewhat flamboyant taste. The furniture stared back at him, disdaining its seedy surroundings, the worn buff carpet, the porridge-coloured walls, the cheap folkweave curtains and the peeling paint. If it was going to make its home here he'd have to spruce the place up a bit. Muriel, his ex-wife, would have loved it as she loved all cool, elegant, expensive things.

Why had she come into his mind at a time like this when he already had quite enough to think about? Because that damned suite reminded him of her, he thought wearily. Because she had always chosen the decor of their homes, engaged enthusiastically in the choosing of colours, the intricacies of matching fabrics, the exact placing of objects so that contours harmonized, the artistic ideal accomplished. She'd taken a course in interior design. It had been one of her fads, for a time. Of course it cost money. Everything Muriel wanted cost money. So the need for it had risen in her like a tide she couldn't stop flowing, and that need became greater than the money itself until she was engulfed by it. Gambling. What a stupid, irrational, and finally incurable disease. He had watched helplessly as it took hold of her, like a drug he could not prevent, an addiction he could not even understand.

He aimed a kick at the calm, yielding leather of the armchair as he made his way to the kitchen. It was time he concentrated on devising means of making supper with one hand.

THE NEXT DAY Kemp was back at his office desk; if his recovery could be put down to good medical treatment it was also accelerated by the power of straight old-fashioned anger. He accepted the mingled commiseration and congratulation of the staff rather absently, and looked at his diary to confirm he had only been absent a mere four days. It seemed much longer.

'Mr Kemp?' There had been no knock on the door. The man who entered looked as if he'd never knocked on a door in his life. He had a pinched white face, narrow all-seeing eyes cut exactly in half moons, the effect of bi-focal glasses which shone at a disconcerting angle.

'Ah, Mr Proctor? You and your colleague are here on an audit, I understand.'

'Could we trouble you for a moment—we have a query.'

The room at the end of the passage was unused save for storage files in the limbo between 'costs paid' and ultimate oblivion. It contained a large table, several chairs and an outdated photocopier shelved in favour of this year's cute new model. Today the place looked like an industrial complex. All the firm's books, ledgers and accounts were either piled neatly on the table or strewn about the floor as if someone were planning an obstacle race for mice. Kemp threaded his way through to where Carruthers sat with his hands spread on the open day-book.

'What's the trouble?'

Carruthers didn't look up. The young man beside him, pin-striped suit but in shirtsleeves, gave Kemp a brief nod.

'There's an item here of your personal expenditure, Mr Kemp, for which we require an explanation.' Proctor's voice was without inflection, merely stating a fact about which he had already made a foregone conclusion.

'What is it, Peter?' Kemp leaned over on the other side of the cashier. 'I take no personal expenses out of the firm other than my salary. You know that.'

'I don't understand it either, Lennox. But it looks this way: you saw a client for Mr Lambert last Monday.' He turned the pages of a file in front of him. 'Name of Albert Burgess?'

Kemp nodded.

'That's right. Buying a maisonette. Contracts about to be exchanged.'

'You took his cheque for the deposit?'

'Part deposit—he'd already paid £1500 to the agents. The contract price is £25,000 if I remember correctly. I took his cheque for the remainder of the ten percent—£1000. I made out the slip for you with the details of the transaction.'

'I have the slip.' Carruthers extracted it. His hands were shaking. 'But there was no cheque attached to it.'

Kemp frowned. 'I put them both on your desk Monday afternoon—just before I left for the Halstead property.'

'I didn't get the cheque. I asked Elvira if it was still in the file but it wasn't. We searched the office but it didn't turn up. By then it was too late for banking so I held over the matter till the next morning to ask you about it . . .'

'But I didn't come in. Haven't you found it?'

'Yes, it's been found.' Proctor had come up behind them. He carefully placed a cheque on the table. 'Endorsed by yourself, Mr Kemp, and paid into your private account at the National Midland in Newtown.'

Kemp picked up the cheque. Made out by one Albert Burgess to Gillorns. He turned it over. His signature; he peered at it, unbelieving—it looked like his signature—on the back. Proctor's thin bloodless hand appeared and laid down another piece of paper—a paying-in slip, again signed 'Lennox Kemp' for £1000 to his own National Midland Account and also dated Monday.

'But this is nonsense! I don't do my banking that way. That slip didn't come from my paying-in book.'

'They're always available at the Bank, Mr Kemp.' Proctor sounded tired. 'You may not have had your paying-in book with you.'

'It's still nonsense. Why on earth should I pay clients' money into my own account?'

The man beside Carruthers smiled faintly. 'We've run a Bank check, Mr Kemp. Your private account was running a bit low and you didn't have the wherewithal to pay for that expensive new suite you'd just ordered.'

'Hold on a minute, George,' said Proctor as if the young man had spoken out of turn. 'You see, Mr Kemp, your little—er—transaction made us curious. So we asked the Bank about recent withdrawals and what comes up? This comes up.'

He handed Kemp a receipted bill of sale, headed 'Cousin's Furniture': 'One leather Clarendon Suite, £999.79p. to be delivered to Flat 4a, Berryfields, Newtown.' It too was dated Monday.

'You didn't waste much time paying for the goods, did you? I suppose you thought you'd reimburse the client's account before your little lapse was discovered. Easy enough—given a few days' grace and a word with your obliging Bank Manager about an overdraft. You'd have got it all right—he says your credit's good. And you would have given some story to Mr Carruthers here about having mislaid the original cheque... That's the way it would have gone, but unhappily for you things didn't work out as you'd planned. You had the misfortune to be injured and you were not in a position to repay the money. Now you know the reason why we are concerned. I don't have to spell out the implications...'

Peter Carruthers raised his eyes to Kemp's for the first time. They were troubled and full of doubt.

'You called the auditors in, Peter? Because of a missing cheque?'

The cashier shook his head. 'No, of course I didn't. These gentlemen arrived out of the blue...' He made a helpless gesture.

'You are aware that auditors sometimes make spot checks, Mr Kemp,' said Proctor smoothly. 'You have simply been unlucky.'

'Why didn't they send Mr Eliot and Mr Rogers?'

'Come, come. You know as well as I do that Eliots employ different accountants from time to time. I think if you were to telephone Mr Eliot you will find he will vouch for us. It looks as if it's just as well we came when we did. There may be further irregularities to be brought to light...'

Peter Carruthers turned to Kemp. 'Sit down, old man, you look terrible.'

Kemp pulled up a chair and put his legs under it. They felt weak.

'I just can't believe this is happening,' he muttered.

But of course he did believe it. He knew if he phoned Eliots they would confirm Proctor's bona fides; the Intelligence Service had plenty of investigative accountants. He knew if he tried phoning Cousin's Furniture they would say what they had been told to say. It was neat, very neat. A complicated mechanism had been set in motion and would trundle on to the bitter end, and he was under the wheels.

'Thank you, Mr Carruthers, I think we should like a word with Mr Kemp in private.' Proctor dismissed the cashier and closed the door behind him.

He came back to the table and stood looking down at Kemp as if his unpleasant duty bothered him although his cold eyes gave no hint that it was other than routine.

'I understand you have been injured. Concussion, Dr Walters said. Naturally we've spoken to the hospital. You appear to have discharged yourself—very foolish of you in my opinion. Lost memory might go towards mitigation. My advice to you is to go home. Obviously you cannot continue in this office while we prepare our report.'

'Who to?'

'In the first instance, to the head of your firm, Mr Archibald Gillorn.'

'And then the Law Society?'

Proctor smiled thinly.

'You have your past experience of that, Mr Kemp. This is not the first time you've tampered with clients' funds—if I may be blunt...' He glanced at his younger colleague. 'You didn't hear me say that, George.'

George obligingly shuffled papers but he wasn't deaf.

'I should take at least a week or two off, Mr Kemp,' Proctor went on in a level monotone, 'while the matter is being considered by your superiors.'

'Or yours?'

Anger glinted from behind the half-moons.

'Have a care, Mr Kemp. You're in no position to make comments like that. If you defy my order, then whatever Mr

Gillorn says I shall see to it personally that the Law Society is informed, and with your past record you'll be finished in your profession.'

'Defying orders? You make it sound like a threat, Mr Proctor—that's not the kind of talk one usually hears from the lips of ordinary accountants. But then you're not an ordinary accountant, are you?'

Proctor took a step forward. 'That's enough of that. You're in deep trouble. I'm telling you to get out of your office immediately and go home.

'You can always relax on that Clarendon suite,' put in the young man called George with a grin. Kemp could have knocked him down with one swipe of his plastered arm. Instead he got to his feet.

Proctor hadn't finished. 'You will not have any communication whatsoever with any member of this firm, nor any client of this firm, and you will take no part in any business being conducted by this firm...'

Kemp held up his hand. 'Hold on. I've already got the message. I'll go quietly.'

He didn't make a good exit. He caught his shoulder on the door jamb as he groped for the handle and pain shot along the nerves. Neither man assisted him; he didn't expect them to.

He cleared his desk. No one came in. The office seemed unnaturally quiet, and there was no sign of Elvira, but her shorthand notebook was lying on the chair. He could do a bit of Pitman's himself.

He closed the street door of Gillorns, Solicitors, behind him and glanced up at the gold lettering on the windows. What had Rose Amaury said all that long time ago?' 'I like your up-to-date surroundings, Mr Kemp.' He heard her sweetly sharp voice in his ears as he turned away. Dear, dear Rose, he thought, what trouble you have brought me.

SEVENTEEN

WHEN HE RETURNED to the flat the suite looked at him with the bland indifference shop-window furniture accords to passers-by in the street. 'Damned conspirator!' he told it on his way to the kitchen. He managed to scramble eggs, fry bacon and make coffee, childishly pleased at his developing dexterity. Unused to being at home in the daytime, he was at a loss what to do next so he tidied up what was already tidy, then sat down on the pale leather sofa and put his feet up on it to show he didn't care either. The soft yielding cushions made him uneasy; on analysing the feeling he found himself caught up in advertising slogans: 'This too can be in your home for a modest deposit' ...'For such-and-such a month you too can be the owner of this high-class luxury' ...For the first time in years he felt dissatisfaction with his environment. The apartment was shabby, a cheapskate dwelling, second-rate and sliding rapidly downhill. Like himself? He pondered on this. He was forty-four and beginning to look older; men of his age and of less ability were housed in Hampstead mock-tudors with summerhouses in their leafy gardens, and trellised roses, or commuting sedately between the City and the green fields of Kent where wives and faithful cars waited at small stations—home to dinner and the kids.

Orderly thought would not come; it was the wrong time of day. His thinking time was in the evening and that was a long way off. He got up and went over to the window. It was raining now, a fine relentless drizzle shrouding the rooftops in grey haze, making a murky aquarium of the streets below through which the cars and lorries swam like silvered fish.

Kemp dropped the curtains, got out a large notebook and went into the kitchen; threadbare surroundings suited him better than cosseted splendour. He sat down at the table and endeavoured to put his mental house in order. But it was no good; a tide of emotion rose and clouded his judgement. The lengths to which certain forces had already gone, and seemed prepared to go even further to threaten him with ultimate discredit, was frightening. Not only had warning been given that he was not to meddle, action had gone forward to ensure he would be given no chance to try. Professional misconduct—for the second time in his career—had implications far beyond mere speculation as to how, or why, it had been contrived.

For there was now no doubt in his mind that if he, Kemp, did not do as he was told, lie low and docilely accept the situation, those who had given Mr Proctor his orders would carry out their scarcely veiled purpose to disgrace him absolutely. That it had all been effectively planned that way made no difference; the charge would never be put in open court—it would be discreetly done behind closed doors.

In impotent rage he got up and stalked up and down the flat trying to shake off his blind, frustrated anger. Never before had his life been out of his own control. Never before had he been made to feel a puppet manipulated by strings in the hands of others. Even at the time of Muriel's crisis he had remained calmly in command. His act then, dipping into Trust Funds for money to save her from the threats of the gambling syndicate into whose clutches she had fallen—a willing victim of her addiction—had been a deliberate one, foreseeing the consequences if he were caught (which he had been), and bowing to the inevitable. He had weighed up the risk, taken it in his stride and, when punishment came, taken that too.

Muriel had escaped. After the divorce she had married one of her gambling friends, and disappeared out to the States, where she might still be seeking the adrenalin she needed under the glare of Las Vegas lights.

But this was different, although the powers that prowled like the hosts of Midian would assuredly use that episode of more than eight years ago as further proof of his unreliability.

There was no one to whom he could turn. Wryly he recalled his promise to Mr Archibald—not to go running to him if he got into trouble.

He was alone. All he had were his wits.

With an effort of will he went back to the bare kitchen and his notebook and pen. He began to write.

First, the assault upon himself—the physical one.

Who? Why would come later as cause and effect slotted into each other.

Ted Roding and his mates? He put that aside; if Elvira had picked up his shorthand there might be an answer soon despite a watch on his flat.

The Warrenders and the Cavendishes? Cavaliers and Roundheads, which was which and who had the greater power? He bracketed them together for the time being, and meditated on the historical perspective which probably had no relevance. It was evident that Roger and Torvil did not take kindly to his friendship with Lettice but surely the days were gone when young men drew swords in defence of their maiden relatives? More to the point, Lettice had let the cat out of the bag to Julian Cavendish over a week ago by asking him if his aunt did any typing for her grandmother. He would come back to that later.

The elder generation of Warrenders Kemp crossed off his list; he believed Lettice's estimation of her parents. After a moment's thought he also deleted the Reverend Clive—not so much on account of his cloth as his age, although he was left wondering whether the Vicar had faith enough in Divine Providence to leave his sister to that heavenly concept. Could he perhaps have been an unwitting instigator: 'Who will rid me of this turbulent lawyer—' an absent-minded remark thrown off in a misguided moment of desperation like its royal precedent, and heard, as then, by more brutish ears.

Tullia Cavendish. That irksome anomaly, the married spinster. She was the key figure if only he could get at her, but she was for the moment unattainable, hidden away like a princess in a tower, guarded by a vague illness in which no one believed. She had typed Rose Amaury's story, of that Kemp was certain. Had she been searching for the original notes when he found her with the suitcase? Had they been already torn out by somebody else? He could have sworn she hadn't had time to hide them when he disturbed her. He wrote the word 'fingerprints' and put a query. Too late now, even had he access to police facilities.

That story—and the notes for it—there was the vital ingredient, the spice that made the whole course smack of danger. Rose Amaury herself had been unaware of what she had put into the recipe, the sinister element she had introduced which had caused the broth to ferment and turn sour.

It must be something serious; no mere female gossip, fanciful conjecture, fictional characters or imagined situations would have called forth such determined powers to prevent disclosure, unless somewhere, somehow they were based on fact.

He sprang up and dragged out Rose's suitcase from under the box of dusters and vacuum cleaner attachments in his broom cupboard. He hadn't deliberately hidden it; simply answered an instinct not to have it in open view. If they'd searched his flat, they didn't know what to look for. Only Richard, Lettice and, possibly, Tullia knew he still had it. He'd placed his own sheaf of notes in the brown envelope. They hadn't been disturbed. He took out the letter from the literary agency. No one had seen it except himself and Lettice and he didn't think she would have remembered the name. He looked reflectively at the telephone. He knew very little about bugging—such devices were frowned upon at McCready's—apart from their illegality to all save those authorized by warrant. Unscrewing the mouthpiece as he'd seen it done in films was quite beyond his one-handed clumsiness, even had he known what to look for. If they were tapping his line, it was a chance he had to take. He listened carefully as he picked up the phone, and dialled, but there seemed to be no suspicious noise—only the ringing tone.

'Preskel's Literary Agency.' It was a female who answered.

Kemp glanced down at the signature. 'Could I speak to Mr Jacob Preskel?'

'One moment, please. Who shall I say is calling?'

'It would convey nothing to him, but I have an urgent personal message for Mr Preskel.'

There was a click, then a deep voice.

'Jacob Preskel speaking.'

'I'm sorry to bother you, Mr Preskel. My name is Lennox Kemp and I'm a solicitor in Newtown. I'm acting as executor in the estate of an elderly lady who died recently. Among her effects I have found a letter from you regarding some short stories she sent you some months ago.'

'What was her name?'

'Mrs Rose Amaury of The Bungalow, Castleton House, here in Newtown.'

'I don't recall the name. You say it was some months ago?'

'Yes. It was just that in clearing up her affairs I did wonder if she'd sent you anything else. You did return her stories. May I refer to your letter dated February 11th this year?'

'Just a moment, and I'll have a look at my index.'

It sounded like a small business, fortunately; possibly run by one man and his secretary-telephonist.

There was a long silence. Kemp contrived to light a cigarette, a manoevre he had not yet perfected. The phone crackled.

'I've got my copy letter. Nothing else has come in from the lady. You say she's died?'

'Yes, quite recently. Do you remember anything about the stories she sent you?'

'I get hundreds of stories sent in, Mr Kemp. You can't expect me to remember them all, particularly when they're not good enough for me to place. I see I recommended that she work on one of them, and that she has manuscripts typed in future... Really, these ladies who expect us to plough through their spidery handwriting...'

'Yes, yes, that one called *The Bystander*. Can you possibly recall what it was about?'

'I get so many stories from all kinds of people with literary ambitions...' It was a mellow voice, now becoming slightly querulous. 'They're all pretty run-of-the-mill stuff.'

'I appreciate that. But something about this one must have struck you to make you write as you did. Your letter was kind and somewhat encouraging.'

'It's months ago... Let me think...' Again there was a silence before Jacob Preskel came back on the line.

'Oddly enough, Mr Kemp, I am beginning to remember. Not because of the story itself but something struck me at the time. Of course it needed re-writing, it was rather jejune, but there was something about it...'

Kemp had been holding his breath. He let it out slowly.

'What was it that struck you, Mr Preskel?'

'Well, I knew the place where it was set. That was it. Now I remember. She was describing my homeland...'

There was a pause. 'And where was that, Mr Preskel?' Kemp urged him gently.

'The Harz Mountains. I was born in Goslar, Mr Kemp. As you may have gathered from my name,' Jacob Preskel went on drily, 'I am Jewish. My family were fortunate in coming out before it was too late... But that was what I remembered about this story. It struck a chord, you understand?'

'Mrs Amaury wrote about that area?'

'Yes. I think there was a leave centre there for Allied troops after the war. At Bad Harzburg. Because I knew the place I found the background to her tale interesting, and, yes, authentic. As a boy I had walked much in those woods...'

'Can you remember what the story was about?'

'I'm afraid not. It was a bit too long and rambling. Very amateurish. But something could have been made of it. I'm sorry... I can't remember more than that. I have to read so many stories, you see. I wouldn't have remembered this one had I not known the place. But the details of it have quite gone out of my head.'

'What period would she have been writing about?'

There was an old man's chuckle.

'A lifetime away, Mr Kemp. Even I know that. She wrote about *die Grenze*, she even used the original word, *die Zonengrenze*...'

'The frontier?'

'That is so. There was no wall then, you understand. Only the marked trees in the forest. It wasn't until the early fifties that our East German comrades began to barricade the border and the barbed wire began to go up... From what I remember of Mrs Amaury's story she was writing about a period before that. Something about someone going over *die Grenze*... Funny, I'd forgotten all about it until now.'

'Who was the bystander of the title?'

'I can't remember. I think the trouble with the story was that the writer had used the first person—so perhaps she saw herself as simply an onlooker. It was all a bit womanish—lacked punch. Wait now, it's coming back to me—she mentioned the Spectre of the Brocken...'

'What's that?'

'It's a local phenomenon caused by cloud on the western slope of the hill at sunset when there's a mist in the valley. You know the Brocken itself is in the Eastern Zone? It enlarges the shadow of someone standing at a certain point so that their reflection appears gigantic when it's thrown on to cloud below. Mrs Amaury did mention it in her story... I'm sorry I can't recall any more. I'd have forgotten it completely had it not been for the location. I'm sorry the lady has died, but if she was writing out of her own experience—and I rather think she was—then she would have been quite elderly.'

If Mr Preskel had to read so much fiction perhaps he didn't have much time to read the papers. More probably the name of Rose Amaury had conveyed nothing to him when the tragedy had been in the headlines.

'I'm obliged to you, Mr Preskel, for your excellent memory. The matter is really of no importance. As her executor I simply had to ascertain that nothing of her writing had been published...'

The literary agent seemed satisfied by Kemp's stilted explanation, and rang off. Kemp put the phone down gently, and returned to the kitchen table and his notes, but with a lighter step. A weight had been lifted from him. He had managed to cut through one of the strings snarling his fingers. Struck by the metaphor, he tried to wiggle those on the end of his injured arm and was rewarded by movement. He was making progress.

He sat down and contemplated the faceless ones behind the screen of recent events, and found them no longer bogeymen. He was well aware—as most people are—of aspects of Government about which one can happily profess ignorance, indeed it is commendable to do so, and that, although such aspects are said to be in the public interest, the interest of the public is not encouraged. 'The security service is, after all, a secret service...that is part of its essence.' He recalled ruefully that quote from Hansard, and now considered it in the light of his own entanglement. Like Mrs Amaury, he had tripped over something, and a wire had twitched—a long way off. Archie Gillorn had given him the hint that the Intelligence Service was involved...

Now that Kemp had discovered their likely sphere of interest they were reduced in size to ordinary mortals going about their legitimate business as if they were brokers dealing shares or greengrocers sorting cabbages. That their commodity might be secrets, and their methods devious, made no essential difference. Even his resentment at their heavy-handed tactics against himself faded to some extent, from white-hot to lukewarm, now that he had discovered the vital connection. This might be time, he thought with a sudden burst of hilarity, to contemplate the true patriot's gratitude to those who are constantly vigilant for traitors within the realm and enemies without. Had a Union Jack hung on his wall he might well have risen and saluted it.

For now that he had the actual location of Rose Amaury's missing story he felt he could breathe more easily inside his own sphere; it moved the whole operation firmly into the orbit of the Secret Intelligence Service. And as far as Kemp was concerned, they were welcome to it. The dark and intricate underworld of espionage, the moles burrowing and the worms turning this way and that beneath the bloodstained soil of Central Europe, was one he had no desire to enter.

Of course he was still curious. That Spectre of the Brocken she had written about must have cast a very long shadow indeed—long enough to span the years before it touched some sensitive spot. That much he knew, and appreciated. The question for him was: should he take it further or leave it where it rightly belonged, in the hands of those appointed guardians of civilization as we know it?

Conscious that he was becoming light-headed again, he went over to the window to find the rain heavier and the sky darkening—a circumstance which instantly depressed him as he fell victim to pathetic fallacy, that falseness in impression of natural things produced by violent feelings. These swooping changes in mood were beginning to worry him, but he put them down to the effects of recent anaesthesia and hospital drugs.

He decided to make some tea but was interrupted in the process by the ringing of his bell.

Bessie Higgins stood dripping on the doorstep like a cormorant flapping wings on a rock.

'Yer secretary girl said you'd be wanting a cleaner,' she announced with her usual truculence as she divested herself of plastic hood, plastic mac, and plastic overboots, laying them down on the hall floor with no ceremony.

'Come in, Bessie, come in.' Kemp was delighted with her.

She marched straight for the kitchen, and the kettle hissing on the stove. 'I'd have thought you'd at least have an electric,' she observed as she lunged for the teapot. She had an immediate grasp of domestic priorities.

'I charge a pound an hour. You can have six hours a week, mornings only—' she looked at his arm—'and make yer dinner the days I come. That's till you can manage yerself...'

'I'm obliged to you, Bessie. That'll be fine.'

She glanced round with disparaging black eyes as she shovelled tea-leaves. 'H'm... Tidy enough but that floor needs a good scrub an' yer nets wants doin'...' She carried in the tray of tea. 'An' when was this place last dusted? Ye'll have a Hoover?'

Kemp assured her she would not lack equipment. 'Sit down, for God's sake, Bessie. We have to talk.'

She looked with disfavour at the blonde suite, and fetched a kitchen chair for herself.

'Reckon I know why you sent that girl, Elvira is it? Fancy name but she knows what she's about. Said to give you this.' She took a crumpled envelope from the pocket of her dark shirt.

Kemp opened it, and took out the note. Elvira had typed it on office quarto but he could see where the type had hit the platen; there would be no carbon copy taken.

Your shorthand needs brushing up, Mr Kemp, but I understood it. Office in a turmoil but nobody says anything. Mr Proctor's been through your files. Like you said, I'm calling round at the Rodings in my lunch-hour to ask if Mrs Higgins will char for you and will give her this note to bring. Then I'll go to Planning, and try to see Miss Warrender. I've got some Searches to make at the Council Offices so that's an excuse. Those auditors keep on following me with their eyes. Don't understand all this secrecy. Mr Lambert says you can't come into the office for a while. Mr Kemp, you know my address—Bill and I will help if we can. Cheerio...'

'Thanks, Bessie. Now what's all this that Ted Roding had to tell me but wouldn't?'

Mrs Higgins reached into the biscuit tin for chocolate bourbons. 'That Ted! You know he's been picked up?'

'By the Newtown police.'

'Naw. In London, by the Met. One of his mates been and told his ma. Suspected of pilfering on a building site. He's only had the job a fortnight. Well, you know Ted... Seems like he's asked for you, Mr Kemp, as his lawyer, like, but the rozzers wouldn't have it... Said they'd get him a lawyer themselves...'

I'll bet, thought Kemp. All would be done properly; they couldn't afford any fuss.

'Ted's safer in custody,' he remarked absently.

Bessie looked at him sharply but said nothing.

'Now, before this happened, when he was still in Newtown, Ted phoned me...'

'I know. He went on about it. How you was going to clear Kevin, and he'd got summat would help. Then he flew off at the deep end when he saw you one day with the Warrender girl—said you wasn't to be trusted no more...'

'So he told me. He's an idiot. What was it he'd found out that would clear Kevin?'

'It weren't in no Scrubs that set-up was planned. It come to Ted there so's he'd put the finger on Kevin but that's not where it started. Ted says he was used too, just like Kev. Proper mad Ted was when he found out...'

'Where did it start, then?'

'Here in Newtown. With the nobs, that's what Ted says now. Somebody high up, somebody with money...'

'They paid to have the place burgled?'

Bessie's shrewd gipsy eyes met his. She nodded.

'How did Ted find this out?'

'He went back to some of his old mates—the ones he knew at the Youth Club afore the trouble there. Seems like someone had been asking about him and Kevin, how they'd done break-ins and all that... And money passed, a lot of money. Well, after Kevin's funeral there'd been a change of heart. The lads were all upset.'

'You mean the word was passed to Ted in the Scrubs to make it look as if the job came from a London gang?'

'That's right. What Ted says is you'd best look local. He'd 'ave told you hisself but for you seein' the Warrender girl. That didn't half put him off you...'

'Now, listen carefully, Bessie. Did Ted mention any name in connection with this someone? Any name at all?'

'Naw. Just says the gentry's in it...' She hesitated, took a great gulp from her cup. 'Says that's why the rozzers were 'appy to blame it all on Kevin. Suited their book, it did.'

Kemp frowned. The 'gentry' would be Bessie's own word, and could cover an entire class of persons; the rest was straight out of Ted's mouth, and added nothing new.

'When did Ted start work in London, Bessie?'

'It's near two weeks now. Our Ted can work hard when he's a mind to it and needs the dough. He was skint. He got the lend of a pick-up truck to take him to London every day.'

'Which he also used to pick up bits on the side...' Kemp grinned understandingly at her.

'Well, we all know our Ted.' Bessie was making no judgement. 'They caught him with some bricks in the back, like...'

'Was he working last Monday afternoon?'

'Course he was. I know what you're thinking, Mr Kemp. That was the day you got beaten up, I'eard, but it weren't

Ted, that's for sure—nor any of his mates. He were at the site every day till yesterday when the foreman called the cops about bricks that kept disappearin'... Said they was in his truck. Ted swears they wasn't... But with his record who's to believe him?'

Who indeed? Another plant, and an easy one this time. Keep Ted out of circulation for a while, and out of Kemp's reach. Neat, if not totally unforeseen.

'Do you believe Ted, Bessie? Oh, not about the bricks—that's of no matter. I mean, do you believe him generally?'

It was a big question, and Bessie answered it to the best of her ability. 'Ted's an awful liar, Mr Kemp, but not when he's angry—and he's flamin' angry now. Says he's got it all worked out what happened that night. Kevin was to break in, but there was someone else around, just waitin'. Ted thinks Kev was used as a—what d'ye call it?—a decoy while somebody else got into the old lady's bedroom at the back. Lookin' for summat, they were. Kev weren't to be too careful about making a noise, so's she'd get up, and Kev were to keep her talking, like... He'd be good at that, our Kev... Give her the old story and plead to be let off. But it all went wrong. She got coshed, and Kev just took off with the small stuff... D'you think that's what happened, Mr Kemp?'

'I don't know. What do you think?'

Bessie brushed crumbs from her lap. She got up and stacked the cups on the tray. On the way to the kitchen she spoke over her shoulder.

'Maggie says Kevin came back that night... for his passport.'

Kemp shot out of his chair.

'Why the hell didn't she say so?'

Bessie put the tray down carefully and turned, hands on broad hips. 'To them rozzers? You must be joking. They'd say she was in it with him.'

'She saw Kevin when he came back?'

'I'm betrayin' a confidence...'

'Long words, Bessie. Whose side do you think I'm on?'

She took the crockery to the sink and started to wash up
as if the running water would cleanse her of this, the ultimate sin, breaking the trust of a friend.

'She never told me at first . . . not till Kev was dead. Then
she made me swear I'd never tell no one. Kev did come back
that night, and his mam woke up. He were in a right state.
He were lookin' for his passport—that's all he'd come for.
He weren't in the house more'n a few minutes . . .'

'What did he say to his mother?'

'She don't remember much . . . It were wild talk, she says.
It comes back to her in fits and starts when she can't sleep.
That's when I sit with her, and that's when she told me. Kev
kept on sayin' he'd be done for the murder if he didn't get
out but he'd never even touched the old lady . . .'

'Did his mother know it was Mrs Amaury who was dead?'

'She never knew that till next mornin' when the police
come. That's what broke her in pieces—when she knew.'

'What else was in this wild talk of Kevin's?'

'He said he'd be looked after all right once he got abroad.
They'd promised him . . . He showed her money . . . a lot of
it. Said he'd send some to her later. He'd see she were all
right. And he kept on about a stick. How'd a stick get on the
floor, he said. She never had no stick. She just fell down.
And he went on about the lights not workin' . . .'

'What did Mrs Roding make of that?'

'She couldn't make head or tail of his talk. She was that
scared because she knew he'd been there . . . Poor soul, she's
near demented with it all . . . But I got to thinkin', Mr Kemp,
so I says to her: "Maggie, did Mrs Amaury always use that
stick after her accident?' and Maggie says, no, she didn't.
She didn't like usin' a stick—took against it, she did, put it
in the stand in the hall and left it there. She'd only got it because Mrs Paula Warrender insisted.'

'The post-mortem showed that she was struck down with
it and the blow killed her,' said Kemp. 'Did you know that?'

'No, I didn't,' replied Bessie huffily. 'That stuff's all official, like—not for the likes of me.'

'Was there anything else Kevin said to his mother that night?'

Bessie shook her head. 'He just threw things about lookin' for his passport. When he got it he were off—with that holdall he was carryin'. Reckon them bits and pieces were in it. Maggie put the place straight when he'd gone. She never told no one. Only me. An' I feel right dirty tellin' you, Mr Kemp. We've allus been close, Maggie and me. She needs lookin' arter...'

'You did right to tell me, Bessie. Believe me.'

But Bessie Higgins wasn't to be comforted by soft talk.

'Sometimes she blames herself, Maggie does. Says if she'd told the police right off, like, then Kev mightn't be dead now.'

'He'd be dead no matter what she'd done,' said Kemp, feeling that grim truth unavoidable.

Bessie drew her brows down in a black scowl, a sign of her deep thought. 'Maggie says Kevin got a letter through the door that mornin'...not by the post. He'd been hangin' about, like, as if he were waitin' for it. Ever so pleased with hisself he were when it come. He never said nothin' to her... Well, Kev was never one for many words...' Bessie stopped; she too had run out of words.

'You've done me a good turn,' said Kemp. 'Try not to fret about your cousin. Just keep your eye on her, and tell her not to worry—it'll all come out right in the end.' His voice trailed off; he hadn't the certainty of that even now.

Bessie turned away with a slouch to her shoulders. 'I don't know the half of what's been goin' on, Mr Kemp, really I don't. As for Ted, what's a bit o' nickin' here and there compared with what some folks'll get up to?' With this nugget of not altogether original wisdom off her chest, she edged her bulk out of the kitchen and collected her plastic rainwear.

'I'll be here nine sharp in the mornin'... You have a nice long lie-in...'

Kemp watched her from the window, stumping head down across the road like a shiny waterproof beetle with stick legs, splashing through the gutters in great black boots.

Then he returned thoughtfully to his notes.

Interesting that he and Ted should have finally reached much the same conclusions; it had simply taken longer for the implications to percolate the wirewool in Ted's skull—despite his advantage of knowing exactly what had passed between the brothers in that last prison conversation. For there Ted had surely lied to Kemp, and even now some clever lawyer could be trying to worm its substance out of Ted. Kemp wished him luck.

Kemp himself was now left wrestling with two strands of a hypothetical situation which flatly contradicted each other: the provision of a getaway car and a hideout on the Continent sounded far-fetched if Kevin Roding's job was to be simple burglary—as did the amount of money rumoured. It was a bit over the top for a mere break-in, as if a tale had been spun to make a buzz round the prison, particularly between Ted's big ears knowing he was having a visit from his brother.

From that vague whisper with all its overtones of high-priced crime only two solid facts had emerged: the place, Newtown, and the timing of the burglary. Someone had been working to a very tight schedule, awaiting opportunity, and Kevin's part was essential.

Why Kevin? Kemp tugged at the other irreconcilable strand. Kevin hadn't taken his passport that night, and there'd been no getaway car, he'd had to steal one after that frantic dash back home. Ergo, Kevin had not been told the whole story. And, again, why Kevin Roding in the first place? The answer to that stared Kemp in the face. Because he knew the bungalow...or was it because Mrs Amaury would know him? The more Kemp thought of that theory, the more he liked it. Kevin was meant to be caught by her, would plead with her, might even get off... Kevin Roding was only a diversion from something bigger, more sinister, that had been planned.

Whatever it was that had been planned, murder was what had happened. And where did the Intelligence Services fit into all this? It was a big and dangerous question. Perhaps the murder had been inadvertent. But when Kemp looked again at his hypothetical flag it appeared to be hanging at half-mast.

EIGHTEEN

THE NEXT MORNING, leaving Bessie to terrorize the fluff round his kitchen stove, Kemp went dutifully to the outpatient's clinic to have his stitches removed.

'How's the concussion?' asked Nurse pertly, as if the hospital had had no other topic of conversation. 'Dr Walters was quite concerned about you.'

Dr Walters was not the only one, reflected Kemp. 'Anything you may have said will be taken down and used as evidence of concussion...' Neat. He wondered if he had in fact rambled under the anaesthetic; if he had, then he'd been robbed. An Englishman's thoughts should be private even if his home were no longer his castle.

Aloud he merely remarked, straight-faced. 'What concussion, Nurse? Can you unstitch it for me? And who is Dr Walters?'

She finished what she was doing, slipped the scissors into a basin, and turned to peer at him, frowning.

'You surely haven't forgotten Dr Walters?'

'The most forgettable character I've ever met,' said Kemp, and left before she'd worked it out for herself.

Later he settled in an empty corner of The Cabbage White and drank two cups of coffee. By twelve o'clock he had begun to wonder if Lettice would come. By half past the hour he had almost given her up, so he got himself a prawn salad and a glass of white wine. The place had filled up but his table was still satisfactorily isolated. Just before one o'clock he saw her come in the door. After a quick glance she went to the counter, without looking at him. He kept his eyes on his plate, heard her quick determined step and watched as she set down her dish and cutlery, stacked her tray and took a seat. Without speaking, he got up and fetched two more glasses of wine.

'I need this—for medicinal purposes. And you're going to need it too.'

'I don't know why I'm here.' Her voice was clipped, her tone brusque. 'Your secretary said you wanted to see me. I cannot think why.' She might have been the head girl admonishing a first-former.

'I thought we had an arrangement—an alliance.'

'Not any more, Mr Kemp.' Lettice cut her wedge of quiche precisely in two, put her knife down and proceeded to demolish the crumbled pastry mixture with the fork, conveying it with delicate accuracy behind her pretty white teeth. Between mouthfuls she continued to address him with severity. 'You have been dishonest with me—as I understand you have been dishonest with others. I am disappointed, but not surprised. I have learned that men like you are plausible liars.' She stopped to butter a roll, tore off small pieces and popped them into her mouth which closed firmly on each as if to give them no chance to escape. 'What are you staring at me like that for?'

'Your eating habits amaze me, Lettice. Did you all do it to the count of ten at that school of yours?'

She dropped her fork with a clatter. Kemp retrieved it for her. Her face flushed, and she looked at him in silence. 'Well,' she said eventually, 'what have you to say for yourself?'

'About what? You accuse me of dishonesty. Then you include me in a generality on the perfidy of certain men. What am I supposed to say? Bow down and kiss your feet, beg your forgiveness?'

'You've taken advantage of me . . .'

'Oh, come off it, Lettice Warrender. We're not in a Victorian novel, nor are you a schoolgirl any more. Grow up, lass, for heaven's sake!'

She nearly left the table at that gibe. He could see her instant resolution, smiled at her as it faltered. She decided on the modern, sophisticated approach. She picked up her glass of wine and sipped, the female executive confronted with a recalcitrant employee—as seen on television board-room drama. She carefully relinquished her glass, pursed her pink lips, then spoke with deliberate candour.

'Mr Kemp. Two men came to Castleton House last night. They talked first with my parents, then with me. They informed us it was their duty to explain why you could no longer act as executor in Grandmother's estate. Uncle Richard had already been told the facts at his London home...'

Kemp brought his palms together in a soundless clap.

'Bravo! Spoken like a true civil servant. Dot the i's, cross the t's, and duck when the shit hits the fan.'

She shrank. It was language she read about but seldom heard. The look on her face made him repent.

'Sorry, Lettice. It's not my usual style, and hurts me as much as it does you. Anyway, why did you come today?'

'For an explanation. You owe me one. You misled me with this tarradiddle about Grandmother's death. What she said to you about her life being threatened. It was all a pack of lies. You're just a dishonest solicitor trying to wheedle your way into our family affairs. I don't know what your motive has been. Just to ingratiate yourself, I've no doubt...'

Kemp offered her a cigarette which she refused, but when he fumbled his one-handed attempt to light it she helped him.

'They said you'd been struck off once. Mother and Father were outraged. If they'd only known.'

'Your grandmother knew.' Grace McCready had been open in reply to Rose Amaury's questions as to why a lawyer should be working for a lowly detective agency.

Lettice showed her astonishment, but she rallied.

'Then Gran was the more fool to trust you.'

'But she did, Lettice,' said Kemp quietly. 'Why do you suppose she did that?'

'She was crazy. That's what they said...'

The shock in Kemp's face registered with Lettice, and she made an abrupt movement, upsetting her glass. 'It's too good to waste,' he said, getting up. 'I'll fetch another.' The pause would do her good. When he returned her face was blank.

'You're doing your grandmother the greatest injustice if you believe that,' he said gently. 'There was no one more in command of her senses than Rose Amaury when she died. Remember that. Don't let yourself be fooled.'

'But what those men said about you... You never told me that you'd been struck off by the Law Society for dishonesty.'

'You never asked.' Kemp shrugged. 'It's not something one volunteers. Anyway, it's got nothing to do with your problem.'

'I haven't got a problem.'

'Oh yes you have. Otherwise you wouldn't be here. You don't know whether to believe what these men told you or to believe me. Your grandmother was murdered, and not by Kevin Roding. Kevin Roding was set up—do you know what that means?'

She put her hands over her ears. 'I don't want to hear any more.'

'It means she was killed by a person or persons unknown, and you don't give a damn who did it...'

'They said you'd try this... That you'd try anything. And Julian said...'

'Was Julian Cavendish there when these men came?'

'He brought me home last night. We'd been to a concert.'

'And what did Julian say?'

'That people like you... people who'd gone under... were embittered against society, and would try and get back at those in... established positions. Oh, Julian wasn't being nasty. In fact he was very sympathetic. Said he understood how you probably felt... This hitting back at

those in positions of authority, it would be the natural reaction of someone like you...'

Kemp took a deep breath. Where the stitches had come
out the skin seemed to burn, and he put his fingers on the
scar tissue. God save us from the sociology experts, he
thought. Commiseration and half-baked psychoanalytic
rubbish from Julian Cavendish was just about the last straw.
The weight of it made his voice heavy.

'So you've decided that all is well in the best of all possible worlds so long as the subversive elements are kept in
their place?'

'Who's talking generalities now?'

'A specific person who's fed up to the teeth with one
particular aspect of the status quo... and who is... bloody
angry.' When Kemp forsook his rational self, an underlying
violence surfaced visibly which could alarm an onlooker
more than he realized. Lettice was shaken by the blaze in his
normally vague eyes, the obstinate lines which took the
roundness from his cheeks, the set of an otherwise inconspicuous jaw. It was as if a cuddly toy had suddenly turned
into a tiger. Her first leaping thought was truly feminine:
My God, I'd thought him only interesting, he's really at-
tractive!

'Why should you be so angry?' she faltered, 'Gran was
nothing to you... and she can't be brought back to life.'

'Injustice makes me angry. Did any of your family spare
a thought for Margaret Roding? Her son's dead, and la-
belled a murderer in the eyes of the world. Is that justice?'

She looked away, and stared out of the window where the
sun was sweeping the morning's rain clouds from the sky.
At last she said: 'The police have brought back some of the
things he stole. The Dutch authorities traced the market
stalls he'd been to before...'

'I hope they fitted the inventory,' said Kemp drily.

'It's proof he was there,' she said fiercely.

'Oh, he was there all right,' said Kemp, 'the poor sod. He
was meant to be.'

She winced at the hardness in his voice. But she dived into her bag and brought out a folded piece of graph paper.

'I'm not altogether a ninny,' she said gruffly. 'I wasn't going to show you this but maybe I should... When I found Gran that morning I simply stood and stared. I was so shocked I went numb. But I did know what to do. I didn't touch anything, only leant over her and saw that she was quite dead. I phoned the police and the doctor. But afterward I tried to remember the scene in every detail. You know my way. I'm a good draughtswoman so I drew a sketch plan of the room as I found it. Oh, I realize it was done from memory but I was trained to be observant. Anyway, the police didn't want it, they make their own sketches. But I kept it.'

She spread it on the table, methodically clearing the dishes to make space. It was a good drawing, clear and accurate. Kemp remembered the little parlour. He studied the position of the body, just inside the door, the outline of a stick lying beside the head. The furniture was depicted as on a stage set, the cabinet door swung open, and upset vase of daffodils on the carpet, a round object half under a chair. Lettice put a finger down on it. 'I saw it, but didn't see it, if you know what I mean,' she said. 'It was only later when I thought about it, and after I'd talked to you, that I realized what it was. Granny's torch. She always kept it by her bed since power cuts all those winters ago.'

'But the police found her bedside lamp on in the morning. Why did she need a torch?'

'Her bedroom light was on. I could see it from the hall when I went in at the front door... The broken lock and that lamp being on were the first signs that something was dreadfully wrong. The police explained to me later that she must have switched on the lamp when she was disturbed.'

'Well, it fitted their theory that she was wakened by a noise in the front room—that vase smashing—and she put on her lamp, took up her stick and came down the passage. She recognized Kevin, he snatched the stick and struck her with it. I didn't know about the torch but I suppose the police thought it just fell from her hand and rolled under that chair.'

'But Gran couldn't have managed to carry both a torch and her stick! I know it's only a small torch but she had arthritis in her left hand—she couldn't grip properly.'

'And Kevin Roding said there wasn't a stick. He also said the lights wouldn't go on...' Kemp was talking to himself. 'He'd have his own torch—no self-respecting burglar should be without one. Why should he want to put the lights on? And why didn't they go on? Because someone had already thrown the main switch. But they put that right afterwards—when they searched her bedroom, when they took what they'd wanted...' He looked at the sketch. 'That vase of flowers. The day I called to see your grandmother, it stood on the little table by the window. Was it always there?'

Lettice nodded.

'It wasn't near the desk, or the cabinet. Kevin had no reason to touch it. It wasn't valuable and far too big for him to carry off. And the table it was on is a long way from where Mrs Amaury fell. He deliberately smashed it to make a noise. She heard it, tried to put on her lamp but it failed. She picked up her torch and made her way to the sitting-room. Somebody followed her, took the stick out of the hallstand and...'

Lettice was white, staring at him.

'Is that what you think happened?'

'I don't know. I'm only trying to piece things together. Kevin Roding talked to his mother that night. Wild talk, but it's beginning to make sense.'

'You said "they"...that they'd got what they wanted. What was it, Lennox?' Her voice had sunk to a whisper.

The patch of sunshine lying on the table between them stained yellow the white paper of her drawing. A shadow fell across the line of light. Instinctively Kemp covered the diagram, folding it over. He ran a finger down the crease before looking up at Julian Cavendish.

'Well, well. The Spectre of the Brocken...'

He couldn't think why he said the words. The juxtaposition of sun and shadow had brought them, unbidden, into his mind but he was unprepared for their effect on the man who had approached so silently. Cavendish had rested a hand on the table edge, and now the glassware shivered and the crockery went into a crazy dance. Kemp continued to watch the schoolmaster's face as the hand was hastily withdrawn and thrust, still shaking, into the pocket of his leather jacket. It was a fine jacket, custom-made, showing off Julian's thickset manliness and his self-identification as a relic of the swinging 'sixties. He did not look as if he was swinging now. Struggling to regain composure, he deliberately turned his broad back on Kemp, and spoke to Lettice.

'You said you'd be here. I was to come and pick you up in case this man was making trouble.'

'Yeah. She needs rescuing.' Kemp was playing his anger for all it was worth; it seemed to be getting results. 'I'm glad you came, Mr Cavendish. I wanted to have a word with you. It concerns your aunt. I'd like to see her.'

Julian Cavendish stepped to one side, and looked down at Kemp coldly. Light on his feet, thought Kemp, taking in the suede shoes, and a soft treader; I should have guessed.

'Mr Kemp. I do have some sympathy with your position. It is an unenviable one and you may well have reason to be bitter. But to try to hit back at society by insinuating yourself into the confidences of elderly ladies is simply despicable. I have no intention of allowing you to see Miss Cavendish. And right now you can stop bothering Lettice.'

'Protector of young maidens, too?' sneered Kemp, 'You take your scholastic duties a mite seriously—she's out of the classroom now.'

It was a nasty little exchange and Kemp felt no better for it as Lettice got to her feet hastily. But she pushed Julian's arm away when he put it round her shoulder.

'I'm quite capable of getting back to my office on my own feet, thank you, Julian.' She strode off down the restaurant with Cavendish following close at her heels. At the door she turned and looked back at Kemp.

He put the sketch plan to his lips in a silencing gesture, and was relieved to see her give the slightest nod.

NINETEEN

LENNOX KEMP left The Cabbage White and went to the Newtown police station. Inspector Upshire wasn't pleased to see him.

'You've no business here. In fact you've no business anywhere at the moment, from what I hear. But I don't listen to rumour, and I don't ask questions unless I have to. You're out of things for the present, and it'll do you good to take a rest. No, we've come up with nothing on the assault—except that it wasn't Ted Roding.'

'Even I know that. He was busy pinching materials from a building site following his natural bent—or so they say. That's not why I'm here.' Kemp laid the sketch plan on the Inspector's desk and sat down, ignoring the expression which had come over that officer's chubby features, the look of a choirboy about to be shown unhealthy pictures.

Kemp marshalled his thoughts carefully, and proceeded to state his case as if in Court, putting forward cogent argument, theorizing only from facts and setting these firmly brick by brick on top of one another as if laying a wall.

John Upshire had a high regard for Kemp's legal abilities, and was not himself a man easily satisfied. When Kemp had finished Upshire sat silent for a while; he rubbed his face as he considered what he had heard, his wide blue eyes reserving judgement.

'What do you hope to achieve?' he asked.

'Some consideration for the Rodings. A further inquiry into that very convenient death in Amsterdam. Surely at least that can be done without rocking whatever boat other people have at sea?'

Upshire shook his head. 'It'll only stir things up. Anyway, I haven't the authority.'

'You could try. Have a word with Superintendent Quennell—in view of this.' Kemp brought his hand down on Lettice Warrender's sketch. 'And what I've told you.'

'I don't like it, Lennox. What if it was one of their men who was at the bungalow that night?'

'What if it were? Don't they have to answer to somebody? Look, John, I don't give a damn who they were or what they were up to, but, believe me, I won't let it stop here. I'll go to the Press...'

Upshire got to his feet abruptly. 'You wouldn't dare. Think of your own position—you'd be ruined.'

'I've been ruined before. I keep bobbing up—and I'll keep bobbing up until there's been some justice done to that family.'

'The Rodings? What about the other families involved?'

'They've got enough clout to look after themselves. They've done all right so far...'

A smile slipped over Upshire's face. 'You're bad for me, Lennox Kemp. A terrible influence, you are. You appeal to my baser instincts. All right. Tell you what I'll do. I'm in London tomorrow. I'll go and see Quennell. Make some excuse. It won't be official, mind. Just a word in his ear over a drink. It's the best I can do.'

'Tell him what you like. Say you've got a raving maniac on your hands—the result of that blow on the head. But make sure he knows that I'll make trouble if I don't get some answers. There's a lot to be said for a spot of concussion, clears the grey matter in the frontal lobes wonderfully—like a dose of ECT.'

Upshire looked at him somberly. 'It's no joke. You're asking to be put away.'

'That had occurred to me, but it's a mad world we're in.'

Satisfied that he had at least cast his bread upon the waters, Kemp went home and did what everyone had advised him to do. He went to bed and slept the clock round. Mrs

Higgins made his meals, bustled about the flat, and said she would stave off callers. There were none. Neither did the telephone ring.

Kemp spent two days in blissful isolation, switched off from all thought, and felt more relaxed than he had been since the death of Rose Amaury. His arm was healing. He could move not only his fingers but his whole hand. Perhaps Dr Walters might be good enough to remove the plaster.

'I'd better go down to that hospital,' he told Bessie as she cleaned the lunch dishes on the third afternoon. 'No need for you to stay. I'll bring in my own supper.'

'None of that nasty takeaway stuff—there's a good pie in the oven. I'd best get back to Maggie.' She sniffed. 'They don't do nothin' for her, those doctors. It's pills and pills all the time. She don't need no pills. Any rate, I doles them out to her in ones and hide the rest. There's no tellin' what she might do in one of her moods.'

Kemp looked startled. 'As bad as that? Keep your eye on her, Bessie. We'll get it sorted out.' But he spoke with more confidence than he felt.

'She's frettin' herself into her grave, that's what she's doin', Bessie said darkly. 'But no use talkin'. See you look arter yourself, Mr Kemp. I'll be in in the mornin' same as usual.'

Half an hour after she'd gone the bell rang. Kemp glanced through the curtains. A large black car stood at the kerb. Well, well, he thought, going to the door, who have I drawn now in life's little lottery?

'Why, Mr Gillorn! This is an unexpected honour. Do come in, sir.'

'How're you, Lennox? Good to see you up and about. Oh, this is Mr—ah—Perigord.' No further explanation came.

The tall man in the elephant grey suit followed them into the sitting-room. He shook hands with Kemp, a firm non-committal grip, as his eyes expressed neither pleasure at their meeting nor concern for its outcome; whatever he was about was in the line of duty.

Having settled his guest comfortably in the new suite, Kemp offered hospitality which Mr Perigord politely refused.

'I'd like some coffee, if I may,' said Archibald Gillorn, sinking into an armchair. 'Wasn't given time after lunch. Rushed out here. Well, that's as may be... I don't object to the powdered stuff if it's all you've got. And if you've a brandy?'

'I can give you real coffee, and a good cognac.' Kemp was delighted with the old man, and gauged a wary friendliness in his manner. He brought coffee, a half-bottle of Remy Martin he'd been keeping against better times, his finest Waterford glass on a silver tray given to his father on his retirement—and felt an elation of spirit as he placed it within reach of Mr Gillorn's hand. He had been conscious while in the kitchen that neither of his visitors conversed in his absence.

'Well, Lennox, Mr Perigord here has a word to say to you. I have no wish to hear it. My part is finished in that I have brought him to you. You are to talk in private. I see you have a music thingummy... What's it? A radiogram? If I could have some quiet music...?'

'Debussy, perhaps?' Kemp put on a record and closed the lid.

'Very soothing. I might even doze off. Don't mind me. You two go ahead.'

'The kitchen would be best,' said Kemp, leading the way, 'if you don't mind a hard seat.'

'I'm used to them.' Perigord sat down at the deal table, fresh-scrubbed by Mrs Higgins.

'I'm sure you are.' Kemp closed the door and took the other chair.

'Now, Mr Kemp, I'm sure you know why I'm here.'

Kemp nodded. Mr Perigord wore his hand-sewn lapels, grey silk necktie modestly spotted in pale blue, and his clean smooth countenance as if they were but trappings.

'You are causing us a lot of trouble, Mr Kemp. We have done our best to keep you silent.' He raised a hand like a white wand. 'I make no excuses for that. It was necessary. It does not seem to have worked. Superintendent Quennell is alarmed. We are alarmed.'

Kemp said nothing. He took out a packet of cigarettes and offered it.

'I don't, thanks.'

Kemp lit his own. It was a manoevre he had mastered.

'There are certain aspects of this case which must be kept quiet for a time. I'm sure you understand.'

'You say "for a time." Just what do you mean by that?'

'Exactly what I say. We need time. We want you to give us time.'

'How long is "time"?'

Perigord shrugged. 'That I can't say. It is a very delicate situation.'

'What is?'

'My dear Mr Kemp, there's no need for courtroom tactics. You must accept what I say.'

'Look, Mr Perigord. I don't know who you are but I can guess. I've been physically assaulted. I've been threatened with professional ruin. I've been shamefully treated in front of my own staff, and all you can say is you need time.'

'My department had nothing to do with any assault upon your person, Mr Kemp. I can assure you quite categorically on that point. As for your professional future, that will be taken care of—which is the reason for Mr Gillorn's presence with me today.'

'That's all very well. But dirt sticks, Mr Perigord, and I am vulnerable, as you well know. The word has already gone around as to my unreliability. It's just not good enough to say your people want time. Time may be on your side—it's certainly not on mine.'

Perigord spread his hands as if pushing away trivialities.

'I can assure you, your reputation will be cleared if you will but wait. Reparation will be made should it be necessary.'

'I don't want reparation. I've been insulted before, Mr Perigord. Don't push it now.'

His visitor looked surprised at the show of anger.

'You are indeed a difficult man, Mr Kemp. You don't accept easily. What is it you really want?'

Kemp looked straight into the cold eyes. This was a man who had heard everything, seen everything and remained unimpressed, or was it simply that he had been so stunned by experiences beyond the normal ken that he had become a hollow man, denied even the blessing of surprise?

'I want justice,' he replied quietly. 'Not for myself. This isn't a just world. But for some the smallest measure of that abstract concept would be sufficient.'

'H'm, very idealistic.'

'Idealistic be damned! They have nothing, they look for nothing, why take away the very shreds they live by?'

Perigord put his chin on his hand, and gently massaged his lower lip. He was silent for a few moments.

'It will be made up to them...'

'In time, I suppose? She could be dead by then!'

'You are of course talking of Mrs Roding, the mother of that unfortunate youth. It's a risk they take, Mr Kemp, letting their sons get into crime...'

'Stuff that for a moral! Why can't she be told now that her son was no murderer?'

'There are circumstances. Delicate matters to be resolved.'

Kemp got up blindly, banging his plastered arm on the table edge.

'To hell with your circumstances, the woman's going out of her mind...' He went to the sink and poured himself a glass of water. Perigord moved his chair back slightly.

'Come and sit down. You really are a most touchy fellow.' He sighed. 'Well, perhaps I have to take you into our confidence. There seems no other way to keep you quiet.'

'If you think I can be trusted.'

There was a glimmer of amusement behind the eyes.

'Oh, I trust you, Mr Kemp. Implicitly. And in return you must trust me. Let me tell you a story. In 1947 an officer in the British Army volunteered to go over to the Eastern part of Germany—the Russian Zone as it was then called. He was a good linguist and had already worked in Army Intelligence. What he proposed interested our people at the time. It wasn't difficult then to cross the frontier, though the majority were coming the other way. His idea was that he should go as a defector. He had a German girlfriend whose family were Communists living near Leipzig and she wanted to rejoin them. It would be an excellent cover from our point of view. To make it the more plausible he stole money from Mess funds, and the military police had been alerted. The story given out was that he was a fugitive from the Army who'd fallen for the German fräulein and, with her help, taken the easy way out. He settled in her home town, and made his living as a translator and teacher of English. The plan was for him to lie low for a while before infiltrating their centres and relaying information back to us through our other agents. There was a great deal we wanted to know about the set-up in what was to become the German Democratic Republic.' Perigord paused. 'I wouldn't mind a cup of that coffee now.'

Kemp made the coffee and brought it to the table.

'The Spectre of the Brocken,' he remarked, pouring out two cups.

Perigord looked up sharply. 'How'd you hear about that?'

'It's a well-known geographical phenomenon.'

'H'm. Perhaps we'll come back to that later. We did receive quite interesting reports from time to time from—shall we call him Major Prentis? Then for some reason or other they tailed off. Naturally we checked. He was still there in the same small town, living quietly, getting on with the neighbours and accepted by the community. The German girlfriend had died but he went on lodging with her family.'

'Perhaps he was happy. He'd be getting into middle age. Perhaps he liked it there.'

Perigord looked grim. 'Agents are not supposed to like where they are. But, yes, we did suspect something like that had happened, especially when he was sending us nothing that was of much use, and by then we had other sources of intelligence that were better.'

'You thought he'd gone over to the other side?'

'Not precisely. That would have been very dangerous. But the risk was there. We wanted to bring him out. He refused.'

'So the mole went to sleep?'

'Something like that. His excuse was that he was more use to us where he was. If something important cropped up he was on the spot. We didn't like it but we had no option but to leave him there. For years we heard nothing until recently.' Perigord paused, took some coffee and wiped his lips with a large white monogrammed handkerchief. 'A few months ago he got a message through to us that he was ill, he suspected it was cancer and the prognosis wasn't good. In short, he said he was dying and he wanted out. Said he wanted to die in England.'

'A sentimental agent? Well, I suppose it takes all kinds.'

Perigord ignored the flippancy. 'Major Prentis has brought pressure on our people to aid his repatriation. He's a clever man. He may have gone quiet but he hasn't been asleep. He knows too much. We want him out as much as he wants to come. We can't afford not to help him. He's already had far too much access to our own networks.'

'So he's coming over?'

'It's not easy. He has to keep up his original cover as a defector, a traitor if you like. Otherwise he's blown, and if interrogated in his present state of health he might just

talk... So we're using the sentimental angle, and so is he.
He still has a wife in England and he wrote to her, quite
openly, saying he was not ashamed of his past but that he
was ill and wanted to come home to die. Her instructions—'

'From your department, of course?'

'Naturally we contacted her. Her instructions were to reply to him that she forgave him, and that she would appeal
to the Foreign Office and ask that he be repatriated.'

'And did she?'

'Oh yes, she's been most cooperative. Makes endless pleas
to our authorities which have been passed on by diplomatic
means to the other side of the Iron Curtain. Her letters have
been quite heart-breaking...'

'After over thirty years? Is this a movie?'

Perigord gave him a glazed look. 'Broken hearts are old
hat in Central Europe,' he observed blandly.

The quick snap into his own assumed lingo was sufficient rebuke to shock Kemp into a more sober approach.

'Then what's the difficulty?' he asked on a different note.

'It should be obvious. Prentis is now a citizen of the People's Republic. That was all part of his original plan. He had
given out that he had Communist sympathies, had no time
for his native land. To make his cover stick he had to go the
whole hog. Besides, although it's over thirty years ago,
questions about him get asked in the House from time to
time... The Press ran a story about him in the 'sixties.
Someone at a Leipzig Trade Fair had run into him. I'll give
Prentis his due, he fielded that one like a pro—told the man
he'd never regretted his defection, said he was still only interested in teaching students languages as an aid to the uni-
versal brotherhood in which he believed. Naturally, his
desire to return to his native land has put the East German
authorities on inquiry. But they are sympathetic because of
his illness. What we cannot afford is any hint that his original defection was other than for his own personal reasons,

and to further his purported adherence to the Communist cause.'

'What point have the negotiations reached?'

Perigord sighed.

'About two months ago we would have said we were home and dry—a pleasing metaphor, don't you think, if applied to Major Prentis? He had had himself admitted to a hospital in Leipzig and been thoroughly investigated. It was cancer all right, an inoperable tumour resistant to chemotherapy and any other form of treatment. We have their medical certificate. The East Germans were satisfied that the wife's appeal for his return was sincere. Naturally their Russian masters exhumed their files on Prentis. Remember, he had been billed as a hero to them on his defection—a British officer who had seen the red dawn and all that. Even they were satisfied that he'd only about half a year to live. It only remained to issue him an exit visa. As you well know, bureaucracy over there moves by stealth and takes time. Prentis is still awaiting that vital piece of paper...'

'What's holding it up?'

Mr Perigord shrugged a graceful shoulder. 'We don't know. It could be simple bureaucracy. It could be something else... I have to take you back to the beginning. In that September of '47 Prentis, having rigged the Mess accounts, went to the Forces' leave centre at Bad Harzburg where his German girlfriend, Ilse Brunner, worked as a chambermaid. The frontier was close, just a swathe of de-forested area and marked trees. Easy enough to slip across if you knew the way, and Ilse Brunner did. At that time the British Frontier section was a Provost Company of the military police, and they were given orders not to stop either of them. Presumably the girl had made sure they wouldn't be stopped on the other side. At sunset one evening when there was a thick mist they simply walked over. I understand from the reports that the girl was to be allowed to go first, and Prentis was to follow after a short interval. That delay was fatal.

A soldier in our Frontier Service challenged Prentis and there had to be a hurried consultation with an officer in the Provost Company before he was let through. A real military cock-up, that was...' Perigord made a *moue* of disapproval.

'Which a bystander witnessed? Someone who had gone out that evening hoping to see the Spectre of the Brocken...'

Perigord gave a wry smile. 'What she did see in fact was a British officer saluting a man in lederhosen with a pack on his back slipping away in the direction of the frontier in the wake of a German girl with a battered suitcase—and she knew them both.'

Kemp gave a whistle of astonishment. 'As bad as that, eh?'

Perigord nodded. 'I see you are with me, Mr Kemp. Have you read the story?'

Kemp shook his head. 'Have you?'

'Unfortunately, no. We have not yet found it.'

The two men looked at each other warily, both reassembling their thoughts, and their next cautious words. Perigord took longer.

'Then how do you know about it?' asked Kemp.

'By another plaguey coincidence that story came into the hands of an—er—interested party who gave us a garbled, incoherent account of it but was unable to hand the damned thing over to us. That was a nuisance... Let me assure you on one point. The writer of the story seems to have been quite innocent. She had initially strayed into a situation she didn't understand, though she guessed a lot. She had told no one, not even her husband when the Prentis defection was publicized, nor earlier when he was first missing and rumour was rife at Rhine Army headquarters where they were all stationed.'

'But she did know it was Prentis?'

'Oh yes. She and her husband had met him in the bar the previous night. She also knew Ilse Brunner who had taken a job as chambermaid at the Hof where they were staying, and she had got interested in the girl. Officers' wives tittle-tattled no end to their servants, I suppose... It must have been a fairly closed world out there for some of them.' Perigord got up and mopped his brow. 'It was all so damned coincidental...'

'Coincidences do happen in small communities. It's not only in fiction that they help the wheels of action to turn. Mrs Amaury just used her imagination to link them...' Perigord sat down again.

'Trouble is that she got it right—from what I hear of that story.' He slapped his hand hard on the table top. 'She kept it in her head for nearly thirty years, then out it pops at the worst possible time. We heard about it and had to take action.'

'What action?'

'Use your brain. If this story was published even in the most modest way there was the risk it might get picked up by the wrong people, and bang would go all hopes of getting Prentis out. One breath of this in certain quarters while our negotiations were going on and the Reds—German or Russian—would have him gutted like a dead fish.'

'I can see that. I still want to know what action you took.'

Perigord shifted uneasily in his chair. 'We were on a very tight time schedule...'

'Why didn't you take the straight path—speak to Mrs Amaury herself? She'd have understood the dilemma. I knew her. Your people would have had nothing to fear from her. She'd have been immensely intrigued, I've no doubt, but she'd have kept silent.'

Perigord nodded. 'I believe you. But I didn't know the lady. We couldn't take that chance. She was elderly, she might have been indiscreet...perhaps got overexcited if she knew how important her story had become. She could have blabbed to anybody. We were presented with a simpler suggestion. The Major's case officer—you're familiar with the phrase?—who'd been running him over the years had some—ah—personal information about him which could be

put to use. The matter was urgent, not just in days but
hours...'

Perigord paused, and mopped his brow.

'One hint of this story getting out and the whole repatriation exercise would blow up in our faces. Our method
therefore for retrieval of the manuscript had to be—er—you
might say, unorthodox.'

'Burglary? I'm sure it's been done before.' Kemp could
not forbear a sardonic element in his tone.

'Rarely. Only when it's strictly necessary, and in the
national interest.' Perigord's words carried rebuke.

'I'll accept that. But in this case you didn't get what you
were looking for?'

'Pages from her notebook were extracted but the original
manuscript had disappeared, as had the typescript.'

'Surely your informer had them both?'

'No. It had been read—which is why we were apprised of
its contents—but it had been returned to Mrs Amaury along
with the one typed copy so that she could have no suspicion
as to its importance. But you must see that by then time was
of the essence. She could have sent it off anywhere...'

'So the break-in was arranged at the earliest possible moment...and botched.'

Perigord bristled at the word; it was probably inadmissi-
ble in his field.

'These are delicate matters, Mr Kemp, which the ordinary citizen does not always comprehend.'

'We can all comprehend murder when it happens, Mr
Perigord.'

The grey man eyed him with speculation. Then he said,
coldly: 'I have read the report on the incidents that night and
I can assure you that Mrs Amaury's unfortunate death was
quite satisfactorily explained therein.'

'Let me get this straight,' said Kemp, breathing hard as he
felt his way through the verbiage of officialese scarcely
lightened by the halo of secrecy which encircled Perigord's
brow like an aura of sanctity. It was difficult to get any-

thing factual in this context—he could only try. 'Let me get
this straight,' he said again. 'Someone entered the house
before Kevin Roding broke in, or they went along with him.
They threw the main switch. They waited till he smashed a
vase to alert the old lady so that she left her bedroom. Then
they nipped in, found the suitcase and the notes—they seem
to have been excellently well-informed—but nothing else.
What did the report say happened next?'

'I understand Mrs Amaury's fall was heard. Unhappily
she was already dead when they rushed to her aid, and the
young man Roding had disappeared into the night before he
could be stopped.'

'In fact they didn't try,' said Kemp bitterly. 'He'd have
been a right embarrassment had he been picked up.'

Perigord wore his pained expression. 'You must understand, Mr Kemp, there are circumstances in which certain
persons have to be given a free hand... The arrangements
that night were not of my making. That is not the way we
work. I do not inquire into the methods used...'

'The end justifies the means, eh?'

'Quite so.' Mr Perigord did not seem disposed to enter
into any arguments on an ethical basis.

'And Kevin Roding got away—at least as far as Holland.'

The other man made no comment.

'Where he was casually ditched,' went on Kemp. 'Had
your people anything to do with that?'

Perigord looked shocked. 'I see your line of thought. Superintendent Quennell made it very clear to me that you
want the matter pursued. You must remember we did not
have the benefit of the information you have since ac-
quired...'

'Damn it, you know very well young Roding wasn't guilty
of the murder!'

'I do not know it. Your so-called evidence on that point
is mere conjecture, but it will be looked into as you have

brought it to our notice. In fact, I'm willing to do a trade with you, Mr Kemp.'

Perigord put his elbows on the table and his fingertips together. It was as if unpleasantly cluttered ground had been cleared, and the time had come for commercial proposition to be got under way.

He dropped his tight-lipped, touch-me-not manner, and became the merchant ready for a deal.

'When Major Prentis is safely in this country, we are prepared to assist a full police investigation into the part played in this melancholy affair by Kevin Roding, including the circumstances of his own demise. If such investigation leads to the conclusion that he did not murder Mrs Amaury a public statement will be made to that effect, and reparation will be made to his family.'

Kemp took out a cigarette. This time Perigord leaned forward and lit it for him. The gesture marked the change in their relationship.

And what, Kemp wondered as he listened, does this man want from me in return? Surely he can't be inviting me to join his merry band? He wished he hadn't read so many spy novels in his spare time; they'd always made his stomach queasy.

TWENTY

WHEN HE WAS once more alone in his flat Kemp finished the brandy. Later he might face up to Bessie's supper offering. At the moment he wasn't hungry and he wanted to think. His flat had suddenly become unreal. Only an hour ago he had closed the door behind Mr Gillorn who had waited till Perigord was downstairs before he spoke on a personal note.

'You look shaken up, laddie. If it's your work you're worried about, that's taken care of.' He laid a gnarled finger along the side of his nose. 'Mum's the word... Whatever arcane nonsense that lot's up to, I'll see you're all right.'

'Thanks, sir. But I've already had that assurance from His Nibs.'

'Humph. They're a secretive bunch. Don't trust them myself but then I've never become involved, thank God. Get yourself well, Lennox, and then a little holiday, eh? Things will pass. They always do. Time, like an ever-rolling stream...'

Kemp grinned at him. 'Good of you to come, sir. Careful on those stairs.'

He felt a lump in his throat as he cleared the tray; the old man had taken only a tiny drink and had been comfortably asleep when they'd finished their talk in the kitchen. He had smiled as he woke, and accepted Kemp's arm to raise him from the chair.

'You two finished your palaver? Let's get back to London, then...'

The old man had seemed a rock in the midst of shifting sands, and when he had gone even the walls looked infirm and the window-curtains insubstantial material floating in space. And this even before he'd touched a drink, reflected

Kemp, reaching for the bottle. He felt drained, and he knew why. He had talked himself to a standstill. Now he knew what they meant by brainwashing; his had been pumped clear to the last puddle.

Why were there all those jokes about them having ways to make you talk? They weren't even funny when you thought about it. And it wasn't natural for Kemp to talk so much, he usually left that to others and preferred to listen. But Mr Perigord was obviously an expert in a field Kemp had considered his own specialty. How had it been done?

By a mixture of gentle persuasion, almost brotherly concern, and chat between equals—or so Perigord had made it seem—plus of course the bargain struck: everything you know, Kemp, including your theories, in exchange for the chance to clear Roding's name. During the remainder of the interview the whole character of the man in grey had undergone a metamorphosis. The icy eyes thawed into smiling conspiracy, the patrician angularity of his face softened, even the tailored perfection of his suit crumpled into the baggy homeliness of any commuter on the Central Line. All this happened in front of Kemp's eyes, himself only gradually aware that he was in the process of being wrung dry.

Some things surprised him, certainly. He had imagined the Intelligence Services omnipotent in their knowledge but they hadn't heard of Jacob Preskel...

'Didn't they see the letter from the Agency?' (Between them, "they" had become a generic term for "your man, who shall remain anonymous" ... Further than that Perigord would not deign to go: 'In my line we must maintain confidence, Mr Kemp.')

Now Perigord said, 'You'll remember the searcher was disturbed by hearing Mrs Amaury fall. Tell me about this Preskel...'

Kemp told him, and Perigord made a note. 'You were smart on that one. I like your methods...' Kemp was beginning to recognize such flattery was part of the game.

Finally, he had asked outright: 'Who do you think took the manuscript and the typed copy? And why? Have they still got them, or have they been passed on?'

At that point Perigord had risen, buttoned his jacket and smoothed his lapels.

'I would like you to find that out for us, Mr Kemp, and do it if you can without sinking the ship. Certain avenues will be open to you that were—ah—temporarily closed...'

Just like that. Another part of the bargain.

Perigord opened the kitchen door, signalling that the interview was at an end.

'I'd like to brush up. Where's the whatsit?'

Kemp showed him. When Mr Perigord returned he was again the grey uncompromising servant of the State, his lips as tight shut as a security file—and one not, apparently, to be at Kemp's disposal.

Very well, he'd open his own. He got out his notes and wrote for an hour, with pauses for speculative thought. Having thus cleared his mind, he tackled the oven pie and was finished the remains when the phone rang.

The Reverend Clive Cavendish was one of those who regard the telephone as an uncertain mode of communication and so pitch their voices an octave higher than necessary in order to assist it. It seemed to Kemp therefore that the Vicar was speaking to him out of a cloud high above the earth.

'My sister and I were much distressed to hear that you had sustained an injury, Mr Kemp. We have just heard and—um—hope it is not serious... An accident, was it?'

'Not entirely,' said Kemp, 'but fortunately not too serious.'

'I'm glad to hear it. We were wondering if you were well enough to—ah—take coffee with us in the morning? Are you able to drive to the Vicarage?'

'That is very kind of you both. I should like to come, and yes, I am able to drive.'

'Capital, my dear chap. We shall look forward to seeing you.' As the instrument had proved adequate Clive Caven-dish's voice dropped to his normal hearty tone. 'Capital,' he said again before ringing off.

News seemed to travel both fast and slow in Newtown, depending on the mood of the recipients. The friendly in-quiry as to Kemp's health had been late in coming from his clerical acquaintance, but swift upon his re-entry into re-spectable society. Tullia Cavendish and he appeared to have recovered almost simultaneously; perhaps it was the heal-ing power of the Security Services that was responsible rather than those of the National Health.

Certainly the latter was not responding as vigorously to-wards Kemp's reinstatement when he called at the out-patients' clinic first thing in the morning. He was told curtly that Dr Walters was not available, and without his say-so the plaster must remain. Sister was unimpressed by Kemp's demonstration of his ability to waggle his fingers. He had to drive slowly and carefully to the Vicarage, where he left his car at the gate and proceeded up the overgrown drive to the front door, still hampered by the unwieldy limb.

However, his appearance there as more or less walking wounded served to cover any initial embarrassment his host and hostess might be feeling, and as a topic of conversa-tion, accidents in general and fractures in particular, his arm satisfactorily bridged the unease of all concerned. By the time coffee and biscuits were produced even Tullia had set-tled down, stopped weaving indecisively between kitchen and parlour, seated herself before the round table where the lace tablecloth hung a little off-centre, and begun to give Kemp her full attention. The Vicar still hovered, cup in hand.

'I'll leave you, if I may. Some parish business to attend to. I'll be in the study, my dear... Look in before you go, Mr Kemp...'

Another aged person opting out from the burden of State secrets? Or perhaps the matter did not concern him? That,

Kemp could scarcely believe; the Cavendishes were an old family, the glue of history must have welded them by now into an unbreakable unity. Touch one, you touch all.

He looked at Tullia Cavendish. She wore a nondescript frock of a blue as vague as her eyes, and an ill-fitting cardigan. Yet her overall appearance radiated a stern competence. Perhaps it was the stiff back, the rigid set of bony shoulders, the long legs neatly crossed at the ankles. Kemp remembered those legs, and the episode of the spilt kettle. Tullia looked composed enough now.

'More coffee, Mr Kemp?'

'Thank you. It's very good.'

She poured out his cup, her hand shaking ever so slightly. But it could have been from the weight of the silver pot.

'You must be wondering why you are here.'

Kemp made a deprecating movement.

'I understand you know much of my lamentable history,' she went on, 'Mr Perigord, whom you have met, has told me that you are in his confidence. So I suppose I have to accept that. I've had to accept a great many things lately...'

There was a weariness in her voice despite the clipped accent and quality of command he had first noticed about it.

'I'm sure you have. It can't have been easy for you.'

'It was such a shock. Hearing from Patrick after all these years. I have lived so quietly, trying to help Clive here in the parish. And I have been happy. It is the kind of life for which I was raised. To be of service to others in the only way I know. My marriage was an aberration—a mistake. But it happened so long ago and it lasted such a short time that I've almost forgotten all about it. Nor did I want to be reminded in view of what he did...'

'Did you not know he went as an agent?'

'Of course not. It was Patrick's wish that I shouldn't be told. And naturally it suited them. They don't trust wives, and a man whose main reason for going was to escape from a misguided marriage'—she winced, drawing down the corners of a mouth grown thin with the years—'that was an offer they couldn't refuse!'

'I didn't know that,' Kemp murmured, smothering sudden pity.

'I never divorced him. He was never married to Ilse Brunner. Originally, that eased the pain in a way. A man would call it vindictive but I couldn't help it. And then...time passed and it no longer mattered. There were— how shall I put it—compensations that came to me, in time.'

Kemp considered the remark. Tullia Cavendish was not a worldly woman, neither did she seem excessively spiritual; compensations must have taken another form.

'How do you feel about your husband coming back?'

She rose and put a few small coals on the fire. It flickered briefly before subsiding once more into a kind of smouldering resentment.

'At first I really didn't care whether he came or not. Oh, I knew why he wanted to die in England. He was always a sentimentalist at heart, Patrick. He was not well-bred, you know...' With a little smile which explained everything. 'But then I was contacted by those people, and they stressed the importance to them of Patrick's return.'

'It must have made a difference to your feelings when you learned he'd not been a defector?'

'Patriotism, you mean? Yes, of course, on one level it did. But it was unforgivable of Patrick not to have told me—to let me suffer the shame, the humiliation . . . I had to give up calling myself by my married name—otherwise the Press would have hounded me. It was unbearable.' She stroked the crêpey skin of her neck, stained now by a flush which went down into the folds of her collar. A bitter woman, still. Under the ladylike demeanour Kemp sensed the iron of self-esteem. That was where it had hurt.

'But you did what they wanted you to do—you wrote to him and you appealed to the Foreign Office?'

'I did what was my duty, Mr Kemp. The sentiments I expressed were not my own, but I'm not a fool. I recognized his importance to others . . . and my duty to my country.' In anyone else the last words might have sounded pretentious; in Tullia Cavendish they were the simple truth.

'And then Mrs Amaury gave you that story to type?'

'I knew she did some writing—trivial stuff. Romantic fiction—not at all my kind of thing, but she liked that sort of frivolity, poor Rose... Then one day she got excited about one of her stories, said she might get it published if it were typed. I offered to do it for her . . .' Tullia broke off, moved dishes on the table aimlessly. 'It had been a normal day till then... I remember I had gone to Rose for some little cakes she had made for our W.I. bazaar in the afternoon. She gave me bunches of snowdrops to sell, tied with green wool . . .' The tiniest details were etched in her memory. 'Naturally, I had many other things on my mind . . . Patrick's return was not going to be easy although they had assured me there would be no publicity, it would all be done quietly. But it was out of my hands, and my everyday work in the parish had to go on. I am not one given to moping . . .' She straightened her back as if shifting an old burden.

'When did you read the story, Miss Cavendish?' Kemp prompted her.

'I had items for our magazine to type in the evening. It was then I took out that . . . that manuscript. I could not believe what I was reading. It was too horrible. Yet so much of it could have been true.' Her voice now held a wondering note. 'Patrick did come home from the Middle East that summer, and he said he'd been posted to Germany. He said he was leaving me anyway. He was so casual about it, as though it were of no importance . . . the marriage was finished as far as he was concerned . . . Oh, it was just the stuff for that trashy kind of story all right,' she ended bitterly, and, picking up the poker which lay along the tiled hearth, she attacked the poor fire with unnecessary violence.

'But it confirmed your husband was no traitor?'

She glared at him. 'He was a traitor to me... It was a terrible story. At first I didn't take in the implications about that Army patrol...there was so much else. You haven't read it, Mr Kemp? It's not been found?'

Kemp shook his head.

'I'm glad.' Apparently patriotism in Tullia Cavendish had its limits, or animosity towards her husband had none.

'But the story could put him in danger, Miss Cavendish.'

'I'm aware of that. After some very sleepless nights I put my personal feelings aside, and telephoned the number I had been given—they prefer to deal with one at a distance. I was put on to Mr Perigord, and I gave him the gist of the story. The rest I understand you know.'

'You say you spent sleepless nights. Did it not occur to you to speak to Rose yourself?'

'And let her know who I was? There had been nothing to connect her reminiscences with me. All she knew was that I'd had a broken marriage and that my husband had been in the Army. But that was a common enough experience. I could not have borne her pity... Even had I not been under instructions to keep silent, I could not have told her. Not when she knew so much. She had even used Ilse Brunner's real name. She'd talked to her, gossiped with a German servant girl—about me! Patrick had told that little Communist slut about our marriage—the most intimate details...' A dry sob rattled in her throat.

Kemp paused, then asked slowly, 'And you have no idea where the manuscript is now?'

'I was told to type it out and return it to Rose. She had already been pressing me for it. She had such hopes of it. I kept putting her off, saying I was busy... But to delay longer they said might make her suspicious.'

'Did you return it before she had that fall in the garden?'

For the first time, Tullia looked flustered. 'I can't remember. I'd nothing to do with that.' It wasn't a question Kemp had asked.

'That day you found me in her bedroom I was looking for her notes. You disturbed me...'

'It didn't matter. They found them. They're very thorough. But the story itself is still missing—and Rose Amaury is dead.'

She put a hand to her head. 'That dreadful thing... A common burglar and to think how good Rose had been to his mother! He deserved his death. May God forgive him.'

'Amen to that.' Kemp made no further comment. If Miss Cavendish still believed in Kevin Roding's guilt, so be it. Time would tell.

'When you were typing *The Bystander*, as Mrs Amaury called it, could anyone else have read it?'

'Certainly not.' She was fierce. 'I could not have brought myself to show it to anyone. The awful things Patrick had said...'

'I cannot believe they could have been so very terrible about you, Miss Cavendish.'

'That's because you're a man, Mr Kemp. You wouldn't understand. You see, early in our marriage it was found that I could not have children. Patrick was not... sympathetic. I was very young. You cannot imagine... And he told that to Ilse Brunner. Said his wife in England was a barren husk...' She had closed her eyes as memory flooded them.

Profoundly embarrassed, Kemp rose.

'I'm sorry, Miss Cavendish. I didn't mean to pry.'

'At least you listened. They were interested in the story apart from the bit about Patrick being saluted by the Army officer before he followed that German girl into the forest.' She dried her face with a scrap of handkerchief from which the lace hung in shreds. Like a young woman's life, thought Kemp as he held out his hand and brought her to her feet.

'Your brother, he knows about the story?'

'Naturally he knows the circumstances but he has not read it. I have consulted him throughout. I have needed his prayers. His advice has always been that it is our duty to assist in Patrick's return, and to cooperate with the authorities. That we have done. He and Julian have been my support in this terrible time.'

'Julian, too?'

'Of course. We are a family, Mr Kemp, but my brother is not young and events have been a strain upon him. We confided in Julian—with the consent of Mr Perigord—and I understand he has been of practical help to the security officers. Now I am tired. If you will excuse me...'

Kemp left her. He knocked at the door of the Vicar's study.

'Ah—you're on your way, Mr Kemp. I must hasten to my sister. I hope she is not too much distressed? It was Mr Perigord's desire that you should have a talk with her.'

'He works in strange ways, Mr Cavendish. It is a thing outside my scope.'

'And mine. I only met Patrick briefly at their marriage. It brought Tullia to great sorrow. We can only trust in God to bring that unhappy man home so that he may sleep peacefully at last under an English heaven. I have thought wickedly of him these past thirty years—may I be forgiven. But I was not to know the truth till now.'

'And this tale of Rose Amaury's—you have never seen it?'

'It would not have been right. My sister would divulge nothing of its content to either myself or my nephew. She will not have us speak of it, Mr Kemp, and her wish must be observed. She is a good woman, and she has suffered enough.'

TWENTY-ONE

KEMP ALSO HAD been given a number to ring. When he got back to his flat he looked at the telephone reluctantly. To hell with it, he thought, not yet...

In the early evening he had the caller he had hoped for: Lettice Warrender.

'I don't understand anything,' she announced, plumping herself down on the sofa. 'Why, you've got a new suite. How very luxurious. Have you come into money?'

'Not to my knowledge. What don't you understand?'

'All this to-ing and fro-ing. Uncle Richard came out for lunch at Castleton today and told Mother that you are to continue as his co-executor. Your senior partner explained to him there'd been a mix-up. Of course nobody tells me anything.'

Pleased though he was to see her, Kemp wasn't inclined to undo that particular tangle for her benefit. 'But it was true that you were struck off some years ago,' she went on. 'What exactly did you do?'

Kemp told her.

'That was just silly,' she said with her usual forthrightness. 'No woman's worth it. And she left you afterwards, anyway, didn't she?'

Kemp came round the end of the sofa and sat in the armchair. In passing, he patted the top of her shining hair. 'You like everything to be cut and dried, Lettice, like contours on land, site lines on plans. But you can't map out people's lives nor the way they'll use them. You'll find that out as you get older.'

She made an impatient movement. 'Stop treating me like a schoolgirl. You're as bad as Julian.'

'I hope not,' said Kemp fervently under his breath. Aloud he asked: 'And what has your childhood mentor been saying to you? He wasn't very pleased with me when we met the other day.'

Lettice played with the cushion fringe. 'I expect he was a bit jealous. He's been very attentive of late. I've been seeing a lot of him ...'

'With any object in view?'

'As a matter of fact, yes,' she said coolly. 'I think he'd like us to become engaged. There's no need to look so surprised. It's been on the cards—as they say—for a long time. The parents would be pleased. They weren't so keen a few years ago when Julian was going through what they considered to be his drop-out phase ... But now he's settled down and has a responsible job I think they're rather keen.'

'And of course a nice upper-class girl like you takes heed of her parents' approval?'

'There's no need to be so sarcastic, Lennox. Sometimes I think I preferred him as he was ...'

'Why's that?'

'Oh, I suppose it seemed romantic. He was full of ideas, and he had such interesting chums from his student days. They did exciting sort of things—at least they seemed exciting to me when he told me about them in the hols. Made my school seem like a flat, stale, unprofitable prison ... Julian appealed to the rebel in me, I suppose.'

'What kind of exciting things?'

'You know, going abroad and all that. The most we got were carefully conducted tours of French châteaux. He followed the hippy trail, as he called it. Overland to Nepal, wandering around Europe, that kind of thing. He had lots of foreign friends. Now of course he shepherds schoolboys on just the sort of disciplined parties that we had. It all seems rather a come-down.'

'He still goes abroad, then?'

'Well, it's part of his work, isn't it? Teaching them languages and, as he puts it, "expanding their infant minds".'

He's got another trip coming up at half-term, taking Scouts to Austria.' Lettice paused, examining her fingernails. 'He mentioned that when we talked about marriage plans. Said we might announce our engagement when he came back if that would suit me...'

'I may be wrong, Lettice, but you don't sound as ecstatic as you should. You've had a crush on Julian Cavendish since you were a kid, and now here he is proposing marriage. You ought to be all dewy-eyed, and falling into his arms with joy.'

'I'm not a shopgirl. We don't behave like that. There's nothing so old-fashioned as a proposal these days, just mutual plans. It's not such an emotional thing, getting married.'

Kemp exploded. 'Then it damned well should be. Shall I tell you what I think?'

'You have my full attention.' She stopped looking coy, which hadn't suited her anyway, and looked straight at him.

'I don't think you're in love with Julian. I don't think you've even discovered what love is. You've found your Byronic hero—the Childe Harold of your girlhood—has dwindled into a near middle-aged schoolmaster for whom you have only the affection of long acquaintance...'

'I didn't say I'd said yes to the marriage plan,' she said, her hazel eyes watchful but not noticeably hostile. 'I'm giving it my consideration.'

'You sound like a councillor confronted with a building scheme that smells. But I'm glad to hear it. Am I right about your feelings for Julian?'

'Perhaps. He's changed certainly. But recently there's something else. Something I don't quite understand...'

Kemp listened. Women's talk, their quick sensibility, the way the female antennae pick up signals, translate nuances of behaviour and speech into messages only they understand, intrigued him. So much could be learnt from listening to them, and observing, as now with Lettice, the changing expression that played across their features. She was, he noted, somewhat lukewarm today when she spoke of her beloved. Perhaps the game being won, the prize had lost its savour.

'He used to be so light-hearted,' she was saying, as if taking a view of Julian from a long way off. 'Now he has these moods, pretty sombre ones sometimes...'

'He doesn't look like either his uncle or his aunt. What's his parentage—as I'm sure all girls of your sort must ask?'

'Really, Lennox, you're the most class-conscious man I've ever met! Anyway, Julian's always been there. Clive Cavendish had a brother—High Commissioner in an outlandish spot of Empire. He and his wife died in some catastrophe, and Tullia and Clive adopted their little boy—at least that's the story. You're very curious about Julian, aren't you?'

'Yes. I'd like to meet him again. Bring him round for a celebratory drink.'

'I didn't say we'd anything to celebrate—yet. Besides, he'll be busy preparing for his boys' trip, the half-term starts on Friday. But, yes, I'll ask him.'

THE MOMENT LETTICE had gone, Kemp did not hesitate to pick up the phone. At least Perigord didn't keep to regular office hours. He listened, then was brusque.

'We know all that. Don't try teaching us our business.' The voice was sharp enough to cut the wires; Kemp moved the receiver another inch from his ear.

'He assaulted me. He and the Warrender boys—probably told them I'd been pestering their young Lettice. But that wasn't the real reason...'

'He has been a great help to us.'

'I'm sure he has. But he goes his own way about it. He wanted to stop me interfering.'

'So did we, Mr Kemp, and he knew our purpose.'

'Oh, he did, did he? You take some very odd people into your confidence.'

'No odder than yourself, Mr Kemp, when necessity dictates. Besides, he's a Cavendish. He's family.'

'Oh yeah? Well, I think he has friends in Amsterdam. The old hippy drug trail. And it was to these friends he despatched young Roding.'

Perigord gave a small cough. 'Not on the telephone, if you please. And as I've already said, don't teach us our job. All I asked you to do was to find any trace of that missing manuscript. Have you succeeded?'

'Oh, you can stop bothering about that. It's been destroyed.' Kemp felt some satisfaction at the long silence which ensued.

'Are you sure?'

'Yes, I'm sure. It ended up in a small fire in a small grate.'

Again silence. Then Perigord said, 'We must have a meeting. I'll send a car.'

'I'M NOT USED to these late hours,' Kemp murmured when finally ushered into the presence of Mr Perigord. 'Nor to trotting down such corridors of power.'

'Thank you, Charters. I'll call you when Mr Kemp is ready to leave.'

Kemp's guide closed the door with a soft snap like the breaking of a ginger biscuit.

It was a charmless room, adequately furnished to demonstrate its occupant's status in the hierarchy, with here and there touches of a more mandarin taste, a few watercolours of the Norwich School on one wall, a Chinese screen in the shadows.

'Drink?'

'Scotch, if you please.' Kemp sat himself in a worn leather chair across from Perigord's desk. The green-shaded lamp cast an amber circle round the liquid in his glass.

'What do you mean, the manuscript has been destroyed?'

Kemp told him.

'And that's all you've got to come to that conclusion?'

'It's enough.'

'Expert in female psychology, are you?'

'No. Simply observant. The story was distasteful to her. She's a fastidious creature, so she burned it.'

'She has the habit of obedience to authority. You told her to type it out and return both the manuscript and the finished typescript to Mrs Amaury. She couldn't even bear to type it. You just took it for granted she'd given the story back. If you'd asked her direct, she wouldn't have lied. But you people are so used to having your instructions obeyed to the letter...'

Perigord tapped his fingers on the desk.

'And she didn't show it to anyone?'

'That was the last thing she'd do.'

'So no one else has seen it?'

'I didn't say that.'

'Her brother?'

Kemp shook his head.

'Then who...?'

Kemp sipped his drink, and settled back in his chair.

'It's obvious, isn't it? When Tullia Cavendish brought that story back to the Vicarage she'd no reason to hide it. It was just a piece of romantic fiction her friend Rose had concocted. It wasn't all that important. She probably popped it into her basket along with flowers and things for the W.I. bazaar that afternoon. She didn't do any typing till the evening, and it was only then that she read it. It was lying around in that house for hours... And nephew Julian is a prowler. He tends to know everything his aunt does. Maybe he was just curious...'

'You think he found it?'

'I'm damned sure he did. And what is more he knew immediately that it was dynamite. I want to know why he knew. Was he already acting for your people?'

'Certainly not. There was no need for such involvement at that stage; the repatriation was being handled quite properly by Major Prentis's case officer, with the coopera-

tion of the Foreign Office... It was only when this story
came to light that—er—more local arrangements had to be
made.'

'And Julian Cavendish was brought into the conspiracy?
I cannot say I applaud your methods—or your choice of
accomplice.'

Perigord frowned.

'And I deplore your choice of words, Mr Kemp. There
were perfectly cogent reasons why Julian Cavendish should
be told of the Major's impending return and why Mrs
Amaury's story had to be stamped on before it got any further.'

'Cogent reasons?'

'He appreciated what was at stake. He was the natural
choice.'

'But he didn't tell you he'd read the story?'

'It's only your surmise that he had.'

Kemp changed his tack. 'If you'd checked him out—is
that the phrase?—you would know of his skittish youth and
possible Marxist leanings?'

'A common enough aberration in students of his generation, but quite irrelevant in his case. He is a highly respected schoolmaster and devoted to his aunt. He, more
than anyone, wanted the Major's safe return.'

Kemp listened to this special pleading with some scepti-
cism, and voiced it. 'Why?' he asked.

Perigord spread his white hands like giant moths in the
pool of lamplight.

'It would be the natural thing. He realized the delicacy of
the matter, how much it meant to this aunt that her husband should be brought back to this country speedily and
safely...'

'Bosh! Tullia Cavendish didn't care whether Prentis lived
or died. She only did what you wanted out of an old-
fashioned idea of patriotism—ironic when you consider
what her husband's patriotic gesture did to her those long

years ago. I suppose you'll say that Julian Cavendish has
been acting from the same high-minded motive?'

'There's nothing wrong with patriotism,' Perigord observed, stiffly, but without much conviction. 'Mr Cavendish was only too eager to assist us.'

'Too eager by half. Strikes me he was in his element. I
suppose it was he who gave you your fall guy, Kevin Roding. He knew Ted and his brother through the local Youth
Club.'

'Those—er—arrangements were his, yes. We had good
reason to trust him . . .'

Kemp felt a tingling sensation behind his ears. He picked
up his whisky and let the warm spirit swamp his throat while
he waited for the other man to expand on the last statement. But Perigord had closed his lips firmly, and there was
silence.

'I see,' said Kemp finally, but it was merely a phrase with
no truth behind it. 'You had good reason to trust him...but
did he trust you? Apparently not enough to tell you he'd
read Rose Amaury's story. Don't you think you ought to ask
him about that—before he goes away again?'

'Is he going away?'

Kemp drained his glass and looked at his watch. 'It's not
for the likes of me to teach you your job, Mr Perigord—and
it's long past my bedtime.'

The phone on the desk purred gently. Perigord took it up
and held it to his ear as if both were fragile and shock might
fracture either of them. He listened impassively.

'Yes. Yes. Good. When? Any other activity? I see. Fine.'

He cradled the receiver with precision and looked at
Kemp.

'Major Prentis has his exit documents. He will be flown
home within the next few days.'

'So all's well that ends well—and the end has justified the
means?'

'If you like to put it that way . . .'

'And there has been no snag at the other end?'

'Apparently not.' Perigord sat still, pushed his glasses up on his forehead and rubbed his eyes. It was the only sign he showed of relief after strain. 'Of course this news is for your ears alone at this juncture, Mr Kemp. I hardly need to remind you of that.'

'Message received and understood. Until the gallant Major is safely in your hands, I presume? Now there's a phrase that touches a chord . . .'

'He won't be the gallant Major till we have him,' said Perigord sourly, 'and maybe not even then.'

'So there'll be no hero's welcome, no banners flying?'

Perigord's mouth turned down. 'Use your common sense, Mr Kemp. The matter will be handled with discretion. The less people know of Major Prentis, the better. He will come home quietly, and be allowed to spend whatever time he has left in peace.'

'The peace that passeth all understanding? When your lot has finished with him.'

Perigord coughed. 'There will necessarily have to be some debriefing, but that is outside my scope. And as far as you are concerned, you will say nothing. You know that was part of our bargain.'

'If you will keep your side of the agreement. A full inquiry into the circumstances of Kevin Roding's involvement, and the apprehension of his murderers?'

'It may take some time, Mr Kemp. We shall have to await the findings of the Dutch police.'

'Then I'll settle for the murderer of Mrs Amaury.'

'Don't try to push us, Mr Kemp. Perhaps that death, though unfortunate, was irrelevant.'

Kemp was shocked, and it showed in his face. As if to soften the effect of his last words. Perigord changed the subject.

'By the way, we checked Mr Jacob Preskel and his secretary. Nothing there. He was never aware of the significance of that manuscript—and still isn't, I hasten to add. Our men were very discreet.'

'I told you Preskel had no idea,' remarked Kemp with some asperity, 'but you wouldn't take my word for it. I only hope your men were careful as well as discreet. They managed to frighten the life out of Mrs Amaury, didn't they?'

Perigord sucked in his lips. 'I imagine you're referring to our surveillance of her, and the incident of the car. She was in no danger. She surprised them by coming out of her garden door, and they may have accelerated rather quickly. You told me of the incident, and I have their report. You also told me some tale about a wire across a path. Have you solved that one?'

'Oh, that was easy enough. Miss Cavendish was in a panic. She hadn't returned Rose's story and was making excuses for her delay in typing it. She didn't mean any real harm to come to Rose, just a little accident. Like you people, she was playing for time. But if it hadn't been for those two incidents I wouldn't be in the case at all ... By the way, I should like to have a look at those notes your men pinched from Mrs Amaury's house that night. I am still her executor and have the right.'

Perigord hesitated. 'I cannot release any papers to you yet, but there is no reason why you cannot see them. They are no longer relevant if, as you say, the original story has been destroyed.'

He opened a drawer in the desk and produced a folder. It fairly bulged with documents so that the slender sheaf of pages he extracted seemed puny by comparison. He slipped them across to Kemp and rose to his feet, but not before carefully locking the file back in the drawer.

'Now I have certain arrangements to make concerning the return of the wanderer so I will leave you for a short while. Do help yourself to another drink.'

Kemp made it a strong one. After all, he was going to be run home at Her Majesty's expense. Nevertheless, he was quite unprepared for the jolt to his senses which the sight of Rose Amaury's girlish handwriting gave him. How easy it can be, he thought, to slip into the ways of this secret world where death has become an irrelevance. Now he remembered her, and the sound of her silvery laugh. He turned the pages slowly.

She obviously had not needed to rely much on notes, it all must have been clear in her memory. Only dates, times, and the names of places had been written down; Harzburg, the Brocken, the Eichfeld, the deforested area and the marked trees, but she had made a note of the ill-fated blunder of that last salute to the man clad in lederhosen with a pack on his back, the man she had recognized. And she had seen the girl carrying a battered suitcase, skirting the trees. Ilse Brunner had intrigued her more than the man himself; she had carefully recalled her conversations with the German chambermaid who spoke good English—Rose's feminine instinct and curiosity had fuelled her interest. Attached to the notes with a rusty paperclip which had left its mark were yellowed newspaper cuttings. From time to time the Press had revived the story of the runaway Major and she had kept them. The latest, from the 'sixties, was an interview Prentis had given in Leipzig when he denied any suggestion that his defection had been in any way sinister; personal conviction had taken him East, and he was not to be shaken in his belief that the system over there offered more hope of a peaceful world than in the capitalist West.

That was all. The mole had gone to sleep for twenty years, and had only been wakened by a threat more malignant than politics, and as fatal to him as discovery or an assassin's bullet.

Kemp put the notes, their ragged edges showing where they had been torn roughly from her book, back on the desk just as Perigord returned.

'Now, Mr Kemp, I have some important calls to make,' he said briskly. 'I shan't require your services any longer, but I'll be in touch. Charters will drive you home.'

Kemp got to his feet, but he was determined on the last word.

'And you propose to do nothing then about our friend?'

'Nothing. And neither will you. There is a time for action and a time for waiting. This is a time for waiting. Please remember that.'

TWENTY-TWO

THE BLACK LIMOUSINE deposited Lennox Kemp on his own doorstep. It was one o'clock in the morning and the lights of Newtown were veiled in a misty drizzle of rain. 'Will you be all right, sir?' inquired Charters courteously as he came round the front of the car.

'Thank you, I'm home and dry,' replied Kemp, but he stood and watched the receding rear light until it turned the corner. Only then did he mount the stairs to his flat. As seemed to be always happening recently, his key had difficulty in turning the lock. He sighed. So much for the Englishman's castle.

He closed the door behind him and switched on the hall light. A voice spoke from the sitting-room: 'You keep very late hours, Mr Kemp, but I waited.'

Julian Cavendish flicked the switch of the lamp. 'I hope you didn't mind?'

'Not at all,' said Kemp, crossing to the kitchen. 'I'm making coffee. I was expecting you anyway...'

He took his time. 'You'll find whisky and soda in that cupboard,' he called out, 'Bring out a couple of glasses, will you? It looks like being a long night.'

'I admire your cool,' remarked Julian when Kemp eventually came in. 'And your taste in spirits.'

Kemp made no comment, poured coffee and pushed a cup towards the schoolmaster who was regarding him with sharp dark eyes at once amused and faintly scathing.

'You don't seem surprised at my being here?'

'It takes a lot to surprise me. Last time you did it was from the rear...and you had your pals to help you.'

'I'm sorry about that. But I was under orders.'

'Like hell you were. You made it a personal thing and that I won't take, Cavendish.'

'Julian, please. I'm not all Cavendish, you know.'

'I'm aware of that. In fact you're not Cavendish at all.'

The other man's eyes narrowed but without losing that hint of suppressed laughter. First thing a schoolteacher learns, thought Kemp, is a waggish insolence to match the worst his little charges can throw at him.

Cavendish leaned over the table and picked up his coffee cup. He drank a little. 'You make good coffee.'

'And you make a rotten assailant. Why'd you not do it on your own? You can box. You're stronger than I am. Why'd you have to involve the Warrenders?'

'Oh, come now, Kemp, there had to be some excuse. It was your own fault for involving poor old Lettice in the first place. You were asking for trouble there. Even her mother thought she was getting into low company.' The suggestion of a sneer was deliberate.

Kemp knew it was an attempt to provoke him; this time it would be 'hands off my fiancée'. He merely remarked, 'Whereas you are safe enough as a suitor despite having no true Cavendish blood?'

Julian raised his tumbler with an affected gesture.

'To the English class system—long may it flourish. Oh, my credentials will be impeccable.'

'Will be? You mean when the conquering hero returns?'

Cavendish sat up. 'You know too damned much, Kemp. It might be expected from a down-at-heel inquiry agent.' His tone had lost its raillery and the words were spat out.

Kemp shrugged. 'No worse an occupation than spying.'

'That depends, doesn't it, on the view taken by our masters?'

Kemp felt too tired for fencing practice; words in a teacher's mouth could conceal as much as communicate, be weapons as well as sources of learning. Better to stab quick and get it over.

'I think you killed Rose Amaury—in fact I know you killed her. I just haven't yet figured out why.'

'Mrs Amaury was struck down—alas with fatal results—by the unfortunate Kevin Roding. That's the official view and will stand.'

'Not while I've anything to do with it.'

Julian carefully refilled his glass, squirted soda, and sighed.

'What a confounded nuisance you've been, Kemp, but your time's up and you can haul your little boat ashore. You're out of your class in this affair. It isn't one of your sleazy little domestic murders in Walthamstow or wherever you plied your trade before coming here. There are more important issues at stake than the killing of an old lady by a bungling young lout—who is himself now beyond recall.'

'Then why are you here?' Kemp got out a cigarette and lit it, watching Julian's face. The man appeared to be in complete command of himself but a small nerve throbbed at his temple where the smooth black hair was brushed back.

'Only to give you warning since you didn't take it the last time. I see your arm has not recovered yet. How would you like the other one broken?'

Although the threat was suavely spoken as if giving out a hundred lines of Latin prose, Kemp felt a spasm of fear; Julian Cavendish meant exactly what he said.

'I don't think you'd dare—not now.'

'Why not? I still have the highest protection for my deeds.'

'So have I.' From the interchange so far, and Julian's insolent calm, Kemp had deduced that the other man was so far unaware that Perigord had taken Kemp into his confidence. It was worth that small divulgence if only to protect himself from another attack.

Julian's eyes blazed as he understood. 'Aha...I did wonder about that black car which brought you home tonight.' He appeared to alter his stance, becoming more thoughtful and eyeing Kemp with new wariness.

'So we're both on the same team and under the same captain,' he said lightly, 'How much have they told you?'

Kemp laughed. 'We may be in the same team, Cavendish, but we're not playing the same game. I have no interest in the return or otherwise of Major Prentis. I'm an outsider, a mere citizen if you like, who wants to see fair play and that means putting you away for the murder of Rose Amaury.'

'I can never be charged with that. They wouldn't allow it.'

Kemp chose his next words with care, and used them with deliberate impact, keeping his eyes fixed on Julian. 'Oh yes, they will—in time. When they've got all they want from your father—Major Prentis is your father, isn't he?—then they'll allow him to die in peace, and you'll be worthless. I think they know by now that you killed Mrs Amaury but they daren't pick you up until they have the Major safe. He wasn't likely to come across at all if he heard his son had been charged with murder. He'd have stayed where he was. He'd have no reason to come home, there'd be no peace in England for him to die in...'

Julian Cavendish sat still as stone, only his eyes alert, but Kemp felt the man was gathering his strength, containing it within him. His devious mind searching for means of escape. When at last he spoke it was in a measured tone, devoid of any emotion.

'Yes, I'm Patrick Prentis's son. I've lived with that knowledge since I was seventeen. I found out the Cavendishes never had a nephew. At first Aunt Tullia made out that I was a refugee child rescued from somewhere in Central Europe—that accounted for the fact that my first language was German—but she's a bad liar and I soon got at the truth. She was upset at the time by reports in the Press about the runaway Major and it didn't take much to put two and two together. Of course I was sworn to secrecy—well, that wasn't difficult, it was scarcely a thing to boast of at my Public School, that I was the son of a renegade Army Officer who'd defected to East Germany because he was a thief! Much better to remain a Cavendish with all the benefits which flowed from that family name.' Again, the sarcastic undertone.

'I wonder how they got you to England,' remarked Kemp with some curiosity. 'Doubtless through the man over here who was running your father over the years.'

'Tullia said I was smuggled out with other children from one of the DP camps, but my guess is that my father begged her to take me. Now we all know the truth about him, yes, it was probably easy for our masters in secrecy... It pleased Tullia to adopt me...gave her a vicarious satisfaction having something precious of his. She's a strange woman, my aunt.'

'I can see it from your father's point of view. He wouldn't want a six-year-old boy around in whatever dangerous activities he was up to—particularly when your own mother had died.'

Julian's face took on a bleak look.

'Leave my mother out of it,' he said sourly. 'It was bad enough hating him all these years for what he'd done. He betrayed people, and he went on doing it...'

'It was his job.'

'I don't mean all that nonsense!' Julian was fierce. 'East and West, what's the difference? It's the same story on both sides—lies and betrayals, the whole pack of them!'

'Rose Amaury's story? You read it, didn't you?'

Kemp was unprepared for the effect of his question. He should have remembered; Julian Cavendish was a man of sudden movements. Now he was on his feet, glaring down, his hands twitching so that Kemp felt himself in danger of immediate assault. Nevertheless, he pressed home the point he had made; if it could galvanize Julian to this extent, then it had implications beyond itself. 'That story mentioned your mother...and it used her real name. Mrs Amaury knew your mother; that was what was so important to you alone in that story, that she knew Ilse Brunner...'

The schoolmaster's cheeks were livid, and the words came from between clenched teeth. 'Don't speak of my mother. Don't say that name to me!'

Kemp stared up at him. 'You did what no one else had the sense to do. While everybody was pussy-footing around scared stiff about the Major's cover being blown, you did the obvious... You went direct to the author!' Dawning enlightenment made Kemp go headlong into the line of his thought, and the words came out in a rush. 'It would be the natural thing... That was the phrase used which put me on to your parentage... But they were thinking of your father, how natural it would be for a son to want his return. They forgot a son would also want to know about his mother. He would barely remember her, and suddenly here was someone who had known her, talked to her, all those years ago...'

Julian turned away, and with rapid steps paced the room as he talked.

'Of course I talked to Mrs Amaury. I was a friend of the family, wasn't I? I never let on what was my real interest. She never suspected a thing... I just mentioned casually that I'd seen the story my aunt had been given to type, and I appreciated its literary merit. A little flattery, a little talk over afternoon tea. Oh, it was quite easy. She talked all right...' He ended savagely.

'It must have been gratifying for you to discover after all that your father had been a British agent,' Kemp observed carefully. 'And how you must have impressed on the Intelligence people your eagerness for his safe return... No wonder they trusted you implicitly. They didn't need anyone else. You wormed out of Rose where she kept her writings. But it had to be made to look like a burglary.'

Julian returned to his chair. He had recovered his control. He sat down and took up his glass. There was only the merest tremor of his hand as he downed the whisky.

'Cloak and dagger stuff,' he said, 'It's the way they like it.'

Kemp leaned back and regarded him warily.

'You didn't find the manuscript but you tore out the pages from the notebook. There must have been a waiting car—Perigord's man—to receive the papers. You gave him the notes, and told him that the burglar had struck down the old lady because she recognized him, then he'd panicked and fled...'

'Quite a consummate reconstruction, Kemp,' Julian remarked, reverting to habitual sarcasm, 'and who is to prove otherwise?'

'But you had your own plan for Kevin Roding's getaway... An address in Amsterdam where you had contacts... Perigord's lot wouldn't want to know about that part of it. You would take care of it...'

Julian only shrugged his shoulders. He was calm now, seemingly invulnerable. Kemp strove to remember at what point he had earlier goaded the man into near violence. He had it.

'Those notes,' he said, 'You didn't have time to read them... But I have. There was another story there which Rose Amaury hadn't written, but she might...some time in the future. She told you about it, didn't she, over that afternoon cup of tea? She knew more about Ilse Brunner... and that was why you killed her!'

Julian Cavendish was on his feet in an instant, hurling back his chair with such force that it crashed into the bookcase, shattering the glass.

Kemp threw himself to one side before the blow landed, and as he twisted away from the flailing fists the door behind him burst open. Charters took one look at the situation and went for Cavendish, who abandoned Kemp and with a boxer's agility aimed a lightning punch at his new adversary. It caught Charters on the side of his head so that he staggered, and was unable to stop Julian reaching the hall. Then they heard the sound of his running feet on the stairs. Charters calmly pulled aside the curtains. 'I was just checking on you when I heard that crash. Sorry. He seems to have got away.'

'Don't tell me that,' observed Kemp bitterly, picking himself off the floor. 'I'm sure those were your orders.'

Charters looked astonished. 'I don't even know who he is. I'm only chauffeur and, when necessary, bodyguard. Looks like you could do with one. Mind if I have a drink? It was bloody cold out there . . .'

Kemp, temporarily speechless, gave him a glass of whisky and went to make himself some strong coffee. Charters followed him and leaned on the kitchen doorpost. 'My instructions were simply to keep a watch on your place,' he said conversationally, 'see if you had any unwelcome visitors, any visitors, in fact. I wasn't to know one had already arrived. I should have come up with you and checked.'

'I won't report you for that. I was damned glad to see you—I'm not much good at one-armed combat. So you've no idea what this is all about?'

Charters shook his head. 'Nor do I want to. But I couldn't ignore the noise I heard. Sudden sort of chap, is he?'

'The worst kind,' said Kemp tersely, 'the kind that jumps.' He came to a decision. 'Are you still going to keep an eye on me all night?'

'Those were my orders, sir. Don't worry about me, I slept most of the day.'

'I didn't,' said Kemp, 'but you can keep an eye on me in your car. You're going to drive me right back to your boss. There's something I want from him and I want it tonight.'

Charters looked shocked. 'He's not going to like it.'

'I don't give a damn whether he likes it or not. Come on, the waiting game is over.'

TWENTY-THREE

THE WARRENDER FAMILY were in the dining-room at
Castleton House when the surly parlourmaid entered to announce that Mr Lennox Kemp wished to see Miss Lettice.

'Says it's urgent.' She sniffed and went about her business of bearing dishes as if her duties were of more importance. Kemp was forced to stand aside as she swept through
the door. He closed it behind her with a wry smile, and
turned towards the startled people at the table under the red
shades of the candlebra.

Paula looked pained at this interruption to the proper
ritual of mealtimes, but good manners prevailed.

'It's rather inconvenient, Mr Kemp, but may I offer you
some refreshment?' It was said with the stiff propriety she
could not help, given her nature, but acerbity crept in as she
added: 'I'm sure you must have good reason for a visit at
this hour but I do find the disturbance singularly ill-judged.
No, Lettice—' as her daughter pushed back her chair—
'whatever Mr Kemp has to say can surely be said to all of
us...'

'Oh, Mother!' Lettice rose with an impatient gesture.

Lionel wiped his mouth with a napkin which he crumpled and tossed down. 'Come on, out with it, Mr Kemp.
There are no secrets here.'

No one had asked Kemp to sit down. It seemed a pity to
break up such a peaceful domestic scene. He saw Roger's
quick glance at the plaster still on his arm. The young man's
face reddened, and he looked away as Kemp gave him a grin
which contained warning as much as amusement.

'My words are for the ears of Lettice alone,' he said, taking her arm and guiding her to the door. As he opened it he

added, over his shoulder: 'And there's really no need to worry—it's not a proposal of marriage.' He shut out their shocked faces and hurried his captive through the hall and down the stone steps between the grey urns.

She shook herself out of his grasp and faced him like a spitting cat. 'That remark was in your usual bad taste, and quite unnecessary.'

'You sound just like your mother.' Then Kemp dropped his bantering tone, and spoke gravely. 'What I have to say to you is serious, Lettice. When your ancestors had to discuss important matters they paced the terrace, or walked in the shrubberies for an hour or two. We may have to do both since this is going to take some time.'

LATER, THEY SAT on a mossy wall at the far end of the gardens from where the mansion glimmered through the summer foliage against the darkening sky. Lettice stared, without seeing.

'Roger and Torvil! How could they!'

'Don't blame them, they were only camouflage. Julian has a way of spinning a tale... He probably told them I was out to seduce you, and needed to be brought down a peg. To them it was just a bit of a lark until I was on the ground and Julian started in earnest. They were scared, and they ran off. I think they've been ashamed of themselves ever since, and frightened of saying anything; they couldn't know that Julian had another motive—a very real one—for putting me out of the way. And don't forget that for a space of time he considered himself above the law.'

She put her head in her hands, then raised it, her features blanched of all colour. 'Where is he now?'

'He's being held on a charge of grievous bodily harm.' Kemp was grim. 'I was forced to bring that up to get the information I wanted the night before last—threatened I'd swear the warrant myself if they didn't let me see that dossier on Major Prentis. It's only a matter of time before Julian faces a more serious charge. Coming to my flat was a great mistake but he couldn't resist having another go at me. And I provoked him into doing something really stupid—trying to pre-empt his Austrian trip by booking an earlier flight out of Heathrow. Of course they were waiting for him—he'd been watched ever since I alerted them...'

'Did he intend to come back from that trip?'

'Who knows? It was a convenient bolt-hole if the sky dropped on him. He would simply have disappeared over there. That was one plan.'

'And the other?'

'You mean if I hadn't interfered? Well, the Amaury case would have remained closed. He'd have come back and married you, dear Lettice Warrender...'

She turned her clear hazel eyes on him. 'Don't,' she said, 'because it isn't true. I wasn't going to marry Julian Cavendish. You were right. I'd got over my schoolgirl crush.'

Kemp breathed a sigh of relief. Telling Lettice the truth had seemed to him to be the hardest part, yet he had insisted on its priority. In Perigord's office that afternoon, waiting for a certain call, he had said:

'She has a right to be told. He asked her to marry him. I don't know what her feelings for him are... For God's sake! After all, everybody's going to know sooner or later.'

When the call had finally come through, Perigord gave a weary assent. 'Tell her,' he said. Kemp had raised his eyebrows at the phone. 'Yes,' Perigord answered the unspoken query. 'Major Prentis has arrived in the West. The doctors felt his heart could not stand the strain of a flight so he was brought out by ambulance at one of our checkpoints an hour ago. They say he's a dying man.'

'And Julian Cavendish?'

'He'll be charged with the murder of Mrs Amaury. Now get out of here. I've work to do.'

'I can't think of him as other than Julian Cavendish,' Lettice was saying now, 'I don't suppose we'll ever know his real name.'

'He was quite properly adopted by the Cavendishes. As to his real father, who knows?'

'And names matter so much to us,' she was almost whispering, 'How sad it all is...'

'I think that's what touched your grandmother's heart—what she heard from her German chambermaid. You see, she hadn't put it all into her story, but it was there in the notes. The story certainly had the truth in it—that Ilse Brunner was pregnant when she went over the frontier with the Major—and everyone assumed it was his child she was carrying. It was simply another reason for him to flee from the West. And Julian was born to Ilse in Leipzig some months later—and the name of the father given as Prentis.'

'So even he thought it was his child?'

'Only the galloping Major knows the answer to that. But she was his girlfriend, and he used her because she had family to go to in East Germany—it was the perfect cover for him. Ironically perhaps, she also used him...to give her child a father. Ilse could always say the baby was premature. Men like Prentis with other more important things on their minds aren't very good on women's matters... I believe he really thought it was his son and he had a conscience about him, so he had the child sent to Tullia.'

'You must have been very sure of all this?'

'Not until I saw the records. Major Prentis only arrived in BAOR in late July 1947. He was in the Middle East until then. That's one thing about the Army—you can always check where people are at a given date. Even if the Major had met and bedded Ilse that July—no baby of his could be moving in the womb by September. Quickening doesn't happen until at least the fourth month.'

'It moved?'

'Women's talk. Ilse had become very friendly with your grandmother who was a sympathetic listener. She'd just had a baby of her own and was interested in such things. Her father had been a doctor, and so was her husband. Ilse told her she was having a child, put Mrs Amaury's hand on her stomach, and said, 'Ach, you feel it too!' The note said she felt the fluttering quite distinctly. She was happy for the girl... Ilse had chattered a lot. She was a pretty girl, she'd had many lovers. There was a kitchen porter who'd refused to marry her, and there was this British officer who was fed up with a strait-laced wife in England who wouldn't, or couldn't, have children... Oh, Ilse had prattled away all right, and your grandmother remembered. The conversations were all in the notes. The seeds of romantic fiction— that's all the Intelligence people thought they were; they were more concerned with the scene in the forest.'

'And when Julian talked to Granny about her story she told him all this? How awful for him—just when he'd learned the man he'd always believed to be his father might become a national hero!'

'I don't suppose our security people are likely to go that far, but yes, there would have been some quiet glory.'

'Granny would have known the truth.' Lettice stared into the twilight, tears glistening in her eyes. 'She would be the only one to know that Julian might be the son of a kitchen porter!'

'And she would not have minded, that's the terrible thing. If only he'd known her better, trusted her... If only he'd not been so caught up himself by then in secrecy and deception... But they gave him the opportunity and he jumped at it. What was it he said to me? "It's all lies and betrayals...the whole story's a pack of lies." That's what he hoped it was. I don't think he really cared whether his father was a patriot or a spy but he was curious about his mother. He knew her name was Ilse Brunner so he went straight to Mrs Amaury and wheedled the truth from her. Then he kept quiet. I think he probably guessed that his aunt had burnt the story. That danger had passed, the danger to him lay in the future. When the Major was home and the whole matter no longer a secret, only your grandmother would know the darker side. He could not bear that thought...'

'I cannot bear that he killed her.'

'You've already been through that—when you thought
she had been struck down by young Roding. Does it make
so much difference now when you know it was one of your
own kind?'

'That's cruel!' she burst out. 'That's a hard thing to say.'

'It would have been a harder thing if it had been allowed
to rest with Kevin's death.' Kemp pulled the girl gently to her
feet. 'Come on, young Lettice, you'll get over it. You'll
think your way through it, and recognize a sort of justice.'

She was silent as they made their way across the lawns.

Kemp's car was on the terrace. He stopped.

'I'm not coming in with you,' he said. 'Your people will
have to be told, of course. The Cavendishes know it all by
now—they are in the forefront. Do what you can for Tullia—she still has the hardest part to face. She loved Julian,
too.'

He drove off in the direction of Rummymede Crescent,
and as he did so the hymn again came into his mind:

> 'The rich man in his castle,
> The poor man at his gate,
> God made them, high or lowly,
> And order'd their estate.'

Winner of the Grand Master Award from the Mystery
Writers of America, Dorothy Salisbury Davis "...has few
equals in setting up a puzzle, complete with misdirection
and surprises."

DOROTHY SALISBURY DAVIS
LULLABY OF MURDER

A Julie Hayes Mystery

When the infamous New York gossip columnist, Tony
Alexander, is found murdered, reporter Julie Hayes starts
digging and discovers a lot of people are happier with Tony
dead! As murder takes center stage, Julie finds herself caught in
a web of hate, deceit and revenge, dirty deals and small-town
scandals.

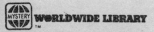

From the author of the spellbinding STAGES comes this contemporary mystery-romance set in the cutthroat world of a New York advertising agency.

MADISON AVENUE MURDER

Gillian Hall

A young woman investigates the brutal murder of a successful art director and comes to understand the chilling flip side of passionate love . . . and the lowly places to which the highest ambitions can fall.

Worldwide Mysteries means superlative suspense from award-winning authors.

HANG THE CONSEQUENCES—M. R. D. Meek $3.50   ☐
Private investigator Lennox Kemp gets more than he bargained
for when he is hired to locate a client's missing husband. He
soon finds himself involved in blackmail, adultery
and . . . murder!

FOOL'S GOLD—Ted Wood $3.50   ☐
Police officer Reid Bennett investigates the violent murder of a
geologist and finds that his presence not only triggers additional
killings but attempts on his life.

PAINT HER FACE DEAD—Jane Johnston $3.50   ☐
A reporter becomes implicated in murder while researching a
story on a fraudulent encounter group.

MURDER IN C MAJOR—Sara Hoskinson Frommer $3.50   ☐
A woman becomes caught in the middle of a complicated and
dangerous investigation when two members of the symphony she
has joined are murdered in successive rehearsals.

	Total Amount	$ _____
	Plus 75¢ Postage	.75
	Payment enclosed	$ _____

Take 2 books & a surprise gift FREE

SPECIAL LIMITED-TIME OFFER

Mail to: The Mystery Library
901 Fuhrmann Blvd.
P.O. Box 1867
Buffalo, N.Y. 14269-1867

YES! Please send me 2 free books from the Mystery Library and my free surprise gift. Then send me 2 mystery books, first time in paperback, every month. Bill me only $3.50 per book. There is *no* extra charge for shipping and handling! There is no minimum number of books I must purchase. I can always return a shipment and cancel at any time. Even if I never buy another book from The Mystery Library, the 2 free books and the surprise gift are mine to keep forever.

414 BPY BPS9

Name   (PLEASE PRINT)

Address   Apt. No.

City   State   Zip

This offer is limited to one order per household and not valid to present subscribers. Terms and prices subject to change without notice.

MYS-BPA5